John, wesley Hanson

Famous American Men and Women A Complete Portrait Gallery

of Celebrated People, Whose Names are Prominent in the Annals

of the Time, Each Portrait Accompanied by an Authentic

Biographical Sketch, Secured by Personal Interviewthe Whole

Forming a Text

John, wesley Hanson

Famous American Men and Women A Complete Portrait Gallery of Celebrated People, Whose Names are Prominent in the Annals of the Time, Each Portrait Accompanied by an Authentic Biographical Sketch, Secured by Personal Interviewthe Whole Forming a Text

ISBN/EAN: 9783741190414

Manufactured in Europe, USA, Canada, Australia, Japa

Cover: Foto ©Andreas Hilbeck / pixelio.de

Manufactured and distributed by brebook publishing software (www.brebook.com)

John, wesley Hanson

Famous American Men and Women A Complete Portrait Gallery of Celebrated People, Whose Names are Prominent in the Annals of the Time, Each Portrait Accompanied by an Authentic Biographical Sketch, Secured by Personal Interviewthe Whole Forming a Text

INTRODUCTION.

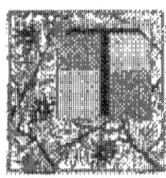HERE is an irresistible attraction in reading the lives of celebrated people which enchains the hearts of young and old alike. The study of individual character as represented by men and women whose names are graven on the imperishable tablets of Fame, is not only fascinating but instructive.

Strange as it may seem we know less of living celebrities, who by thought and action are now molding the destiny of the nation, than we do of the immortal dead whose epitaphs are written in the sacred archives of history.

This work is a record of noted Americans now living, and of the important events they have created. It contains the portraits of famous persons whose names are prominent in the annals of the times. Each portrait is reproduced from a recent photograph, and is accompanied by a biographical sketch obtained in nearly all cases by personal interview. The work is therefore of untold value as a text book of national character, an authentic account of modern progress and development, and the influence of master minds upon American history.

Hon. Benjamin Harrison, Ex-President of the United States, has said:

"If we would strengthen our country, we should cultivate a love for it in our hearts and in the hearts of our children and neighbors; and this love for civil institutions, for a land, for a flag, if they are worthy and great and have a glorious history, is widened and deepened by a fuller knowledge of them."

Biography is not alone the history of individuals, it is the history of a Nation.

The influence of truly great men upon humanity cannot be estimated. The diplomacy and stanch patriotism of Grover Cleveland, the statesmanship of William McKinley, the forensic ability of Melville W. Fuller, the rare scholarship of Edward Everett Hale, and the broad liberality of Archbishop Ireland, have been important factors in shaping the course of human events.

The scientific discoveries of Thomas A. Edison have resulted in untold benefit to Americans and to the world.

The poetic genius of Thomas Bailey Aldrich, the oratory of Chauncey M. Depew, and the humor of Mark Twain, have left an indelible impress upon mankind.

"One touch of nature makes the whole world kin," whether it be the princely charity of John D. Rockefeller, or the devotion of Neal Dow to the cause of temperance.

The world loves to read of great deeds of bravery and the heroism of Ida Lewis, the lighthouse-keeper who risks her life, in an open boat, during a terrible storm, to rescue drowning sailors, or the courage of Dr. Charles Parkhurst, battling against the forces of evil, calls for the admiration of all.

America has produced many celebrated men who have risen from humble stations to occupy exalted positions. Levi P. Morton started in life as an humble clerk; Robert Collyer was a blacksmith; John Wanamaker, a messenger boy; Lyman J. Gage, a night watchman; James Whitcomb Riley, a wandering sign painter; William B. Allison, a farmer boy; George M. Pullman, a house mover; Richard J. Oglesby, a carpenter, and Francis Bret Harte, a printer. These and many others began the battle of life under discouraging conditions, but finally overcame all obstacles and rose to eminence and honor.

This work is of especial importance in view of the approaching presidential campaign. Soon a new pilot will stand at the helm to guide the Ship of State through the shoals and shallows of doubt and danger. Many able statesmen have spent their lives in vain pursuit of this coveted honor, while others, more fortunate, have secured the prize. The biographies and portraits of all possible candidates for president and aspirants for other political honors are found in this book.

The work is an invaluable cyclopedia of names and a portrait gallery of the most prominent men and women of the day. Its value to the young is unquestioned, as it teaches them to emulate the deeds of those who are living examples of deserving fame.

The work necessarily contains the portraits and biographies of many who have seen long years of service, but who wear their age "like a lusty winter, frosty but kindly." And when the summons comes for any one of these grand old heroes to rise to a higher and a better life we can say from our hearts:

> " Weep not for him,
> Who departing leaves millions in tears ;
> Not for him—
> Who has died full of honor and years ;
> Not for him—
> Who ascended Fame's ladder so high,
> From the round at the top
> He has stepped to the sky."

MELVILLE W. FULLER.

A LESS modest man of equal abilities would probably have risen to public prominence earlier in life than did Mr. Fuller. Not until 1888, when he was appointed Chief Justice of the United States Supreme Court, did he become known to the country as a great jurist, though he had long been recognized as such in Illinois. Melville W. Fuller was born in Augusta, Maine, February 11, 1833. After graduating at Bowdoin College in 1853 he began the study of law at Harvard, and in 1855 entered upon the practice of his profession in his native city. Here he edited the Augusta "Age," became president of the common council, and in 1856 was elected city attorney. In the last-named year he removed to Chicago, where for thirty-two years he conducted a highly successful law practice. Mr. Fuller was a member of the Illinois Constitutional Convention in 1862, and of the Illinois House of Representatives in 1863. A strong Democrat, he served as a delegate to all the national conventions, from 1864 to 1880 inclusive, and was always prominent in the councils of his party, where his word had the greatest influence. When President Cleveland selected him to fill the vacancy on the Supreme bench of the United States, caused by the death of Chief Justice Waite, the choice was pronounced a wise one by those who knew Mr. Fuller best. He was confirmed by the Senate July 20, 1888, and took the oath of office on the 8th of October following. The degree of LL. D. has been conferred upon him by Bowdoin College and the Northwestern University.

MELVILLE W. FULLER
7

THOMAS ALVA EDISON.

IT may be truthfully said that the current history of this country contains no brighter page than that which recites the achievements of Thomas A. Edison. This great inventor first saw the light of day at Alva, Ohio, February 11, 1847. As a boy he became particularly interested in the study of chemistry. While employed as a newsboy on a railway train he took up the study of telegraphy, and pursued it so persistently by sitting up late at nights in a railway station that he was soon an expert operator. He worked at this trade in a number of places, and while at Adrian, Mich., opened a shop for repairing telegraph instruments and the making of new machinery. He then went to Indianapolis, where he invented his automatic repeater. Later, he was stationed in Cincinnati, with an established reputation as an inventor, and from there went to Boston, where he perfected his duplex telegraph. Shortly thereafter Mr. Edison was made superintendent of the New York Gold Indicator Company, and transferred his shops to Newark, N. J. In 1876 he resigned this position and established himself permanently at Menlo Park, N. J., devoting his entire time to research and invention. Among the productions of his brain are the phonograph, the microphone, the electric pen, the quadruplex and sextuplex transmitter, improvement in the electric light and the telephone, the kinetoscope and kinetograph. Mr. Edison is of a modest, retiring disposition, an indefatigable worker, and when occupied in perfecting a new invention scarcely takes time to eat or sleep until it is completed. Remarkable as have been many of his achievements in the past, he expects to produce still greater results from recent experiments, and the public has great confidence in his forecasts of coming miracles.

THOMAS ALVA EDISON.

9

ELIZABETH CADY STANTON.

AMONG the women of the United States who have devoted their lives to the work of correcting existing evils in the social conditions of their sex, there is none now living who is better known or more highly honored for the good she has accomplished than Elizabeth Cady Stanton. This popular lady was born in Johnstown, N. Y., November 12, 1815, and was graduated at Mrs. Emma Willard's Seminary, in Troy, N. Y., in 1832. In 1840 she was married to Henry Brewster Stanton, and in the same year, while attending the World's Anti-Slavery Convention, in London, she met Lucretia Mott, with whom she was in sympathy, and with whom she signed the call for the first Women's Rights Convention. This was held at her home in Seneca Falls, July 19 and 20, 1848. She addressed the New York Legislature on the rights of married women in 1854, and in advocacy of divorce for drunkenness in 1860, and in 1867 spoke before the Legislature and the Constitutional Convention, maintaining that during the revision of the constitution the state was resolved into its original elements and that citizens of both sexes had a right to vote for members of that convention. She canvassed Kansas in 1867 and Michigan in 1874, when the question of woman suffrage was submitted to the people of those states. Since 1869 she has addressed many congressional committees and conventions, and delivered numerous lectures on this subject, and for ten years she was president of the National Woman Suffrage Association. In 1868 she was a candidate for Congress. She was an editor with Susan B. Anthony and Parker Pillsbury of "The Revolution," founded in 1868, and is joint author of "History of Woman's Suffrage."

ELIZABETH CADY STANTON.

11

GROVER CLEVELAND.

STEPPING from comparative obscurity into the highest position in the gift of the American people, it is safe to say that no man was ever more favored by fortuitous circumstances than President Cleveland. He was born in Caldwell, Essex County, N. J., March 18, 1837. His father was a Presbyterian clergyman. After his father's death Grover became a clerk and assistant teacher in the New York Institution for the Blind, but in 1855 he settled in Buffalo with his uncle, and studied law in the office of Rogers, Bowen & Rogers. He was admitted to the bar in 1859, and from 1863 until 1866 was district attorney of Erie County. He became the law partner of Isaac V. Vanderpool, and in 1869 a member of the firm of Lanning, Cleveland & Folsom, practicing until 1870, when he was made sheriff of Erie County. The firm of Bass, Cleveland & Bissell was formed in 1873, and in 1881 Mr. Cleveland was elected mayor of Buffalo. In 1882, favored by a factional fight in the Republican party, he was made governor of New York, and in 1884 the Democratic party nominated him for President of the United States, and elected him on a platform of tariff reform. He was defeated for a second term by the Republican candidate, Benjamin Harrison, but in 1892 he in turn defeated Mr. Harrison, and again became President. Mr. Cleveland is a man of well-balanced temperament, a hard worker, persistent almost to obstinacy, and devoted to economical reforms. He was married in the White House, in 1886, to Miss Frances Folsom, daughter of his former law partner. He stands forth a very sturdy figure in the line of Presidents.

GROVER CLEVELAND.
13

FRANCES FOLSOM CLEVELAND.

NEVER did a fairer type of American womanhood preside over the domestic affairs of the White House than she who has been twice called to the proud position of "the first lady in the land." Mrs. Cleveland, only a few years ago, was the charming Miss Frances Folsom, of Buffalo, N. Y., where she was born in 1864. Her father was at one time Mr. Cleveland's law partner and the two men were close friends up to the time of Mr. Folsom's death, in 1875. After that sad event Mr. Cleveland was appointed guardian of his late friend's daughter, and she was taken to the home of her grandmother in Medina, N. Y., where she attended high-school. She was regarded as one of the brightest pupils in her class, and upon finishing her course in the high-school she entered the sophomore class of Wells College, where she graduated with high honors. As a girl, Miss Folsom was a general favorite, admired for her beauty and charming vivacity, as well as for her many accomplishments. After leaving college she visited Europe with her mother, and soon after her return she became the mistress of the executive mansion at Washington. She was married to Grover Cleveland, in the White House, May 28, 1886, and at once became the most popular lady in America. Under her leadership Washington society acquired great brilliancy. With a grace and dignity all her own, coupled with a charming cordiality and simplicity of manner that commanded the admiration of the whole country, she bore the responsibilities of her trying position like one to the manor born. She has proved a loving mother as well as a devoted wife. Mr. and Mrs. Cleveland have three beautiful children, Ruth, Esther and Marion.

FRANCES FOLSOM CLEVELAND.

WILLIAM B. ALLISON.

WITH a broad and breezy style of statesmanship that at once stamps him as a product of the great West, Senator Allison, of Iowa, must be enrolled among those eminent Americans whose abilities have forced them into prominence from the obscurity of the farm. His early years were spent on the farm at Perry, Wayne County, Ohio, where he was born March 2, 1829. He was educated at Allegheny College, Pennsylvania, and at the Western Reserve College, Ohio, after which he took up the study of law, and practiced his profession in Ohio until 1857. He then went to Dubuque, Iowa, which city has since been his home. He was a delegate to the Chicago convention that nominated Abraham Lincoln for the presidency in 1860, and in the following year became a member of the staff of the governor of Iowa, in which capacity he rendered valuable service in raising troops and organizing volunteer regiments for the war. In 1862 Mr. Allison was elected to the Thirty-eighth Congress as a Republican, and was re-elected to the three succeeding Congresses, serving continuously as a member of that body from December 7, 1863, until March 3, 1871. In 1873 he was elected United States Senator to succeed James Harlan, and he has been three times re-elected. His present term of service will expire in 1897. Senator Allison has long been recognized as one of the strongest men in the Republican party, a natural leader and organizer, combining the shrewdness of the politician with the broad-minded patriotism of the statesman, and with personal influence second to that of no man in Washington. He has been a prominent candidate for the presidential nomination in more than one Republican convention.

16

WILLIAM B. ALLISON.

17

DAVID BENNETT HILL

IN stature rather below than above the average height, and somewhat
sparsely built, Senator Hill is, nevertheless, a giant among the representatives of that wing of the Democratic party that has no patience
with the so-called reform methods of the Cleveland administration. He
was born in Havana, Chemung (now Schuyler) County, New York,
August 29, 1843. His first employment was as a clerk in a lawyer's
office in his native village, and he afterward studied law in Elmira,
and was admitted to the bar in 1864. He was appointed city attorney, and later was many times a delegate to the Democratic State
Conventions, being president of those held in 1877 and 1881. He was
also prominent in the Democratic National Conventions of 1876 and
1884; was a member of the New York Legislature of 1870 and 1871;
was elected Mayor of Elmira in 1882, and in the same year was
elected lieutenant-governor on the ticket headed by Grover Cleveland.
When Mr. Cleveland resigned in 1884, to become President of the
United States, Mr. Hill succeeded him as Governor of New York, and
in 1885 he was elected Governor for the full term of three years. In
1888 he was re-elected over Warner Miller, and in 1891 he was
chosen United States Senator to succeed William M. Evarts. As a
champion of Tammany, Senator Hill was opposed to the nomination
of Grover Cleveland for a second presidential term in 1892, and has
since vigorously antagonized the administration by his vote and influence in the Senate, defeating the President's favorite nominations. His
bitterest political opponents admit his shrewdness and courage.

DAVID BENNETT HILL

19

THOMAS BRACKETT REED.

A MAN of forceful ideas and a happy gift of expressing them — a man who thinks for himself, and displays remarkable originality of thought in looking at any subject — Thomas B. Reed, of Maine, is a recognized leader of the Republicans in the National House of Representatives. Mr. Reed was born in Maine, October 18, 1839, and was graduated at Bowdoin College in 1860, after which he studied law. In 1864 he entered the Navy as acting assistant paymaster, but after one year of service he resumed his profession. He was elected a member of the lower branch of the Maine Legislature in 1868, and was state senator the following session. For two years he was attorney-general of the state, and was city solicitor for Portland for a term of four years. In 1876 he was elected a member of Congress, and has since been continuously re-elected. In the Fifty-first Congress Mr. Reed was elected Speaker of the House, and the vigor of his administration, and his fearless departure from the usage of years in his rulings, attracted widespread attention, as well as a storm of criticism. He was assailed in every way that party indignation could invent or the bitterness of defeat devise, yet his acts may be said to have been vindicated. It is admitted even by Mr. Reed's political opponents that he is a man of honor and patriotism — an American throughout — with a force of intellect and character, and a training and education which make all Americans proud to have him in the forefront of our public life. In the Fifty-fourth Congress Mr. Reed was again elected Speaker of the House. The revival of the Monroe Doctrine, by a controversy between England and the United States over the question of territorial rights in Venezuela, was the most important event of this Congress.

THOMAS BRACKETT REED.

23

JOHN SHERMAN.

POSSESSING in an eminent degree the essential qualifications of a statesman, combined with a positive genius for solving the financial problems in the affairs of government, the United States Senator from Ohio presents one of the most imposing figures in public life. John Sherman was born in Lancaster, Ohio, May 10, 1823. After receiving an education he studied law with a brother at Mansfield, where he afterward practiced for ten years. In 1855 he was elected to the Thirty-fourth Congress in the interest of the Free-Soil party, and was re-elected to the three succeeding Congresses. He became a power on the floor and in committees, and was recognized as the foremost man in the House, particularly in matters affecting finance. In 1861 he was sent to the United States Senate, where he at once became a leader. After the close of the Civil war he and Thaddeus Stevens prepared the bill for the reconstruction of the Southern States, which was passed by Congress in the winter of 1866 67. President Hayes appointed Mr. Sherman Secretary of the Treasury in 1877, and it was due to his management while at the head of that department that the resumption of specie payment was effected in 1879 without disturbance to the financial or commercial interests of the country. In 1881 he re-entered the Senate, of which he is still a leading member. Senator Sherman was a prominent candidate for the Republican presidential nomination in 1880, and again in 1888. His present term in the Senate will expire in 1899. He is a member of the committee on finance, the committee on foreign relations, and several select committees requiring the exercise of his superior judgment and knowledge of affairs.

JOHN SHERMAN.

JOHN GRIFFIN CARLISLE.

KENTUCKY enjoys the distinction of being the birthplace of many noted men. Among those who have been before the public for a long term of years, and whose fame is so national in its scope that they can scarcely be said to belong to any state, is John G. Carlisle, appointed Secretary of the Treasury in 1893. He was born in Campbell (now Kenton) County, Kentucky, September 5, 1835, and now resides in Covington, in the same state. He was occupied as a public school teacher while studying law, and in 1858 was admitted to the bar. Mr. Carlisle was elected a member of the Kentucky Legislature in 1859, and in 1864 he was nominated as presidential elector on the Democratic ticket, but declined to serve. He afterward served two terms in the senate of his native state, resigning his seat upon being nominated for lieutenant-governor, to which office he was elected in 1871. He was subsequently elected to Congress, and served with distinction in the House of Representatives, a portion of the time as Speaker, until he was elected United States Senator from Kentucky to succeed the late Senator Beck. He later resigned his seat in the Senate to enter President Cleveland's Cabinet as Secretary of the Treasury. Mr. Carlisle is a leading representative of that branch of the Democracy which advocates a low tariff, and in his public speeches he has presented many forcible arguments against the policy of protection. Personally, he is a man of generous impulses and charitable inclinations, and is one of the most popular officials at Washington. Mr. Carlisle is a vigorous advocate of a sound financial policy. His views are always openly and freely expressed, and he is an unflinching opponent of any measure that threatens the safety of the currency.

JOHN GRIFFIN CARLISLE
25

WILLIAM McKINLEY.

HIS sturdy advocacy of the principle of protection, coupled with abilities of the highest order, have made William McKinley, of Ohio, a leader of his party, and one of the foremost figures in American politics. Born in Niles, Ohio, in 1843, he inherited the indomitable energy, perseverance and intellectual brilliancy characteristic of the Scotch-Irish and German blood that flowed in the veins of his parents. After completing an academic course Mr. McKinley entered upon the career of a school-teacher, but abandoned that calling on the breaking out of the Civil war to enlist as a private in the Twenty-third Ohio Regiment. He was repeatedly promoted for gallant service, attaining the rank of captain in 1864, and was breveted major at the close of the war. He then studied law, and in 1871 established himself in Canton, Ohio, where he was married to Miss Ida Saxton. His rise in the legal profession was rapid, and in 1876 Major McKinley was elected to Congress, where he remained four terms by successive re-elections. It was during this period that he became famous as the author of the measure known as the "McKinley bill," which subsequently became so great a factor in national elections. He was first elected Governor of Ohio in 1891. In 1893 he was re-elected by a plurality of over eighty thousand votes, mainly upon the issue of protection. This remarkable record has greatly enhanced his chances of receiving presidential honors, and has caused the Republican party to look upon him as its leader. Mr. McKinley has been likened to Napoleon in his personal appearance, though he is of larger physique than the famous general. As an orator and debater he has great power and influence.

WILLIAM McKINLEY.

SHELBY M. CULLOM.

A VERY shrewd politician is Shelby M. Cullom. He was born in Wayne County, Kentucky, November 22, 1829. His family moved to Illinois when he was but a mere child, and he grew up among the pioneers. He worked on the farm in summer and attended the district school in winter. Subsequently, as has been the experience of so many of the strong men of the country, he taught the district school himself, and afterward entered the office of a law firm at Springfield, Ill., and, it so chanced, used the very books that were used by Abraham Lincoln when he studied law. Mr. Cullom rapidly acquired prominence after being admitted to practice. He was elected city attorney at Springfield, and in 1856 was elected to the Legislature and was voted for by the Fillmore adherents as Speaker of the House. In 1862 he had become a man of prominence in Illinois, and was appointed by President Lincoln on the commission with George Boutwell, of Massachusetts, and Chas. A. Dana to oppose important claims against the government, arising from the accounts with quartermasters and others, dating from the Civil war. In 1864 he was elected to Congress as a Republican from a Democratic district. He remained in the House for years, and in 1872 returned to the Illinois House of Representatives, was elected Speaker, and in 1874 served another term in the Legislature. In 1876 he was elected governor of Illinois, and was re-elected in 1880, serving in that capacity until 1883, when he resigned to take his seat in the United States Senate, made vacant by the death of the Hon. David Davis. As a political organizer, Senator Cullom has few superiors, and as an experienced lawmaker his rank is among the highest.

SHELBY M. CULLOM.

HENRY WATTERSON.

IDENTIFIED with the revenue reform movement of the Democratic party, as an aggressive advocate of free trade ideas, the editor of the Louisville "Courier-Journal" is a man of remarkable force and influence, whose advice is sought by the leaders of his party. Henry Watterson, whose father was a native of Tennessee, was born in Washington, D. C., February 16, 1840, and was educated there by private tutors. He entered the profession of journalism in Washington in 1858, and in 1861 went to Nashville, Tenn., where he edited the "Republican Banner." During the Civil war he served on the Confederate side, a portion of the time as staff officer, and later as chief of scouts in Gen. Joseph E. Johnston's army. Soon after the war he went to Louisville, Ky., to reside, and in 1867 succeeded George D. Prentice as editor of the "Journal." In the year following he united the "Courier" and the "Times" with that paper, and in connection with Walter N. Haldeman founded the "Courier-Journal," of which he has since been the editor. He was a member of Congress from August 12, 1876, until March 3, 1877, being chosen to fill a vacancy, but with this exception he has always declined public office. He is usually a delegate to the National Democratic Conventions, and presided over the one at St. Louis in 1876. At others he has served as chairman of the platform committee. Mr. Watterson was a personal friend and resolute follower of Samuel J. Tilden. He is prominent as an orator and political speaker; has contributed freely to periodicals, and in 1882 edited "Oddities of Southern Life and Character." As an editor he is easily the leading man in Southern journalism, and under his management the "Courier-Journal" has become a great power.

HENRY WATTERSON.

LEVI P. MORTON.

—— ··

TO have been a successful business man, a legislator, a diplomat, a vice-president of the United States; to return quietly to business as an ordinary citizen, and then, at the age of seventy, to be looked upon as the probable candidate of his party for governor of his state, with a sharp struggle in prospect, is a record to be talked of, and is what Levi P. Morton has made. He was born in Shoreham, Vt., May 16, 1824, a direct descendant of George Morton, one of the Puritan fathers. He acquired the ordinary common school education, became a clerk in a store in Hanover, and showed such capability as to become a partner before he was twenty-one years of age. In 1849 he went into business in Boston, and, in 1854, went to New York, where he established the dry goods firm of Morton & Grinnell. Later he established the banking house of Morton, Rose & Co., with a branch in London, the firms becoming widely known through their connection with the settlement of the Geneva and Halifax awards. In 1878 Mr. Morton was elected to Congress, and was re-elected in 1880. He refused the chance of nomination for vice-president on the Republican ticket the same year, and President Garfield gave him the choice between being Secretary of the Navy or Minister to France. He chose the latter place, and proved a most capable representative of this government. He was defeated by Mr. Hiscock as the Republican nominee for United States senator in 1887, but was nominated for vice-president in 1888 and elected with Mr. Harrison. At the end of his term he resumed attention to his business affairs, but in 1894 he became the candidate for governor of New York and was elected by a large majority.

LEVI P. MORTON.

RUSSELL ALEXANDER ALGER.

M ORE than once has the name and record of the soldier-statesman
of Michigan been seriously considered by the Republican party
when casting about for an available candidate for President of the
United States. Gen. Russell A. Alger has been a successful man, both
in political and commercial life. He was born in Lafayette, Ohio, February 27, 1836, and after receiving a liberal education, adopted the profession of law. He was admitted to the bar in 1859, but two years
later, at the breaking out of the war, he entered the volunteer service
as captain of the Second Michigan Cavalry. He came out as a brevet
major-general, having won promotion by his gallantry on many battle-
fields, and especially at Gettysburg and in the Shenandoah Valley,
where he greatly distinguished himself for coolness and bravery under
the most trying circumstances. After the war he was engaged for a
number of years in the lumber business in Detroit, where he amassed
a large fortune. In 1884 the Republicans of Michigan elected him
governor of the state, and he served two years. He takes an active
interest in the affairs of the Grand Army of the Republic, and was
chosen commander-in-chief of that organization in 1890. General Alger
has rendered valuable service to his party in various state and national
campaigns, and has gained a reputation as an enthusiastic worker in
the political field. Only his loyalty to other candidates prevented him,
on one or two occasions, from allowing his name to be urged for the
presidential nomination, and, indeed, he received a handsome vote in
the convention of 1888. He has many friends in both political parties, and is recognized as a man of unblemished character and marked
ability.

RUSSELL ALEXANDER ALGER
36

LYMAN J. GAGE.

IT was while employed as night watchman in a Chicago lumber yard that the opportunity of his life came to Lyman J. Gage. He was offered the position of bookkeeper for the Merchants' Savings, Loan and Trust Company, and accepting it, he began a career which eventually led him to the highest position in connection with any such financial institution, the presidency of the First National Bank, of Chicago. Born in De Ruyter, Madison County, N. Y., June 28, 1836, Mr. Gage came to Chicago in the fall of 1855, very poor but full of energy and pluck. Accepting the first employment that offered, he became a man of all work in a planing mill and lumber yard, being reduced to the station of night watchman in 1858, when the Merchants' Loan and Trust Company gave him a chance. He rose rapidly to the office of cashier, and in 1868 he went to the First National Bank to occupy a similar position. He became vice-president and general manager of that institution in 1882, and was elected president in January, 1891. Mr. Gage was one of the promoters of the World's Columbian Exposition, and was one of four men to practically guarantee that Chicago would redeem its pledge to raise $10,000,000 for the Fair. It was his genius and tact which largely made the great enterprise what it was. He was unanimously elected president of the World's Fair directors, but his duties as president of the bank compelled him to resign. Over ten years ago a high compliment was paid to Mr. Gage's genius for financiering by his election to the presidency of the American Bankers' Association. He is a man of genial disposition and fine personal appearance.

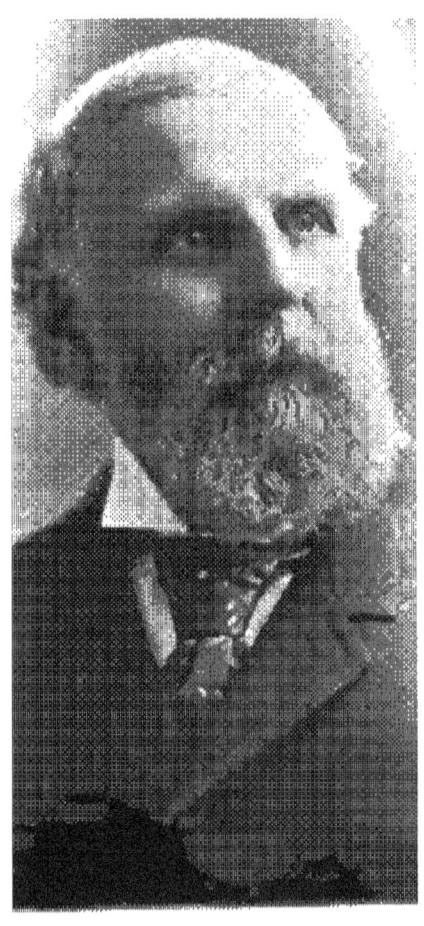

LYMAN J. GAGE
37

HARRIET BEECHER STOWE.

SINCE the publication of "Uncle Tom's Cabin" no book by an American writer, or, perhaps it may be said, by any writer in the world, has reached the standard of popularity and circulation established by it. Its author has produced better things, from a purely literary point of view, but her name and fame are inseparably associated with her first story. Mrs. Harriet Beecher Stowe, who was the sixth child of Rev. Dr. Lyman Beecher, was born in Litchfield, Conn., June 12, 1812, and was educated at the Litchfield Academy. At the age of twelve she wrote compositions on profound themes, and at the age of fourteen taught a class in "Butler's Analogy." In 1832 she removed with her father's family to Cincinnati, where she was married in 1836 to Professor Calvin Ellis Stowe. Subsequently she made several visits to the South, and fugitive slaves were often sheltered in her house and assisted to escape to Canada. In 1849 she published "The Mayflower, or Short Sketches of the Descendants of the Pilgrims," and in 1851, while living at Brunswick, Me., where her husband had a chair in Bowdoin College, she wrote "Uncle Tom's Cabin, or Life Among the Lowly." It was published serially in the "National Era," and in 1852 appeared in book form. Nearly five hundred thousand copies were sold in the United States alone within the five years following its publication. It has been translated into twenty languages and dramatized in various forms. Mrs. Stowe traveled extensively in Europe for several years, and has published a number of other books, among them "The Minister's Wooing," "Dred; a Tale of the Great Dismal Swamp," "Old Town Folks," "The True Story of Lady Byron's Life," and "Lady Byron Vindicated."

HARRIET BEECHER STOWE
41

THEODORE ROOSEVELT.

VERY few men in the United States have made such a record at such an age as has Theodore Roosevelt. No other young man of the old New York families inheriting wealth and position has done anything to compare with him. He was born in New York City, October 27, 1858. He graduated from Harvard, and the next year was elected to the New York Assembly, on the Republican ticket. Young as he was he led the minority in 1882. He was re-elected, and, in the face of bitter opposition, carried through the state civil service reform law and other measures equally important, securing, among other things, a great improvement in the management of city affairs. He was chairman of the New York delegation to the National Republican Convention in 1884, and an unsuccessful candidate for mayor of New York in 1886. In 1889 he was appointed a member of the United States Civil Service Commission, and by his tact, fearless honesty and force of character, made civil service reform something real and tangible. As police commissioner he was instrumental in effecting the recent reconstruction of the police system of New York City. He has been advancing steadily in the literary world as in the political. He owns a ranch in the northwest, spends a portion of his time there, and his works have in many instances the flavor of that region in them. Among his books are: "History of the Naval War of 1812," "Hunting Trips of a Ranchman," "Life of Thomas H. Benton," "Life of Gouverneur Morris," "Ranch Life and the Hunting Trail," "Winning of the West," "The Wilderness Hunter," and "History of New York." He is a splendid young American, one whose career is being watched with interest by a host of people.

THEODORE ROOSEVELT.

THEODORE THOMAS.

THE man to whom, more than to any one else in this country, is due the present appreciation of the modern school of German music is Theodore Thomas. He occupies an exalted and unique position among the musicians of America. Mr. Thomas was born in Essen, Hanover, Germany, October 11, 1835, and received his musical education principally from his father. He first played the violin in public at the age of six. In 1845 he came with his parents to the United States, and for two years played violin solos at concerts in New York. He then traveled for a time in the South, and returning to New York, in 1851, played at concerts and at the opera, at first as one of the principal violinists and afterward as orchestral leader, until 1861. In connection with others, he began a series of chamber concerts in 1855, which were continued until 1869. His first symphony concerts were given in 1864, and extended until he left New York, in 1878, to take the direction of the College of Music at Cincinnati. He remained in Cincinnati until 1880, and then returned to New York, where he continued his work as conductor of the Brooklyn Philharmonic Society and the New York Philharmonic Society, occasionally making concert tours, and giving a series of "summer night" concerts in various cities. He was conductor of the American Opera Company from 1885 to 1887. In 1888, after a successful season in Chicago, he disbanded his orchestra and severed his New York connections, subsequently establishing himself in Chicago, where he organized a new orchestra and where he still remains. He was conductor of the orchestral music at the World's Fair in 1893, where his wide reputation was still further extended.

THEODORE THOMAS.

JOHN IRELAND.

NOTED for his world-wide liberality, and for a patriotism that
embraces humanity, Archbishop Ireland, of St. Paul, is as popular outside his church as he is within its sacred precincts. As an
orator he has gained a national reputation. He was born in Burn-
church County, Kilkenny, Ireland, September 11, 1838. His parents
emigrated to the United States when he was a boy, and settled in
St. Paul, Minn. He went to France in September, 1853, entered the
Petit Seminaire of Meximeux, and finished the course in four years,
half the usual time. After studying theology in the Grand Seminaire,
at Hyeres, he returned to St. Paul in 1861, and was ordained in
December of that year. He served as chaplain of the Fifth Minnesota
regiment during a part of the Civil war, and was afterward appointed
rector of the Cathedral at St. Paul. In 1869 he organized the first
total abstinence society in the state. In 1870 he went to Rome as
the accredited representative of Bishop Grace at the Vatican. After
his consecration as coadjutor bishop of St. Paul in 1875, he undertook
the work of colonization in the Northwest. He made large purchases
of land in Minnesota, which were taken up by nine hundred Roman
Catholic colonists. He then bought twelve thousand acres of land with
equally satisfactory results. In 1887 he visited Rome in the interest
of a Roman Catholic University, and was subsequently appointed archbishop of St. Paul. The Catholics of that diocese are devoted to him,
and he has hosts of warm friends outside the church. Archbishop
Ireland was for several years president of the State Historical Society,
of Minnesota, and has always taken an active interest in the development of the Northwest.

JOHN IRELAND.

15

CHAUNCEY MITCHELL DEPEW.

CURIOUSLY enough, one of the greatest railroad magnates in the country, and a man whose abilities and high standing have even caused him to be talked about as a presidential possibility, is best known to the general public as an after-dinner speaker. Chauncey M. Depew was born in Peekskill, N. Y., April 23, 1834. He was graduated at Yale in 1856, and in a few years was admitted to practice. In 1861 and 1862 he was a member of the New York Assembly, and in 1863 was elected Secretary of State. He held other political offices at a later date, but resigned them to engage in the practice of his profession. From 1866 until 1869 Mr. Depew was attorney for the Harlem Railroad Company, after which he was counsel for the consolidated New York Central & Hudson River Railroad Company until 1882, when he became second vice-president of that corporation. In the meantime, in 1872, he was defeated as a candidate for lieutenant-governor of New York, and in 1874 the legislature appointed him regent of the state university. He was elected president of the New York Central in 1885, and still holds that position, besides being president of the West Shore Railroad Company. Mr. Depew is a man of genial disposition, with a hearty hand-clasp for everybody. He is a delightful conversationalist, a great orator, and a statesman whose views have on more than one occasion been demonstrated as broad and sound. He has infinite tact, a quality so often lacking in public men that its possession may be almost counted an added sense and greatness. A shrewd financier, a diplomat, a brilliant speaker, full "of infinite jest" and humor, an able business man, his versatility has made him a marked man in the affairs of the country.

CHAUNCEY MITCHELL DEPEW.
47

LEW WALLACE.

BLESSED with a happy combination of talents and abundant opportunities for turning them to account, General Lew Wallace, of Indiana, has made his mark as a lawyer, as a soldier, as a politician, as a diplomat, and as a writer. He was born in Brookville, Ind., April 10, 1827, and, after receiving a thorough education, studied law. During the Mexican war he entered the army as first lieutenant. Thereafter he practiced his profession at Covington and Crawfordsville until the beginning of the Civil war, when he was appointed adjutant-general of Indiana, and became colonel of volunteers. Subsequently he was commissioned brigadier-general and then major-general of volunteers. He was at the capture of Fort Donelson and Shiloh, and in 1863 prevented the capture of Cincinnati by the Confederates. His troops were defeated at the battle of Monocracy July 9, 1864, and he was removed from his command by General Halleck, but was reinstated by General Grant. After the war General Wallace was governor of Utah by federal appointment from 1878 to 1881, and United States minister to Turkey from 1881 to 1885. Since that time he has devoted himself to the practice of law and to literature at his home in Crawfordsville. His publications are very popular and have had an enormous sale. They include "The Fair God," 1873; "Ben Hur: a Tale of the Christ," 1880; "The Boyhood of Christ," 1883; and "The Prince of India," 1893. In personal appearance Lew Wallace is the rugged soldier; in social life he is the refined scholar and genial gentleman; in character he is the embodiment of those qualities which go to make the highest type of American manhood. As a lecturer and public speaker he has gained considerable fame.

LEW WALLACE.

JOHN WANAMAKER.

—

ESTEEMED more as a philanthropist, as a reformer, and as an exemplary citizen than for any distinction gained by position or wealth, John Wanamaker is a man whose life furnishes a standard for the emulation of the American youth. Born near Philadelphia, July 11, 1838, he attended a country school until he was fourteen, and then obtained employment in the city as messenger boy in the publishing house of Troutman & Hayes at a small salary. Subsequently the family lived for a time in Kosciusko County, Indiana, but returned to Philadelphia in 1856, where young Wanamaker eventually obtained employment in Tower Hall, the largest clothing house in that city. In 1861 he and the young man who was destined to become his brother-in-law opened a small store, and the business of Wanamaker & Brown was established. It grew to be the largest retail clothing house in America. A second store was started in the city, and, afterward, several branch houses. After the Centennial Exposition of 1876, with the financial management of which he was prominently connected, Mr. Wanamaker opened the great general store in Philadelphia, which continues to be one of the wonders of the age. He has many times declined public office, but in 1889 accepted the portfolio of Postmaster-General in President Harrison's Cabinet, and introduced into the department the most approved business methods. From early youth Mr. Wanamaker has been deeply interested in Sunday-school and temperance work. In 1858 he founded the Sunday-school that has since grown into the famous "Bethany." He was for eight years president of the Philadelphia Young Men's Christian Association, and his gifts to religious and charitable institutions have been numerous and liberal.

JOHN WANAMAKER.

NELSON APPLETON MILES.

—

FOR conspicuous daring, for brilliant displays of coolness and courage, and for remarkable achievements as an Indian fighter, Gen. Nelson A. Miles has made a record of which every patriotic American should be proud. General Miles was born in Westminster, Mass., August 8, 1839. After receiving an academic education he engaged in mercantile pursuits until the beginning of the Civil war, when he entered the volunteer service as lieutenant in the Twenty-second Massachusetts infantry. In 1862 he was commissioned lieutenant-colonel of the Sixty-first New York volunteers, and served with the Army of the Potomac until the close of the war, being steadily promoted for gallantry until he attained the rank of major-general. In 1866 he received an appointment in the Regular army as colonel of the Fortieth infantry, and in 1869 was transferred to the Fifth infantry. He defeated the Cheyenne, Kiowa and Comanche Indians, on the borders of the Staked Plains, in 1875, and in 1876 subjugated the hostile Sioux and other Indians in Montana. In the same year he captured the Nez Perces under Chief Joseph, and in 1878 captured a band of Bannocks near the Yellowstone Park. He was commissioned brigadier-general in 1880, commanded for five years the Department of the Columbia, for one year the Department of the Missouri, and was transferred to Arizona in April, 1886. After a difficult campaign against the Apaches under Geronimo and Natchez, he compelled those chiefs to surrender, September 4, 1886. He was assigned to the Department of the Pacific, promoted to major-general, and later placed in command of the Division of the Missouri. In 1891 he had charge of the Indian war in the Northwest. In 1895 he was appointed commander of the army, in place of Gen. John M. Schofield, retired.

NELSON APPLETON MILES.

53

ADOLPHUS WASHINGTON GREELEY.

IF a taste of adventure be one of the characteristics of the present head of the United States Signal Service, then there must be one man in the world whose taste has been pretty fully gratified. Adolphus Washington Greeley was born in Newburyport, Mass., March 27, 1844, graduated from the Brown High School, and at the beginning of the war enlisted in the Nineteenth Massachusetts Infantry. In 1863 he was promoted to be a lieutenant of colored infantry and arose steadily in the service, until in 1875 he was brevetted major-general of volunteers for faithful service in the field. He received a commission as second lieutenant in the Regular army, was promoted to first lieutenant and attached to the Signal Service. In 1881 he was placed in command of an expedition to the Arctic regions to assist in the establishment of the thirteen circumpolar stations decided upon by the Hamburg Geographical Congress. He sailed in the "Proteus," July 7, 1881, and after great hardships reached a point 81.44 degrees north and 64.45 degrees west. He made important discoveries of lakes and mountains in Grinnell's Land and added much in other ways to our knowledge of the Arctic circle, but found himself without means of returning, the relief expedition promised having failed. Awful suffering ensued. Sixteen of the party died of starvation, one was drowned and one was shot. The third expedition sent to his aid succeeded and those left of the party were rescued when, two days later, they must all have been dead. In 1887 President Cleveland appointed the intrepid explorer, the man who had so endured, to the command of the Signal Service with the rank of brigadier-general, a position he now holds.

ADOLPHUS WASHINGTON GREELEY.

THOMAS NELSON PAGE.

ONE of those who have brought the heart of the South nearer to the heart of the North, just as have Joel Chandler Harris and George W. Cable, is Thomas Nelson Page. His work is known throughout the United States and to a certain extent, abroad. He is a genial and gifted story writer, one who knows the very pulse of a region and has reproduced its heartbeats in his works. He was born in Oakland, Hanover County, Va., April 23, 1853, and grew to manhood on the family plantation, a part of the original grant to his ancestor, Thomas Nelson. He was educated at Washington Lee University and, after graduating, studied law and subsequently engaged in its practice at Richmond, Va. He succeeded in his profession, but that was not to be his chief work. He drifted into the way of writing stories and poems in the negro dialect, and one of the stories, entitled "Marse Chan: a Tale of the Civil War," when published, in 1884, attracted national attention. It was followed by "Meh Lady" and others in the same vein, showing equally the keen perception and sympathy and remarkable gift of expression of the writer. There was but one future for the young lawyer and he has become recognized as one of the brilliant authors of the times. Among his published books are "In Ole Virginia," "Two Little Confederates," and others equally charming. He knows his region and the very heartbeat of its people. He is industrious, but the world has gone well with him, and this man who can tell such delightful and educating stories, as none other can of the country he knew in his childhood, is not working as vigorously as he should just now. But it is in him and he cannot help writing.

THOMAS NELSON PAGE.

WILLIAM DEERING.

A SINGLE generation has worked a complete revolution in agriculture, a revolution that has placed America where it leads the world. In this revolution no name is more prominent than that of William Deering, the head of the Deering Harvester Works, at Chicago, one of the largest manufactories of grain and grass-cutting machinery in the world. Since his birth at South Paris, Me., April 25, 1826, Mr. Deering's whole life has been one of untiring industry. He received a common-school and academic education, and early in life entered the South Paris woolen mills, where he was intrusted with the management of the business soon after reaching his majority. From this he naturally found his way into the wholesale dry goods business, and, later on, established one of the leading dry goods commission houses of New York and Boston, well known as Deering, Milliken & Co. As early as 1870 Mr. Deering became interested financially in the manufacture of the Marsh harvester, invented by the Marsh brothers in central Illinois in the early sixties, and in 1873, in order to protect his capital invested in this business, Mr. Deering came west. He at once took active hold of the business, and by his remarkable ability gave it an impetus that brought it immediately to the forefront. He aided other inventors and increased to their present magnitude the greatness of the works established. Personally, Mr. Deering is of a tall and powerful build, and, though sixty-eight years old, is active, and seems to have lost not a whit of his youthful alertness and vigor. He has given extensively and widely to charities, and is not merely a financier, a bold and fearless manufacturer, but a broad philanthropist and a kindly Christian gentleman.

WILLIAM DEERING.
59

CHARLES ANDERSON DANA.

N OT as a journalist, merely, but also as a critic, historian and
politician, has greatness been achieved by Charles A. Dana, editor of the New York "Sun." His manifold ability and industry have
placed him well in the lead of the newspaper managers of today. Mr.
Dana was born at Hinsdale, N. H., August 8, 1819. He was educated at Harvard, and in 1842 joined the Brook Farm Community in
its socialistic venture. Two years later he took the management of
the "Harbinger," a weekly paper devoted to social reform and literature, and in 1847 became connected with the staff of the New York
"Tribune." He attained the position of managing editor of that paper,
and the development of his genius for journalism was largely instrumental in making it the leading organ of anti-slavery sentiment
just before the war, with an extraordinary influence and circulation.
Leaving the "Tribune" in April, 1862, he entered the service of the
government, and from 1863 to 1865 was assistant Secretary of War.
He then became editor of the Chicago "Republican," which failed of
success. In 1868 he organized the stock company that now owns the
New York "Sun," and for over twenty-six years has been actively
and continuously engaged in the management of that successful journal.
Mr. Dana collaborated with Gen. James H. Wilson in writing a "Life
of Ulysses S. Grant." He also edited "The Household Book of
Poetry," and, in connection with Rossiter Johnson, compiled "Fifty Perfect Poems." As an editor, Mr. Dana is trenchant and fearless; as a
critic, able and opinionated; as a politician, aggressive and bitter. The
"Sun" is conducted as an independent Democratic journal, and from a
literary standpoint ranks high.

CHARLES ANDERSON DANA.

JULIA WARD HOWE.

FEW names of women are more widely known than that of Julia Ward Howe, essayist, poetess, philanthropist and public speaker. She was born in New York City, May 27, 1819, her parents being Samuel Ward and Julia Cuttle Ward. Her ancestors included the Huguenot Marions, of South Carolina, Governor Sam Ward, of Rhode Island, and Roger Williams, the apostle of religious tolerance. Her father, a banker, gave her every advantage of a liberal education. She was instructed at home by capable teachers in Greek, German, French and music, and the ambitious and earnest girl improved her opportunities. In 1843 she became the wife of Dr. Samuel G. Howe and went abroad for a season. She had, when only seventeen years of age, produced several clever essays and reviews, and in 1852 published her first volume of poems. A drama in blank verse, written in 1853, was produced in both New York and Boston. Other works followed, and during the war Mrs. Howe became nationally prominent because of her stirring patriotic songs. In 1867 she visited Greece with her husband, where they won the gratitude of the people of that country because of aid extended in the struggle for national independence. In 1868 Mrs. Howe first took part in the suffrage movement. She has since preached, written and lectured much, and, notwithstanding her advanced age, still enjoys a life of almost ceaseless activity. Among her many works the "Battle Hymn of the Republic" is, perhaps, most widely known and most likely to remain a permanently admired masterpiece in American literature, but in all she has written there has been displayed the same earnestness and poetic gift and the same finished scholarship.

JULIA WARD HOWE.

ROBERT COLLYER.

THE story of that remarkable blacksmith, Elihu Burritt, has a parallel in the early life of Dr. Robert Collyer, the eminent Unitarian clergyman. Dr. Collyer was born in Keighly, Yorkshire, England, December 8, 1823. His father was a blacksmith, and the son was compelled to earn his living in a factory. He attended night school for two winters, and at the age of fourteen he was apprenticed to a blacksmith. In 1850 he came to America and worked at his trade in Shoemakerstown, Penn., where he remained nine years. Having become a Methodist he preached the Gospel on Sundays, and his wisdom and glowing eloquence soon raised him above the shop into scholastic and theological circles. As a result of his studies, to which he applied himself most diligently, his religious views changed in the direction of Unitarianism, and after being expelled from the Methodist Conference he became a Unitarian clergyman and removed to Chicago to take charge of a mission among the poor. In 1860 he organized Unity Church, Chicago, of which he was the pastor until 1879, when he went to New York to assume charge of the Church of the Messiah, which post he still holds. Dr. Collyer has written several books, and his lectures have been widely popular, especially his favorite lecture, "Grit." The poetic instinct is developed in him to a degree that makes all his prose merely another form of poetry. Among the best of his published poems, and one that will live to be read and admired by future generations, is a psalm of thanksgiving written after the great Chicago fire of 1871. Dr. Collyer seems to always look on the sunny side of life, and his conversation is full of entertaining and amusing reminiscences. His personality is described in the one word lovable.

ROBERT COLLYER
65

CORNELIUS VANDERBILT.

IN the directory of the financial world the name that stands out most conspicuously is Vanderbilt. The present head of the family of that time, Cornelius Vanderbilt, is the eldest grandson of the famous Cornelius who amassed an enormous fortune by shrewd business ventures, and whose genius as a financier seems to have been inherited by his namesake. Mr. Vanderbilt was born in Staten Island, N. Y., November 27, 1843. He was educated in private schools, and received a thorough business training. From 1867 until 1877 he was treasurer of the New York & Harlem Railroad Company, then served as vice-president until 1886, and afterward as president of that corporation. He was made president of the Canadian Southern Railway in 1883, and after the death of his father, William H. Vanderbilt, in 1885, he became a director in thirty-four different railroad companies. He is a trustee of many of the charitable, religious and educational institutions of New York City, where he resides in one of the handsomest private residences in the world. Among Mr. Vanderbilt's benefactions are the gift of a building in New York City for the use of railroad employes, a contribution of $100,000 for the Protestant Episcopal Cathedral, and a collection of drawings by the old masters and a painting of the Horse Fair, by Rosa Bonheur, to the Metropolitan Museum of Art. Although his wealth is estimated at over a hundred millions, Mr. Vanderbilt applies himself closely to his business, and personally directs the many railroad enterprises of which he is the head. In his everyday life he is quiet but affable, free from affectation, and stands upon the plane of the thorough-going business man. He has undoubtedly inherited the executive ability of his grandfather.

64

CORNELIUS VANDERBILT.

67

ADLAI EWING STEVENSON.

--

IN a great measure, no doubt, the credit of swinging Illinois into the Democratic column, which was one of the astonishing results of the national election in 1892, belongs to Vice-President Stevenson. A man of somewhat retiring disposition, he had nevertheless come to be recognized as a power in his own state, and was even seriously considered for the first place on the presidential ticket, although he was a Cleveland man himself. Mr. Stevenson was born in Christian County, Kentucky, fifty-nine years ago, and was educated at Centre College, Danville. He afterward married the daughter of the president of the college, Dr. Lewis Green, and removed to Bloomington, Ill., whither his family had preceded him. There he studied law in the office of the late David Davis, and after practicing his profession in Metamora and Bloomington until 1874, he was elected to Congress on the Democratic ticket. He failed of re-election in 1876, but was again successful in 1878. In 1880 and 1882 he was defeated by small majorities. In 1885 President Cleveland appointed him First Assistant Postmaster-General, and he became one of the most popular officers of that administration. He was much talked of by western Democrats as a presidential possibility prior to the campaign of 1892, but the great mass of the party looked to Grover Cleveland for deliverance, and Mr. Stevenson was accordingly nominated for the vice-presidency. Mr. Stevenson has been a successful lawyer and business man, and is regarded in his section as a man of uncommon ability and strength of character. He is energetic and decisive in his actions, and while First Assistant Postmaster-General he excited some comment by removing many incumbents from office.

ADLAI EWING STEVENSON.

EDMUND CLARENCE STEDMAN.

ENGLAND had her banker-poet, the learned Samuel Rogers, and America has a celebrity who divides his attention between poetic literature and the New York Stock Exchange. Edmund Clarence Stedman has unquestionably taken a permanent place in the foremost rank of American poets. He was born in Hartford, Conn., October 8, 1833, and while attending Yale College in 1851 his poem of "Westminster Abbey," published in the "Yale Literary Magazine," received a first prize. He became editor of the Norwich "Tribune" in 1852, and of the Winsted "Herald" in 1854, and two years later went to New York City, where for many years he contributed to the leading periodicals. Some of his poems became so popular that he collected and issued them under the title of "Poems, Lyric and Idyllic." After a hard struggle for a competence he joined the editorial staff of the New York "World" in 1860, and was war correspondent until 1863. He then purchased a seat in the Stock Exchange and became a broker, continuing his literary work during his leisure hours. From time to time he issued volumes of his selected poems, including "Alice of Monmouth," "The Blameless Prince," "Poetical Works," etc. In 1874, with Thomas Bailey Aldrich, he edited "Cameos," selected from the works of Walter Savage Landor, and the poems of Austin Dobson. About 1875 Mr. Stedman began to devote his attention to critical writing, and subsequently produced "Victorian Poets" and "Poets of American Literature." He has since compiled and edited the "Library of American Literature," in ten volumes, besides issuing several additional books of his own works. His poems delivered on public occasions have always attracted attention by their excellence.

EDMUND CLARENCE STEDMAN.

SAMUEL LANGHORNE CLEMENS.

BESIDES being the prince of American humorists, and one of the
most fascinating story tellers in the world, Samuel L. Clemens,
better known as "Mark Twain," has established for himself a high
reputation as a man of letters. The story of his life is an interesting
one. Born in Florida, Monroe County, Mo., November 30, 1835, he
was apprenticed to a printer at the age of thirteen, and worked at his
trade in Cincinnati, St. Louis, Philadelphia and New York. In 1851
he became a pilot on the Mississippi River steamboats. In 1861 he
went to Nevada where, in the following year, he became editor of the
Virginia City "Enterprise," and first used the nom de plume that afterward became famous. He went to San Francisco in 1865, and was
for five months a reporter for the "Morning Call." After an unsuccessful venture at gold mining he went to the Hawaiian Islands in
1866, returning six months later to deliver humorous lectures. He
then went East, and published "The Jumping Frog and Other Sketches."
In 1867 he went abroad with a party of tourists, and on his return
published "Innocents Abroad." He next edited the Buffalo "Express."
After his marriage he settled in Hartford, Conn., where he has since
resided. He afterward lectured extensively in this country and in Europe, and in 1872 wrote "Roughing It." Then came "The Gilded
Age," written in conjunction with Charles Dudley Warner, and later
"Tom Sawyer," "A Tramp Abroad," "The Stolen White Elephant,"
"The Prince and the Pauper," "Huckleberry Finn," "Pudd'n-Head
Wilson," and other volumes. In 1884 he established in New York
the publishing house of C. L. Webster & Co., which failed in 1894.
Mr. Clemens' works have been translated into several languages.

CHARLES HENRY PARKHURST.

PERHAPS nothing else in recent years has done so much to create a sentiment against the New York organization known as Tammany Hall, as the persistent and vigorous onslaughts of Rev. Dr. Charles H. Parkhurst, who, in his capacity as president of the Society for the Prevention of Crime, undertook to demonstrate and to break up the system of paid police protection under which, he declared, all kinds of vice, disorder and criminal immorality had abnormally flourished in that city. Dr. Parkhurst was born in Framingham, Mass., April 17, 1842, and was graduated at Amherst in 1866. He studied theology at Halle in 1869, and at Leipsic in 1872 and 1873, during the intervals of which studies he was principal of the High School in Amherst, and professor of Williston Seminary at Easthampton, Mass. From 1874 to 1880 he was pastor of the Congregational Church at Lenox, Mass., and was then called to the Madison Square Presbyterian Church, New York City, where he has since remained. Dr. Parkhurst has contributed to various magazines, and has published several volumes, including "The Forms of the Latin Verb, Illustrated by Sanskrit," "The Blind Man's Creed, and Other Sermons" and "Pattern in the Mount, and Other Sermons." In 1893 he began a personal investigation of the social evil in New York, which resulted in his subsequent crusade against the alleged corrupt organization controlling the police department of that city. Such sustained energy, such high courage in the face of criticism and opposition, and such unswerving persistence as Dr. Parkhurst has shown in this undertaking are not often witnessed. Physically, the doctor is a small man, but morally and intellectually he is a giant.

74

CHARLES HENRY PARKHURST.

SUSAN BROWNELL ANTHONY.

THERE is something that compels admiration in the fearless, persistent and self-sacrificing devotion with which that famous reformer, Susan B. Anthony, has labored for half a century in the cause to which she early dedicated her life. While one may not always recognize the wisdom of her course, there can be no doubt of her sincerity and heroism. Miss Anthony was born at South Adams, Mass., February 15, 1820. Her father was a Quaker. He settled in Rochester, N. Y., in 1646, where his daughter, after teaching school for a number of years, participated in the temperance movement, organizing societies and lecturing throughout the state. About 1857 she became prominent among the agitators for the abolition of slavery. Her energies, however, were chiefly directed to securing equal civil rights for women. In 1854 and 1855 she held conventions in the cause of female suffrage in every county in New York, and since then has addressed annual appeals and petitions to the Legislature. She was active in securing the act of the New York Legislature in 1860, giving to married women possession of their earnings and the guardianship of children. In the same year she started a petition in favor of leaving out the word "male" in the fourteenth amendment to the United States Constitution, and worked with the National Suffrage Association to induce Congress to secure to her sex the right to vote. Between 1870 and 1880 she lectured more than a hundred times a year in all of the Northern and some of the Southern States. She is the author of "The History of Woman Suffrage," in two volumes, in which she was assisted by Elizabeth Cady Stanton and Matilda Joslyn Gage.

SUSAN BROWNELL ANTHONY.

CARL SCHURZ

BY virtue of his intellectual power and oratorical ability the same sentiments that made Carl Schurz a revolutionist and a fugitive in his own country placed him on a high pedestal as a patriot and statesman in America. He was born in Liblar, near Cologne, Prussia, March 2, 1828, and educated at Bonn. As adjutant in the Revolutionary army in 1849 he took part in the defense of Rastadt, and upon the surrender of that fortress escaped to Switzerland. For a time he was a newspaper correspondent in Paris, and afterward a teacher in London, but in 1852 he came to the United States, eventually settling in Watertown, Wis., where in 1856 he began making speeches in German for the Republican party. In the following year he was an unsuccessful candidate for lieutenant-governor of Wisconsin, and soon afterward he began the practice of law in Milwaukee. His first speech in the English language, delivered in 1858, was widely published, and he became a power in Republican conventions and canvasses. President Lincoln appointed him Minister to Spain, but he resigned in December, 1861, to enter the Union army, and served throughout the war, attaining the rank of major-general. After the war he became the Washington correspondent of the New York "Tribune," but in the summer of 1866 he removed to Detroit, where he founded the "Post." In 1867 he became editor of the "Westliche Post," of St. Louis, and in 1869 was chosen United States senator from Missouri. He supported Greeley in 1872 and Hayes in 1876, and the latter appointed him Secretary of the Interior. Upon retiring from that office he became editor of the New York "Evening Post," which position he held until 1884.

CARL SCHURZ

ANNIE JENNESS MILLER.

SOME years ago a young and beautiful woman, highly cultured, began to expound with unquestionable taste and good judgment the principle of correct and artistic dressing. Her name is now a synonym for dress reform. Mrs. Annie Jenness Miller is a native of New Hampshire, where she was born January 28, 1859. She was educated in Boston, and before her marriage won considerable fame in Massachusetts as a woman of letters. Subsequently she took up the question that has given her fame in another direction, and she is now the most prominent and popular of all the leaders in the movement for reform in the matter of woman's dress. She has lectured in all the leading cities of the United States to crowded houses, and wherever she goes is always warmly received. She is one of the owners of a magazine published in New York, which is devoted to the aesthetics of physical development and artistic designs for dresses, and contains articles by the best writers on all topics of interest to women. Mrs. Miller's intelligence, taste and influence are widely acknowledged. She is the author of "Physical Beauty" and "Mother and Babe," the latter a work which furnishes information and patterns upon improved plans for the mother's and baby's wardrobes. She is a finished writer, and skillful in the elucidation of her subjects. All the progressive and reformatory movements of the day appeal to her and have her sympathy and support. Her ultimate hope is to establish at the National Capitol an institution for physical development and the highest art of self-culture, which shall be under the control of able students of anatomy, chemistry, and physical science. With this end in view, Mrs. Miller now makes Washington her home.

BENJAMIN HARRISON.

FROM the humble station of a farmer's son to the exalted position of President of the United States, describes in brief the career of Benjamin Harrison. He is the grandson of a president, General William Henry Harrison, and was born in his grandfather's house at North Bend, Ohio, August 20, 1833. He was graduated at Miami University, studied law in Cincinnati, and in 1854 removed to Indianapolis, which city has since been his home. Entering the war in 1862 as a second lieutenant in an Indiana regiment, he soon received the appointment of colonel, and in January, 1865, was brevetted brigadier-general. After the war he resumed his former office as reporter of the Supreme court at Indianapolis. In 1876 he ran for governor of his state, but was defeated by a small majority by "Blue Jeans" Williams, the Democratic candidate. He was chairman of the Indiana delegation at the National Convention held in Chicago in 1880, when General Garfield was nominated for the presidency. In that year General Harrison was chosen United States senator, which office he held until March 3, 1887. At the National Republican Convention held in Chicago in 1888, he was nominated by his party for the presidency, and subsequently elected. He was a candidate for re-election in 1892, but was buried under the Democratic "landslide" of that year. Among his personal characteristics it may be said that ex-President Harrison, as an impromptu public speaker, has demonstrated a gift of eloquence that is pointed and forcible. He has a faculty for seizing promptly upon a subject, ready-equipped and without loss of time, and presenting it clearly and concisely. He is an American of whom all are proud, regardless of political affiliations.

BENJAMIN HARRISON.
85

WILLIAM DEAN HOWELLS.

U NDOUBTEDLY the leading novelist and exponent of literature as
an art in the United States is the gifted author of "The Rise
of Silas Lapham," "The Lady of the Aroostook," "A Woman's Reason," and many other popular stories of the realistic school. William
Dean Howells was born at Martin's Ferry, Ohio, in 1837. His ancestors on the father's side were Welsh Quakers, and in all the generations, from the great-grandfather down, the family lived in an atmosphere of books and moral and literary refinement. Howells learned
the printer's trade in the office of his father, who conducted a weekly
paper in Hamilton, Ohio, and at the age of twenty-two became the
news editor of the Columbus "State Journal." He wrote a life of
Lincoln after the latter's nomination in 1860, and the President afterward appointed him Consul to Venice, where he resided from 1861 to
1865. Returning to America, he engaged in literary pursuits, and in
1871 became editor of the "Atlantic Monthly," a position which he
held until 1880, when he relinquished it to devote himself exclusively
to writing. In 1886 he made a salaried connection with "Harper's
Magazine," and created the department known as "The Editor's
Study." During recent years, however, he has done but little editorial
work. As a man of letters Mr. Howells is regarded by many as
far in advance of any other writer of the present day. In addition
to his novels he has written many poems, biographies, criticisms and
sketches of travel in foreign countries. During his residence in Venice
he mastered the Italian language and studied the literature of the country. Mr. Howells is recognized as the leader of the realistic school
of literature.

WILLIAM DEAN HOWELLS

FRANCES HODGSON BURNETT.

HAD she never written anything but "Little Lord Fauntleroy" and "That Lass o' Lowrie's," Frances Hodgson Burnett would have become widely known in literature. She was born in Manchester, England, November 24, 1849. She lived in Manchester and became familiar with the characteristics of the people of the Lancashire coal district, a fact which is shown repeatedly in her works. Trouble came to the family, the father died and the mother and children came to the United States and settled in Knoxville, Tenn., and afterward in Newmarket, in the same state. There were two sons and three daughters, and they worked very faithfully to secure the necessary income for the family. Frances had an idea that she might possibly earn something by writing for the magazines, and made the attempt. In 1872 she contributed to "Scribner's Magazine" an article entitled "Surly Tim's Trouble," which was a success. The next year she married Dr. Luan M. Burnett, of Knoxville, but continued her literary work. There were other works and then came what is possibly her greatest success, "Little Lord Fauntleroy," which first appeared as a serial in "St. Nicholas;" and was subsequently published in book form, both in the United States and England. Mrs. Burnett has become famous on two continents. The more prominent of her published works are: "Kathleen Mavourneen," "Lindsay's Luck," "Miss Crespigny," "Pretty Polly Pemberton," "Theo," "Haworth's," "Louisiana," "A Fair Barbarian," "Through One Administration," "Sara Crew," "Editha's Burglar," "Little St. Elizabeth," and other stories. Upon "That Lass o' Lowrie's," though, and "Little Lord Fauntleroy" rests chiefly her reputation.

FRANCES HODGSON BURNETT.

WILLIAM RALLS MORRISON.

INTIMATELY associated with much of the important Congressional legislation of a decade ago, and particularly with the fight for tariff reform that was waged by a wing of the Democratic party in that body, is the name of Col. William R. Morrison, of Illinois, the present chairman of the Interstate Commerce Commission. Colonel Morrison was born in Monroe County, Ill., September 14, 1825. After receiving an education at McKendree College, he served as a private in the Mexican war, and subsequently studied law and was admitted to the bar. He was clerk of Monroe County from 1852 to 1856, served in the Legislature for the next three years, and in 1861 entered the army as colonel of the Forty-ninth Illinois Regiment, and was wounded at Fort Donelson. While in command of his regiment in the field he was elected to Congress as a Democrat, and served from 1863 to 1865, but was defeated for the Thirty-ninth and Fortieth Congresses. He was again chosen in 1872, and served continuously until 1887. Colonel Morrison was the father of the tariff reform measure known as the "horizontal" bill, and did good work on many important committees. In March, 1887, President Cleveland appointed him a member of the Interstate Commerce Commission for five years. At the end of that period he was reappointed, and upon the retirement of Judge Thomas M. Cooley he became chairman of the commission, a post which he has since filled most acceptably. Colonel Morrison's reputation is that of a good lawyer, a brave soldier, a shrewd politician, and an earnest, aggressive legislator. He is a man of rugged constitution, and is as active and vigorous as when he first entered public life.

WILLIAM RALLS MORRISON.

iv

JAMES WHITCOMB RILEY.

PRACTICALLY alone in his occupation of a most interesting field of literature, James Whitcomb Riley has become justly famous as the "Hoosier Poet of America." His incomparable dialect verse presents to us many vivid character studies and pen-pictures of western farm life, permeated with the perfume of old-fashioned roses, the babbling of brooks, the whistle of the "Bob White" and robin, and all the objects, sounds and expressions familiar to those who have lived in the country. Mr. Riley was born in Greenfield, Ind., in 1852. As a boy he traveled much with his father, who was an attorney, and at an early age he left school to adopt the calling of a wandering sign writer. For some time he performed in a theatrical troupe, and became proficient in recasting plays and improvising songs. About 1875 he began to contribute to the Indianapolis papers verses in the Hoosier dialect, using the pen-name, "Benjamin F. Johnson of Boone." He exhibited his imitative powers by writing a piece called "Leonainie," which many literary critics were deluded into accepting as a poem of Edgar Allen Poe. He finally accepted an engagement with the Indianapolis "Journal," and in that paper, and latterly in the magazines, published numerous dialect and serious poems. He has issued a number of volumes, including "The Old Swimmin' Hole," "Afterwhiles," "Neighborly Poems," "Pipes o' Pan," "Green Fields and Running Brooks," "Rhymes of Childhood," "The Flying Islands of the Night," and others. As a public reader from his own works, Mr. Riley has been very successful. Indeed, if he were not a writer he might win as brilliant a reputation as an actor as he now enjoys in a literary capacity.

JAMES WHITCOMB RILEY.

MARY ASHTON RICE LIVERMORE.

—

MARY ASHTON RICE LIVERMORE is a woman of very earnest purpose, of wide information, and of decided force of character. She was born in Boston, Mass., December 19, 1821. She is of Welsh descent, and her father was an active fighter in the navy in the war of 1812. Her mother was a descendant of a well-known English family. The girl received a thorough education in the Boston public schools, then graduated at a female seminary at Charleston, Mass., and acquired, in addition to what an ordinary girl would get, a thorough classical education. She was then engaged as a teacher to go to Virginia, and among her duties was the teaching of a lot of slaves attached to a plantation. She came back a pronounced abolitionist. She taught in a private school near Boston on her return, but had acquired the gift of talking in public and utilized that power for talking against slavery and the slave trade. In 1845 she had become the wife of the Rev. E. P. Livermore, a Universalist minister, and, their tastes and aims being similar, they worked together happily and effectively. In 1857 the couple removed to Chicago, where Mrs. Livermore assisted her husband in the publication of the Universalist organ for the Mississippi valley. She was earnest in all that pertained to assisting the Union troops during the war, and made a most creditable record, which was widely recognized. Since the war Mrs. Livermore has been best known as associated with the woman suffrage movement in the United States. She is the author of a number of works, among which may be mentioned "What Shall We Do With Our Daughters?" and a number of articles in the "Arena," the "Chautauquan," the "Christian Advocate," and "Women's Journal."

MARY ASHTON RICE LIVERMORE

CHARLES FREDERICK CRISP.

POSSESSING in an unusual degree the quick mental grasp, the accurate judgment, the confident self-control, the promptness and firmness of decision, and the practical training which are among the essential qualifications of the successful parliamentarian, Mr. Crisp, as Speaker, became a power in the National House of Representatives. Mr. Crisp was born in Sheffield, England, where his parents were on a visit, January 29, 1845. He received a common-school education in Savannah and Macon, Ga., and in 1861 entered the Confederate Army as a lieutenant. He was a prisoner of war from May, 1864, until June, 1865. After his release he studied law, and practiced first at Ellaville and afterward at Americus, Ga., which is now his home. In 1872 he was appointed solicitor-general of the Southwestern Judicial Circuit, and held that office until the middle of 1877, when he became judge of the Superior Court of the same circuit. He resigned from the bench in September, 1882, to accept the Democratic nomination for Congress. He was permanent president of the Democratic Convention which assembled in Atlanta in April, 1883, to nominate a candidate for governor. Mr. Crisp was elected to the Forty-eighth Congress, and is now serving his sixth successive term in that body. He was elected Speaker of the House for the Fifty-second Congress, and was re-elected for the Fifty-third. In that position he added greatly to his popularity and influence in the House, and even his political opponents agree that his rulings and decisions have at all times shown careful consideration, unbiased by prejudice. He was succeeded in office by Thomas B. Reed, of Maine, who was elected Speaker of the House, for the Fifty-fourth Congress, in 1895.

CHARLES FREDERICK CRISP.

MARY MAPES DODGE.

FEW authors have possessed so happy a knack of combining enter-
tainment with instruction in writing for the young, or of making
the present moment both enjoyable and profitable for readers of any
age, as Mary Mapes Dodge, the talented editor of "St. Nicholas."
Mrs. Dodge is a native of New York City, where she was born January 26, 1838, and is the daughter of Prof. James J. Mapes, the distinguished promoter of scientific farming in the United States. She
was educated by private tutors, and early evinced a talent for literary
composition, as well as for music, drawing and modeling. At an
early age she was married to William Dodge, a lawyer of New York,
and it was after his death that she turned to literature as a means to
earn the money to educate her two sons. She wrote principally short
sketches for children, a volume of which was published in 1864 under
the name of "Irvington Stories." During the following year she published "Hans Brinker, or the Silver Skates." With Donald G. Mitchell
and Harriet Beecher Stowe, she was one of the earliest editors of
"Hearth and Home," conducting for several years the household and
children's department of that journal. In 1873, when the children's
magazine, "St. Nicholas," was started, she became its editor, and still
holds that position. Mrs. Dodge's story, "Hans Brinker," has been
translated into Dutch, French, German, Russian and Italian, and was
awarded a prize of fifteen hundred francs by the French Academy.
She has published a number of other volumes, both of prose and
poetry, and contributes to the "Atlantic Monthly," "Harper's Magazine," "Century," and other periodicals. She has a pleasant home in
New York, which is a literary center.

MARY MAPES DODGE

WADE HAMPTON.

PHYSICAL and mental vigor, unflinching courage in the face of opposition and love for truth and justice are dominant characteristics of that great southern leader, Senator Wade Hampton, of South Carolina. Born in Columbia, S. C., March 28, 1818, Mr. Wade was graduated at the University of South Carolina and afterward studied law, but with no intention of practicing. In early life he served in the legislature of his state, as a national Democrat, and, although a slave-holder, he had little affiliation with secession sentiments. His speech against the reopening of the slave trade was pronounced by the New York "Tribune" "a masterpiece of logic directed by the noblest sentiments of the Christian and patriot." At the beginning of the Civil war he enlisted in the Confederate service as a private, but soon raised a command which was known as "Hampton's Legion," and won distinction in many engagements. He was several times wounded, and attained the rank of lieutenant-general in 1864. After the war he at once engaged in cotton planting, but was not successful. In 1876 he was nominated for governor of South Carolina against Daniel H. Chamberlain. Each claimed to be elected and two governments were organized, but Chamberlain finally yielded his claims, and General Hampton served two years as governor. In 1878 he met with an accident by which he lost a leg, but, while his recovery was in doubt, he was elected to the United States Senate, in which body he served until 1891. In the Senate his course was that of a conservative Democrat. He advocated a sound currency, resisting all inflation, and generally acted in concert with Thomas A. Bayard, whose aspirations for the presidency he supported.

WADE HAMPTON.
99

BRONSON HOWARD.

STRONGLY equipped in the possession of a keen dramatic sense and a full knowledge of the art of the playwright, it is not to be wondered at that Bronson Howard's success has been greater than that of almost any other American dramatist now living. Indeed, it may be said that at the present time he is easily the leading exponent of that particular school of dramatic literature in which he has been engaged for nearly twenty-five years. Mr. Howard was born in Detroit, Mich., October 7, 1842. His education was begun in the public schools and finished in the New Haven Collegiate and Commercial Institute, after which, having developed a taste for writing, he adopted the profession of journalism. During his newspaper experience, which extended over a number of years, the work of the dramatic critic was especially attractive to him, and he finally decided to write a play. His first successful drama was "Saratoga," which was produced in New York in 1870, and was so well received that it was brought out in London in 1874. His next was "Diamonds," produced in 1872, and this was followed by "Hurricanes" in 1878. In the latter year also appeared "The Banker's Daughter," one of the best and most successful of Mr. Howard's plays. His other dramas have all been given a cordial reception by the theater-going public, among the most popular of them being "Wives," "Young Mrs. Winthrop," "One of Our Girls," "Met by Chance," "The Henrietta," "Shenandoah," and "Aristocracy." Mr. Howard is particularly happy in the invention of plots and dramatic situations, and his judgment is never at fault in the devising of scenes intended to work upon the emotions of an audience.

BRONSON HOWARD.

EDGAR WILSON NYE.

HUMOR, like wine, is not all of one brand, but usually, if it is genuine, bears the trade mark of its manufacturer. The particular brand which has the name of "Bill Nye" blown in the bottle is characteristic enough to be readily detected without the signature, and one of its chief virtues seems to be that it loses none of its effervescence and palatableness from being frequently uncorked. Edgar Wilson Nye - to use the name given him by his parents - was born in Shirley, Piscataqua County, Me., August 25, 1850. While he was still a child his family removed to Wisconsin, and he received his education at an academy in River Falls. Subsequently he went to Wyoming and settled at Laramie, where he studied law and was admitted to the bar in 1876. He became justice of the peace, United States Commissioner of Deeds, postmaster, and editor and proprietor of the Laramie "Boomerang," for which he wrote humorous sketches that were copied far and wide. He began to sign the name of Bill Nye to his articles, and soon his droll sayings were being quoted wherever the English language was spoken. He eventually disposed of his paper and his other interests in Wyoming, and established himself in a pleasant home at Hudson, Wis., but continued to contribute to periodicals. This occupation resulted in an engagement with a New York paper, and he eventually removed to that city, where he has since resided. For several years he has written a weekly syndicate letter, published simultaneously in various newspapers, and has lectured during the winter months. He has published in book-form "Bill Nye and the Boomerang," "The Forty Liars," "Baled Hay," "Blossom Rock," "Remarks," and "History of the United States."

EDGAR WILSON NYE.

MATTHEW STANLEY QUAY.

IT is generally admitted that the manager of the National Republican campaign in the year when Harrison was elected to the Presidency is quite capable of taking care of himself in the world. Very few shrewder politicians exist, even in a nation of politicians, than Matthew Stanley Quay, of Pennsylvania. He was born in Dillsburgh, York County, Pa., September 30, 1833. He graduated from Jefferson College in Pennsylvania in 1850, and began the study of law and was admitted to the bar in Pittsburg in 1854. In 1856 he was elected prothonotary of Beaver County and was re-elected in 1859. In 1861 he resigned his office to become a lieutenant in the Tenth Pennsylvania reserves, then became assistant commissary of the state, later private secretary of Governor Curtin, and, in 1862, colonel of the One Hundred and Thirty-fourth Pennsylvania volunteers. He was compelled by impaired health to leave the army, but participated as a volunteer in the assault made on Mary's Heights after he resigned his command. In 1865 Mr. Quay was elected to the Pennsylvania legislature and served until 1867, when he established and edited the Beaver "Radical." He served as secretary of the commonwealth, which office he resigned to accept the appointment of recorder of Philadelphia, but returned to the former position, retaining it until 1882. He became chairman of the Republican National committee in 1888, and conducted the campaign which resulted in the election of Harrison and Morton. In 1885 occurred his election as state treasurer of Pennsylvania by the largest vote ever given a candidate for that office. In 1887 he was elected United States senator for the term ending in 1893 and was re-elected at the expiration of that time.

MATTHEW STANLEY QUAY.

THOMAS BAILEY ALDRICH.

A S the nattily clever, as the graceful, the thorough, the adaptable and capable dealer with words and imaginations, and with an absolute genius, Thomas Bailey Aldrich stands, admittedly, at the head of American writers who presume to be ranked in the class thus designated. He was born in Portsmouth, N. H., November 11, 1836, and prepared for college, but the death of his father changed family plans, and he engaged in the mercantile business in New York City. He acquired a good education of his own impulse, and in the early fifties began contributions to the magazines. He did charming work for "Putnam's Magazine," the "New York Evening Mirror," and for the "Home Journal," in days when those wonderful men, N. P. Willis and William Morris, gave to the publication a national reputation. From 1870 to 1874 he was editor of "Every Saturday" in Boston, and since that date has devoted himself to the writing and publication of his works and to editorial duties. His poetry includes "Babie Bell," "The Dells," "The Course of True Love Never Did Run Smooth," "Pampinea and Other Poems," "Flower and Thorn;" later poems, "Friar Jerome's Beautiful Book," and an edition de luxe of "Lyrics and Sonnets." Among his prose works are "Story of a Bad Boy," "Marjory Daw and Other People," "Prudence Palfry," "The Queen of Sheba," "The Stillwater Tragedy," "From Ponkapog to Pesth," "Mercedes," and very many translations of magazine articles and stories. He is one of the most knowing, the most thoughtful, delicate, and daintiest of writers. To have written "Marjory Daw" alone, that quaint, sweet and adroit piece of work, would stamp a man as a genius.

THOMAS BAILEY ALDRICH.
107

LYMAN ABBOTT.

DISTINGUISHED as a clergyman, and as a successor of Henry Ward Beecher in the pulpit of the famous Plymouth Church, Rev. Lyman Abbott is also well known as an author, literary critic and journalist. The third son of Jacob Abbott; he was born in Roxbury, Mass., December 18, 1835, and graduated at the University of the City of New York in 1853. He studied law and was admitted to the bar in 1856, but soon abandoned law for theology, which he studied with his uncle, Rev. John S. C. Abbott, the author. He entered the ministry in 1860, his first pastoral charge being a Congregational church in Terre Haute, Ind., where he remained until 1865. He then became secretary of the American Union (Freedmen's) Commission, which office called him to New York and occupied him until 1868. In the meantime he was also pastor of the New England Church of that city, but resigned in 1869 to devote himself to literature and journalism. In conjunction with his brothers he wrote two novels, and for several years edited the "Literary Record" of "Harper's Magazine," at the same time conducting the "Illustrated Christian Weekly." He was afterward associated with Rev. Henry Ward Beecher in the editorship of the "Christian Union," and upon Mr. Beecher's retirement became editor-in-chief. Mr. Abbott has written a number of books of devotion and Biblical history, a "Life of Henry Ward Beecher," and has edited Mr. Beecher's sermons and lectures, in addition to his many contributions to periodical literature. In January, 1889, he received a call to the pastorate of Plymouth Church, Brooklyn, so many years identified with Mr. Beecher's labors, and has continued to fill that post to the present time.

CHARLES KENDALL ADAMS.

A MONG the great educators of the present day Charles Kendall
Adams, late president of Cornell University and now president
of the University of Wisconsin, occupies a high rank. He was born
at Derby, Vt., January 24, 1835. In the fall of 1855 he moved to
Iowa, where he prepared for college in the Denmark Academy, Iowa.
He entered the University of Michigan in the fall of 1857, where, after
graduation course of study, he took the Master's degree in 1862, and
immediately thereafter was appointed instructor in Latin and history, in
1863 assistant professor, and in 1867 professor with the privilege of
spending a year and a half in Europe. After hard study abroad he
returned and soon became a prominent figure in university affairs. In
1885 he was called to the presidency of Cornell University, a position
which he occupied until the summer of 1892. During the seven years
of his incumbency of that position the number of students was increased
from five hundred and sixty to more than fifteen hundred, and the
endowment of the university was increased by nearly two million dollars. In 1892 President Adams resigned the presidency of Cornell University, with the purpose of devoting his life henceforth to the writing
of history, but in 1893 accepted the call to the presidency of the University of Wisconsin. He is the author of many important works.
The degree of Doctor of Laws was conferred upon President Adams
by Harvard University in 1886. He is a member of many learned
societies, and in 1890 was president of the American Historical Association, and has earned a high place among the great thinkers, educators
and historians as a scholar of rare attainments and a writer of wonderful power and depth.

CHARLES KENDALL ADAMS.

JAMES BURRILL ANGELL

T O the performance of the duties connected with his responsible office, the president of the University of Michigan brings a vigorous and impressive personality, distinguished alike for moral and intellectual parts. James Burrill Angell was born in Scituate, R. I., January 7, 1829, and is a lineal descendant from Thomas Angell, who was one of the original settlers with Roger Williams of the Providence plantations. Mr. Angell was graduated at Brown University in 1849, and, after a period of travel and study in Europe, was appointed, in 1853, professor of modern languages and literature in that college. In 1860 he accepted the editorship of the Providence "Daily Journal," which place he occupied until 1866, when he was called to the presidency of the University of Vermont. In 1871 he became president of the University of Michigan, an office he has since continued to fill, except during the years 1880 and 1881, which he spent in China as United States Minister, appointed by President Hayes, and also as chairman of a special commission appointed to negotiate a treaty with China. This commission procured a treaty on commercial matters, and also one on Chinese immigration. In 1887 Mr. Angell was appointed by President Cleveland a member of the commission, with Hon. Thomas F. Bayard and Hon. W. L. Putnam, to settle by treaty with the British commissioners the fisheries difficulties on the Atlantic coast of Canada. President Angell is a frequent contributor to reviews and magazines, is a member of various educational societies, and in 1893 was elected president of the American Historical Association. He received from Brown University the degree of LL. D. · President Angell ranks high as an educator.

JAMES BURRILL ANGELL

113

RUSSELL SAGE.

WHATEVER genius a man may have in certain directions could not be developed in some countries as in the United States. A great astronomer or great inventor might make himself heard of in the Republic of Andorra, or in Guatemala, but such distinction could scarcely come to the man in either country whose gift might be only the faculty of doing well on a stock exchange. But Russell Sage, those who know him best say, would have become prominent as a financier wherever he might have been placed. In Patagonia he would have done well in hides. He is almost the representative man of a large and potent class of business men in this country, not the daring speculator—though on occasion bold enough—not the great administrator of huge enterprises, nor the originator of ventures in new fields, but a man of the old New England stock who lives long and builds shrewdly. Born in Oneida County, New York, August 4, 1816. Mr. Sage has been all his life a business man and for a very long time a prominent figure in Wall street. He is unique in his methods. It is not known that he ever manipulated a "corner," and, though he was once famous for his "puts and calls," it is said that he has curtailed even that branch of his business since one notable day in June, 1884, when he was reported to have lost $7,000,000. He is a man who realizes the present value of money. He loans money to banks and corporations and is a director in many things. He has strong friendships, and cried like a child when Jay Gould died. Nearly eighty years of age, he is active almost as a boy and constant at business. Though he dresses plainly he is a gallant of the old school, a courteous man, and has a keen appreciation of what is clever.

RUSSELL SAGE
115

WILLIAM VINCENT ALLEN.

THE junior senator from Nebraska has become widely known of late as one not afraid to assert himself at any time, since he did not hesitate in the Upper House of Congress to support, in a degree, the unpopular cause of the Coxeyites nor to assist in the defense of the leaders in that movement when they were arrested. William Vincent Allen was born in Midway, Madison County, Ohio, January 28, 1847, and removed with his step-father's family to Iowa in 1857. He was educated in the common schools of Iowa, and later attended for a time the Upper Iowa University at Fayette. He enlisted as a private in the Thirty-second Iowa volunteers, and at the close of his service in the army was on the staff of Gen. J. T. Gilbert. He then began the study of law and was admitted to practice in 1869. In 1884 he removed from Iowa to Nebraska, where he engaged in the work of his profession most successfully, and in the fall of 1891 was elected judge of the district court of the Ninth judicial circuit of Nebraska. In 1893 he was elected United States senator to succeed Algernon S. Paddock. His term of service will expire in 1899, so that there still remain some years for further advocacy of what Senator Allen holds to be the people's cause. He is resolute in his course when it is once decided upon, and is earnest and vigorous in debate. His attitude in favor of the various reform movements has made him popular, and he is looked upon as a political possibility of more than ordinary dimensions. He is recognized as having at least the courage of his convictions, a quality the American elector seems to recognize more and more of late as a necessary quality in one sent either to make laws, to interpret them, or to execute them.

WILLIAM VINCENT ALLEN.
117

WILLIAM TAYLOR ADAMS.

THOUSANDS of middle-aged men of today hold in loving remembrance the name of "Oliver Optic;" a name that was associated with their boyhood's pleasures quite as intimately as was that of Santa Claus himself. And "Oliver Optic" is still living, and is the patron saint of the children today, just as he was a generation ago. His real name is William Taylor Adams, and his home is in Boston. Mr. Adams was born in Medway, Mass., July 30, 1822. He was for twenty years a teacher in the public schools of Boston, fourteen years a member of the school committee of Dorchester, and one year a member of the legislature. He has devoted most of his life to writing for young people, with whom he has a warm sympathy. His literary career began in 1850, and he has produced over a thousand stories in newspapers, exclusive of his books. In early life he edited the "Student and Schoolmate," and in 1881 "Our Little Ones," but he is best known as an editor through "Oliver Optic's Magazine for Boys and Girls." His published works, issued mainly in series of several volumes each, include "In-Doors and Out," "Riverdale," "The Boat Club," "Woodville," "Young America Abroad," "Army and Navy," "Starry Flag," "Onward and Upward," "Yacht Club," "Great Western," etc. In fact, he has published about a hundred volumes in all, and the strangest thing about it is, that he is still writing. The fountain from which he draws seems to be inexhaustible, and his latest stories are as fresh and absorbingly interesting as his first. No writer ever exerted a greater or more wholesome influence on the minds and hearts of the young folks. Mr. Adams often says that he never quite got over being a boy himself.

WILLIAM TAYLOR ADAMS.

119

PHILIP D. ARMOUR.

—

ILLUSTRATING as he does the unflagging energy and enterprise that have made Chicago the most wonderful city, in some respects, in the world, as well as the philanthropic spirit that has given it a reputation for munificence, Philip D. Armour is a representative citizen of the western metropolis and a typical American. Born in Stockbridge, N. Y., May 16, 1832, Mr. Armour was educated in the district school. In 1851 he left home and went to California to seek his fortune. He returned in 1856 without having accomplished his purpose, and soon thereafter embarked in the commission business in Milwaukee, Wis. In 1863 he formed a partnership with John Plankington, of Milwaukee, in the packing business, and that arrangement was the beginning of the immense enterprises in which Mr. Armour has since been engaged, and which has made his name known all over the world. The Chicago establishment of P. D. Armour & Co. was founded in 1868, and there are now extensive branch houses in New York and Kansas City. All in all, the packing-houses in which Mr. Armour and his brothers are interested, form one of the most gigantic enterprises in the country. He gives his business his personal supervision, and has a wonderful capacity for work. The Armour Mission, founded by his brother but cherished and substantially endowed by himself, receives his attention every Sunday. Mr. Armour's latest magnificent present to the city of Chicago—the Armour Institute, fully endowed is of comparatively recent occurrence, and is numbered among the most princely gifts of the century on the part of a private citizen. He is a philanthropist in the best sense of the word, giving not only of his money but of his time and labor to the cause of charity.

PHILIP D. ARMOUR.

THOMAS FRANCIS BAYARD.

•

IT fell to the lot of a Democrat of the old school to first bear the
title of American Ambassador to the Court of St. James. President Cleveland was the first executive to confer this diplomatic rank
upon a citizen of the United States, and the appointment was given to
Thomas F. Bayard, of Delaware. Mr. Bayard comes of a family of
statesmen. He was born in Wilmington, Del., October 29, 1828, and
at an early age entered mercantile life, which he soon abandoned for
the study of law. In 1851 he was admitted to the bar, and two
years later was appointed United States District Attorney for Delaware,
but resigned that office in 1854. In 1869 he succeeded his father as
United States senator, and at once became a prominent figure in that
body. He was re-elected in 1875, and again in 1881, retaining his
seat in the Senate until March, 1885, when he entered Mr. Cleveland's
Cabinet as Secretary of State. Mr. Bayard has several times been
proposed as a presidential candidate, but the recollection of a famous
speech delivered by him at Dover, Del., in the early part of 1861, in
which his language was construed to express Southern sentiments, mil-
itated against his chances of election. Nevertheless, at the Democratic
National Convention at Cincinnati, in 1880, he received one hundred
and fifty-three and one-half votes on the first ballot, and in the convention of 1884 he was Mr. Cleveland's principal competitor for the
nomination. After his retirement from the office of Secretary of State,
in 1889, Mr. Bayard held no public office until his appointment as
Ambassador to the Court of St. James, in 1893. He is a man of
imposing presence, a power in debate, and during his career in the
Senate he was the recognized leader of the Democrats.

THOMAS FRANCIS BAYARD.

123

ALEXANDER GRAHAM BELL.

—

OUT of a long and careful study of vocal physiology, prosecuted with a view of improving the methods of instructing deaf-mutes, was developed the telephone, which has made the name of its inventor famous. Prof. A. Graham Bell is a son of the Scotch educator, Alexander Melville Bell. He was born in Edinburgh, Scotland, March 3, 1847, and was educated at the Edinburgh high school and Edinburgh University, receiving special training in his father's system for removing impediments in speech. He entered the University at London in 1867, and in 1870 emigrated with his father to Canada. In 1872 he took up his residence in the United States, introducing with success his father's system of deaf-mute instruction and becoming professor of vocal physiology in Boston University. He had been interested for many years in the transmission of sound by electricity, and had devised many forms of apparatus for the purpose, but his first public exhibition of the telephone was in Philadelphia in 1876. Its complete success has made him wealthy. His invention of the "photophone," in which a vibratory gleam of light is substituted for a wire in conveying speech, has also attracted much attention, but has never been practically used. Professor Bell has put forth the theory that the present system of educating deaf-mutes is wrong, as it tends to restrict them to one another's society, so that marriages between the deaf are common, and therefore the number of deaf-mute children born is on the increase. He is a member of various learned societies, and has published many scientific papers setting forth his theories and the results of his experiments. He has lived for some time in Washington, D. C. Prof. Bell is thoroughly devoted to the cause of science.

ALEXANDER GRAHAM BELL

EDWARD BELLAMY.

UTOPIAN dreams of perfected socialism have not been few during the nineteenth century, but of all the schemes that have been proposed for the reorganization of society, none has attracted so much attention or received such serious consideration, because of its apparent practicability, as that embodied in Edward Bellamy's remarkable story, "Looking Backward." Mr. Bellamy is a writer of marked ability. He was born in Chicopee Falls, Mass., in 1850, and was educated at Union College and in Germany. He studied law and was admitted to the bar, but never practiced that profession, as he preferred a literary life. During 1871 and 1872 he was on the staff of the New York "Evening Post," and for the five years following was an editorial writer and critic for the Springfield "Union." His health failing him, he made a voyage to the Sandwich Islands in 1876, and upon his return in 1877 became one of the founders of the Springfield "News." After two years more of journalism he abandoned it to devote himself entirely to literature. In addition to his many contributions to the magazines, he has published "Six to One: a Nantucket Idyl;" "Dr. Heidenhoff's Process," and "Miss Ludington's Sister." His greatest success, however, has been in his socialistic novel, "Looking Backward," published in 1888, of which more than three hundred thousand copies were sold in America within two years of its first appearance. Mr. Bellamy still resides at Chicopee Falls, and interests himself in advancing the ideas of nationalism advocated in his book. He is thoroughly in earnest in his beliefs, and is known as a profound thinker, as well as one of the most clever and vigorous writers of the age.

EDWARD BELLAMY.

ANDREW ELLICOTT KENNEDY BENHAM.

A NAME that but a short time ago was on every tongue, in connection with a magnificent display of firmness and aggression in protecting American interests in a foreign harbor, is that of Admiral A. E. K. Benham, late commanding the North Atlantic squadron. In firing upon the Brazilian insurgents, who attempted to enforce a blockade in the harbor of Rio de Janeiro, January 30, 1894, and thus interfere with American commerce, this brave naval officer won the applause of the world. Admiral Benham was born on Staten Island, N. Y., April 10, 1832. He entered the navy as midshipman November 24, 1847, and rose to the rank of lieutenant September 16, 1855, having done several years' service on the "St. Mary's," in the Pacific squadron. He was attached to the "Crusader," on the Home station, in 1860 and 1861, and when the Civil war began was made executive officer of the "Bienville," on the South Atlantic blockade, where he participated in the capture of Port Royal, S. C., and in 1863 served on the "Sacramento." He was promoted to lieutenant commander in 1863, and commanded the "Penobscot" in the Western Gulf blockading squadron until the close of the war in 1865. After that he served at various stations, being promoted to commander in 1866, to captain in 1875, and to commodore in 1885. Later he attained the rank of rear admiral, and was commanding the North Atlantic squadron at the time of the Rio bay incident, when he gave the insurgents and the whole world to understand that the American flag would be protected. Admiral Benham was retired from the service in the spring of 1894, having served his allotted forty-five years, and he took with him into his retirement the grateful appreciation of the Nation for his efficient work.

ANDREW ELLICOTT KENNEDY BENHAM.

WILSON SHANNON BISSELL.

THE man who acted as chief groomsman when President Cleveland was married afterward became Postmaster-General in the President's Cabinet. W. S. Bissell was born in Rome, Oneida County, N. Y., December 31, 1847, but since 1853 has been a resident of Buffalo. After receiving a preliminary education in the public schools he took a two years' course in Hopkins' Grammar School at New Haven, Conn., and then entered Yale College, where he was graduated in 1869. He studied law in Buffalo, and in 1872 formed a partnership with Lyman K. Bass for the practice of his profession. At the beginning of 1874 Grover Cleveland became a member of the firm, which was then known as Bass, Cleveland & Bissell. Mr. Bass withdrew, but the other parties retained their association until Mr. Cleveland went to Albany to assume the duties of governor of the state, and subsequently resumed their partnership. A few years after the marriage of his law partner, then President of the United States, Mr. Bissell followed his example, and Mr. and Mrs. Cleveland were the honored guests of the occasion. Mr. Bissell has been an active Democrat all his life, but has always refused to be a candidate for office, except for elector-at-large in 1884. He was earnestly solicited by Mr. Cleveland early in 1885 to take a high official position, but declined, and his acceptance of a place in the Cabinet in 1893 was a great financial sacrifice. His fitness for the place was demonstrated as soon as he had taken charge of the office, and his services gave him a high reputation as a public official, but he was compelled to resign and return to his law practice in Buffalo, where he has the reputation of being a wise and able counsellor.

WILSON SHANNON BISSELL
131

JOSEPH CLAY STYLES BLACKBURN.

THE name of Blackburn has become familiar throughout the United States as representing Kentucky pluck and vigor and statesmanship, and it is largely to the subject of this sketch that the prominence of the name is due. Joseph C. S. Blackburn was born in Woodford County, Kentucky, October 1, 1838. He attended the common schools, receiving private instruction as well, then took a course of study at Sayres Institute, and finally graduated from Centre College, at Danville. He entered at once upon a course of legal study at Lexington, Ky., and was admitted to the bar in 1858, being then only twenty years of age. He looked upon Chicago, Ill., as a promising field, removed to that city at once, and practiced successfully until the beginning of the Civil war. His sympathies were naturally with the South, and he returned to Kentucky and entered the Confederate army, in which he served with distinction. The war over, he returned to his native state and resumed the practice of his profession, making his home eventually in Versailles. He was elected to the Kentucky legislature in 1871, and became conspicuous in that body. He was re-elected, and in 1875 was elected to Congress, in the Lower House of which he served continuously until 1884, when the legislature of his state elected him to the United States Senate. At the expiration of his term in 1891 he was re-elected to the Senate, for the term expiring in 1897. The same energy and force of character which made him a promising lawyer before he was twenty-one years of age, which led him into the army and allowed no circumstances to deter him from his course, have made Senator Blackburn a capable and earnest law-maker. He is a man of recognized force.

JOSEPH CLAY STYLES BLACKBURN.

RICHARD PARKS BLAND.

FROM the outset of his public career Congressman Bland, of Missouri, has been the champion of cheap and plentiful money in every form, and for many years has been the recognized leader in the House of Representatives of the free silver wing. Mr. Bland is essentially a self-made man. He was born near Hartford, Ohio County, Kentucky, August 19, 1835. Orphaned at an early age, he worked during the summer months in order to obtain means with which to attend school in the winter, and thus acquired an academic education. He then studied law and was admitted to the bar. In 1855 he removed to Missouri, and then to California. Subsequently he settled in Virginia City, Nevada, where he became interested in mining operations. Returning to Missouri in 1865, he eventually drifted to Lebanon, in that state, and while practicing law there was elected to Congress as a Democrat in 1873. He has since been regularly re-elected. He introduced in the Forty-fourth Congress the well-known "Bland Bill," which provided that the Secretary of the Treasury should purchase sufficient bullion to coin the minimum amount of $2,000,000 a month in silver dollars of 412½ grains each, and that these dollars should be legal tender. He also introduced in the Fifty-third Congress the "Seigniorage Bill," which was passed by the House, but vetoed by the President. Whatever else may be said of Mr. Bland's legislative career, it is certain that he reflects faithfully the wishes and the opinions of his constituents. Personally he has his cause much at heart, believing firmly in silver and conceiving himself to be the champion of the debtor class and a crusader against a wicked conspiracy of the bankers and the "gold bugs."

RICHARD PARKS BLAND.

137

JEAN BLEWETT.

THROUGH many charming poems and dainty pen-pictures, which somehow never fail to enlist the deepest interest and sympathy of the reader, the name of Jean Blewett has become well and favorably known in connection with the literature of Canada and the United States, and is constantly acquiring a wider recognition. She was born in a country place near Rondeau Bay, Ontario, Canada, November 4, 1864. Her parents were John and Janet McKishney, of Argyleshire, Scotland, and much of her youth was spent with her Scotch grandparents. She received a liberal education, and early manifested the imaginative faculty which caused her to be regarded as an indolent dreamer. At the age of seventeen she wrote a book of prose, which, though showing the amateur, displayed much strength and originality, and gave promise of the better things that were soon to follow. She has since been a contributor to some of the leading magazines of Canada and the United States, and her poems, etchings and life-sketches have found their way to the hearts of thousands of readers in both countries. A keen observation and the faculty of describing what she sees in language that flows naturally from a poetic soul, give her the rare power of making the reader see, hear and feel with her, while the senses are gratified with the music that accompanies the revelation. Her religious verse is characterized by strength and breadth, and has called forth widely favorable comment, while her short stories show remarkable originality and power. Mrs. Blewett was married when quite young to Bassett Blewett, an Englishman, and now resides in a pleasant home, living a quiet life with her husband and two children, at Blenheim, Ontario.

JEAN BLEWETT.

HORACE BOIES.

WHATEVER may have been the other conditions which aided the Democrats in wresting Iowa from the strong grasp of the Republicans in 1889, there is no doubt that their success was largely due to the strength and popularity of their candidate for governor. The choice of Horace Boies to lead the fight against prohibition legislation in that campaign was a fortunate one. Mr. Boies was born on a farm near Buffalo, Erie County, N. Y., in 1827, and until he was sixteen years of age was a hard-working assistant to his father in clearing the timber land of the farm. He went West at seventeen, but after working for a time on a Wisconsin farm he returned to New York, took an academic course, and studied law. In 1852 he began the practice of his profession in Buffalo, and in a few years had established an excellent reputation as a criminal lawyer. Mr. Boies removed to Waterloo, Iowa, in 1867, and there practiced in partnership with H. B. Allen for several years. He was afterward associated with C. F. Couch until that gentleman retired to become a district judge, in 1884. Mr. Boies continued to add to his reputation and influence year after year, and, being a stanch Democrat, he naturally attracted the attention of the party managers in the state. They made him their candidate for governor in 1889, and he led them to victory. He was re-elected in 1891, but was defeated for a third term by F. D. Jackson, though the excellence of his administration was universally admitted. Mr. Boies was the choice of the Iowa and several other state delegations for the Presidency in the Democratic National Convention of 1892. He is extremely popular in his state, and a prime factor in all political movements.

HORACE BOIES.
141

ROBERT BONNER.

TO many thousands of readers a peculiar interest, amounting almost to reverence, attaches to the name of the man who founded the New York "Ledger," that famous story paper that for many years gave to the public the best productions of Mrs. Southworth, Sylvanus Cobb, Jr., Fanny Fern, Alice Cary, and a host of other writers. Robert Bonner was born near Londonderry, Ireland, April 28, 1824. His parents were Scotch-Irish Presbyterians. Coming to the United States at an early age, he learned the printer's trade, and in 1839 was employed in the office of the Hartford "Courant," where he gained the reputation of being the most rapid compositor in Connecticut. In 1844 he removed to New York, and in 1851 purchased the "Ledger," at that time an insignificant sheet. By printing the most popular class of interesting stories he gave the paper a wide circulation, which was further extended by the contributions of James Parton, Fanny Fern, Edward Everett, Henry Ward Beecher, Charles Dickens, and other eminent authors and clergymen. Mr. Bonner has made large gifts of money to Princeton College and to various charities. To gratify his taste for fast horses he has purchased several of the most celebrated trotters in the world, always withdrawing them from the race course. These included "Peerless," "Dexter" and "Maud S." The last named had a record of 2:09¾, afterward reduced to 2:08¾, and was purchased from William H. Vanderbilt for $40,000. Some years ago Mr. Bonner retired from active business life and is now enjoying, in a quiet way, the fruits of his energy and enterprise. Since his retirement the "Ledger" has been successfully conducted by his sons, to whom he surrendered it.

HENRY BILLINGS BROWN.

—

A VERY clean record and admirable as representing intellect, cultivation and a power to look upon things broadly and justly, is
that of Henry Billings Brown, now an associate justice of the Supreme
Court of the United States. He was born in South Lee, Mass.,
March 2, 1836. He received a thorough preliminary education, and
was graduated from Yale College in 1856, after which he studied law
for some time in a private office, and later attended lectures at both
Yale and Harvard law schools. He came west and was admitted to
the bar of Wayne County, Michigan, in July, 1860, and in the spring
of 1861, upon the election of Mr. Lincoln, was appointed United States
Deputy Marshal, and subsequently United States Attorney for the eastern district of Michigan, a position he held until 1868, when he was
appointed judge of the circuit court of Wayne County, to fill a vacancy.
He returned to active practice in partnership with John S. Newberry
and Ashley Pond, of Detroit, each a man prominent in his profession.
In 1875 he was appointed by President Grant United States District
Judge for the eastern district of Michigan, to succeed Hon. John W.
Longyear, and in December, 1890, was appointed associate justice of
the Supreme Court to succeed Judge Samuel F. Miller. He entered
upon the duties of his present office January 5, 1891. Since his
advent in the Supreme Court, he has become recognized as a man of
marked ability and one who is a credit even to that assemblage of
leaders in the law. Honors have come upon him thick and fast.
He was made an LL. D. by the University of Michigan in 1887, while
Yale University conferred the same honor upon him in 1891. He occupies the front rank in his profession.

HENRY BILLINGS BROWN.
143

ROBERT JONES BURDETTE.

METEOR-LIKE in their short-lived brilliance have been the careers of the majority of the newspaper "funny men" whose bright paragraphs made brief reputations for the journals in which they appeared. With Robert J. Burdette this has not been the case, for he is one of the few who possess literary ability of a high order, who are able to depict the pathetic as well as the humorous phases of life, and who write entertainingly on a variety of subjects. Nevertheless, he is essentially a humorist, and not many years ago he was universally designated "The Burlington 'Hawkeye' Man," because his name was so little known. Mr. Burdette was born in Greensborough, Pa., July 30, 1844, but early in life removed to Peoria, Ill., where he was educated in the public schools. He enlisted as a private in the Forty-seventh Illinois volunteers, in 1862, and served until the close of the war. In 1869 he became one of the editors of the Peoria "Transcript," was afterward connected with the "Review," and still later assisted in the founding of a new paper in Peoria, which did not succeed. Subsequently he became associate editor of the Burlington "Hawkeye," and his humorous contributions to that journal, being widely copied, gave him a national reputation. In 1877 he began to deliver public lectures, in which he was very successful, his subjects being "The Rise and Fall of the Moustache," "Home," and "The Pilgrimage of the Funny Man." Several volumes of his humorous writings have been issued. He was connected with the Brooklyn "Eagle" for some time, and continues to contribute much to periodical literature. He also occasionally preaches, being a licensed minister of the Baptist Church.

ROBERT JONES BURDETTE.

145

JOHN BURROUGHS.

————

WHAT other American author writes so charmingly of bird life, green fields, rural fancies and observations, and the impressions of nature, as John Burroughs? The pure, bracing air of the country breathes through almost everything that comes from his gifted pen. Mr. Burroughs was born in Roxbury, N. Y., April 3, 1837. The son of a farmer, he early imbibed a love of the woods and meadows and the society of birds and books. After receiving an academic education he taught school eight or nine years, and then became a journalist in New York. He was a clerk in the treasury department at Washington from 1864 until 1873, after which he was appointed receiver of the Wallkill National Bank, in Middletown, N. Y. In 1874 he settled on a farm at Esopus, N. Y., giving his time principally to fruit culture, except during the months when his duties as bank examiner called him away. He has contributed largely to periodicals, writing mainly upon rural themes and natural history. His published books are: "Wake Robin," "Winter Sunshine," "Birds and Poets," "Locusts and Wild Honey," "Pepacton," "Fresh Fields," "Signs and Seasons," "Indoor Studies," and "Notes on Walt Whitman as Poet and Person." He has also written enough poetry to create a wish among his admirers that he would write more. The thoroughness with which Mr. Burroughs' keen observation absorbs a subject is only equaled by the cleverness with which he describes it, always enlisting the sympathies and interest of his readers where a less entertaining writer would only weary them. As an author and naturalist he is a worthy successor of Thoreau, without Thoreau's personal peculiarities and erratic habits of life.

JOHN BURROUGHS.
147

GEORGE WASHINGTON CABLE.

MANY readers will remember with what delight they devoured those inimitable short stories, "Madame Delphine," "Posson Jone," "Tite Poulette," and "Cafe des Exiles," with which George W. Cable made his advent in the field of literature, and the enthusiasm with which they received his later and more elaborate works. Mr. Cable is a native of New Orleans, born October 12, 1844. He served in the Confederate army from 1863 to 1865, being severely wounded, and after the war returned to New Orleans, penniless. He had a hard struggle for existence for a time, but finally attracted attention through a series of clever articles published in the New Orleans "Picayune," and in 1878 his sketches of Creole life began to appear in "Scribner's Magazine." These made him famous, and his success as an author was immediately assured. He possesses a thorough mastery of the Creole and negro dialects of his native state, and his stories all have the merit of novelty and interest. His keen powers of observation have enabled him to depict the social life of the Louisiana lowlands so vividly that in some cases serious offense has been given to those whose portraits he has drawn. Through his publications he has been the means of effecting reforms in the contract system of convict labor in the Southern States. Among his most popular works are "Old Creole Days," "The Grandissimes," "Bonaventure," "The Creoles of Louisiana," "Dr. Sevier," "The Silent South," "John March, Southerner," etc. Mr. Cable has also been successful in the lecture field, and his readings from his own books give the stories and their characters an added charm through his clever interpretations. In 1885 he established his permanent home at Northampton, Mass.

GEORGE WASHINGTON CABLE.

JULIUS C. BURROWS.

A PROMINENT figure in Congress has been for a long time that
of Julius C. Burrows, who so ably represents the Third Michigan
district. He was born in North East, Erie County, Pa., January
9, 1837. He received a thorough common-school and academic education.
He studied law and was admitted to practice, but, with the
outbreak of the Civil war, entered the Union army, remaining in the
service until 1864. After the war he settled down vigorously to the
practice of his profession, in Kalamazoo, Mich., and was elected prosecuting
attorney. In 1867 he was appointed supervisor of internal revenue
for the states of Michigan and Wisconsin, but declined the office,
preferring the regular career before him. He was elected to the Forty-
third Congress, re-elected to the Forty-sixth and Forty-seventh Congresses,
and in 1884 was appointed Solicitor of the United States Treasury
Department, but declined the office. In the same year he was
elected delegate-at-large from Michigan to the Republican National Convention.
He was elected to the Forty-ninth Congress, and has been
re-elected continuously since. He was twice elected Speaker pro tempore
during the Fifty-first Congress, and is a recognized power in the
Republican party. In his last contest he received a majority of votes
over the Democratic, Populist and Prohibition candidates combined. A
fluent and powerful debater, a statesman of admitted ability, and possessed
of popular qualities, he is looked upon as a not unlikely occupant
of a seat in the United States Senate. He is a fit specimen of the
clear-headed, broad-viewed men, the drift from the east, who have made
Michigan one of the most typically American and progressive states of
the Union.

JULIUS C. BURROWS.
151

JAMES E. CAMPBELL.

ONE of the men who have become factors in the political history of the country within a comparatively recent period, but who have attracted universal attention by reason of inherent greatness, is Ex-Governor Campbell, of Ohio. First in the National House of Representatives, then in the Governor's chair, he distinguished himself as a man of more than ordinary ability, an able legislator, and a wise executive. James E. Campbell was born in Middletown, Ohio, July 7, 1843. He received a thorough education, and adopted the profession of a lawyer. During the Civil war he served in the United States Navy, and after the restoration of peace settled down to the practice of his profession in Hamilton, Ohio, where, in 1876, he became prosecuting attorney, continuing in that office until 1880. In the mean time Mr. Campbell had become so popular throughout his district that in 1882 he was elected to Congress as a Democrat, and he soon became one of the most popular men at the Capitol, as well as a leader in the House. He served in the Forty-eighth and Forty-ninth Congresses, and was re-elected to the Fiftieth, but subsequently resigned his seat to make the race for Governor of Ohio. He made a vigorous and brilliant campaign, and succeeded in defeating his Republican opponent, Governor Foraker. At the end of his term as Governor, he failed of re-election, but his power and influence in his own party have continued to grow, rather than diminish, and he is today a greater man than ever. At the National Democratic Convention of 1892 he was a recognized leader, and was enthusiastically cheered every time his tall, commanding figure was seen in the aisles. He represents the best principles of the Democratic party.

JAMES E. CAMPBELL
153

WILL CARLETON.

EASILY the predecessor of the American poets of the day who are
describing country life—by the way, the greatest life of the nation—
though he used little or no dialect in doing it, stands Will Carleton,
the Michigan poet, author of "Over the Hills to the Poorhouse," and
of similar poems which have touched the hearts of the American public. He was born in Hudson, Lenawee County, Mich., October 21,
1845. He received the ordinary education of a boy of that region of
apple orchards, of good roads winding beside lakes, and of good schools.
He graduated at Hillsdale College in 1869. After his graduation he
visited Europe and repeated the trip, making an earnest study of general European life as compared with the American. He began soon
after his return a series of contributions to periodicals and magazines,
and one day found himself made suddenly famous by contributions published in the east, "Over the Hills to the Poorhouse" and "Betsy and
I are Out" being, doubtless, the most potent in giving him the wide
reputation he so suddenly attained. He has lectured in Great Britain,
Canada and the United States, and has proved an exceedingly popular
man before an audience. His published books include "Poems" (Chicago, 1871), "Farm Ballads" (New York, 1873), "Farm Legends"
(1875), "Young Folks' Centennial," "Rhymes," "Farm Festivals,".
"City Ballads," and others. With a keen perception of what was
about him, and with the gift of language for expressing in words that
which he sees and feels, Mr. Carleton has won fairly the position
he now occupies in the literary world. He is one of the graceful
poetic historians of a great phase of life in the progress of the new
world.

WILL CARLETON.

ANDREW CARNEGIE.

B Y all odds the largest manufacturer of pig-iron, steel rails and coke in the world is Andrew Carnegie. The son of a poor weaver, he was born in Dunfermline, Scotland, November 25, 1835, and came to the United States with his father in 1845, settling in Pittsburg two years later. He learned telegraphy, and was one of the first to read telegraphic signals by sound. Later, while in the employ of the Pennsylvania railroad, he met Mr. Woodruff, the inventor of the sleeping-car, and joined him in his venture, the success of which gave him the nucleus of his wealth. He pooled his profits with the syndicate that purchased the Storey farm on Oil Creek, which cost forty thousand dollars, and yielded in one year over one million dollars in cash dividends. Mr. Carnegie subsequently associated himself with others in the establishment of a rolling mill, and from this has grown the most extensive and complete system of iron and steel industries ever controlled by an individual, embracing the Edgar Thomson Steel Works, the Pittsburg Bessemer Steel Works, the Lucy Furnaces, the Union Iron Mills, the Union Mill (Wilson, Walker & Co.), the Keystone Bridge Works, the Hartman Steel Works, the Frick Coke Company, and the Scotia ore mines. Many times a millionaire, Mr. Carnegie has devoted large sums to public improvements and to benevolent and educational purposes, both in this country and in Scotland. He owns about eighteen newspapers, is a frequent contributor to periodicals, and has published two books: "An American Four-in-Hand in Britain" and "Triumphant Democracy." He has shown a deep interest in the welfare of the working classes, and in all movements designed to improve their condition.

ANDREW CARNEGIE.

MARY HARTWELL CATHERWOOD.

VERY well defined and more than creditable is the position in literature of Mary Hartwell Catherwood. She was born in Luray, Licking County, Ohio, December 16, 1847. Her father, the scion of a long line of Scotch-Irish baronets, came with his family to Illinois when the state was still half wild, and fell a victim to the duties of his profession. The daughter, Mary, received a thorough education and graduated from the Female College at Granville, Ohio, in 1868. In 1888 she became the wife of James S. Catherwood, and has since resided at Hoopeston, Ill. The child, Mary Hartwell, was always given to story making, but it was not until 1881 that the woman was fairly launched on the sea of letters. In that year "Craque-O'-Doom," from her pen, was published in Philadelphia; "Rocky Fork" was published in Boston, in 1882, and then came in succession "Old Caravan Days," "The Secrets at Roseladies," "The Romance of Dollard," which first appeared as a serial in the "Century Magazine," "The Bells of St. Anne," "The Story of Tonty," and other works. As the romantic historian of Canada and the Great Lakes region Mrs. Catherwood has certainly no peer, and as a graceful defender of the conservative ideal against the unadorned realistic in style she has won almost equal prominence. She has a wonderful gift of story telling, and has, furthermore, an earnestness and enthusiasm in her work which reveals itself in the tone of all she writes. She is the graceful pioneer in a field which will yet be enormously and magnificently fruitful. Among western authors she occupies an admittedly high position, the result of no exploitation nor of adventitious circumstance, but of distinguished merit.

MARY HARTWELL CATHERWOOD.

AMELIE RIVES CHANLER

THOUGH yet a young woman, Mrs. Amelie Rives Chanler is
well known in at least two continents. Her fame came swiftly,
but it has remained because of the real strength of the young authoress. Amelie Rives was born in Richmond, Va., August 23, 1863.
She is the granddaughter of the Hon. Wm. C. Rives, who was three
times Minister to France and once a United States senator. Her
youth was passed part of . the time in Mobile, Ala., and part of the
time at Castle Hill, her father's place in Albemarle County, Virginia.
It was not until 1886 that she became known to the world. In that
year she published anonymously, in the "Atlantic Monthly," a story of
the sixteenth century entitled "A Brother to Dragons," which excited
widespread interest and comment. In 1887 "The Farrier Lass o' Pip-
ing Pebworth," a short story in "Lippincott's Magazine," and "Nurse
Crumpet Tells the Story," in "Harper's Magazine," added to the
author's reputation. In 1889 "The Quick or the Dead" appeared in
"Lippincott's Magazine," and reputation was a thing assured. There
was much adverse criticism of the daring story, but its genius was
admitted. In June, 1888, she became the wife of John Armstrong
Chanler, of New York. Her first drama, "Herod and Mariamna,"
was published just before she went abroad. A study of life in the
Latin quarter of Paris, by Mrs. Chanler, entitled "According to St.
John," appeared in the "Cosmopolitan Magazine" as a serial in 1891,
and a second drama, "Athelwold," was published in "Harper's Magazine" in 1892. Mrs. Chanler spends much of her time at Castle Hill,
and there continues her studies in the line of the career which has
been so brilliantly begun.

AMELIE RIVES CHANLER.

161

WILLIAM EATON CHANDLER

ORIGINAL and aggressive, with a mind that grasps quickly and accurately the most complicated questions of government, few men are better fitted to cope with the problems which the progress of legislation and agitation have pressed upon the attention of this generation than Senator Chandler, of New Hampshire. Mr. Chandler first saw the light of day in Concord, N. H., December 28, 1835. After his admission to the bar, in 1856, he was appointed reporter of the New Hampshire supreme court, and in 1862 he was elected by the Republicans to the Legislature. In 1864 he was employed by the United States Navy Department as special counsel to prosecute the Philadelphia navy yard frauds, and in the following year he was appointed first solicitor and judge advocate-general of that department. From June 17, 1865, to November 30, 1867, he was first assistant Secretary of the Treasury. In 1876 he advocated the claims of the Hayes electors in Florida before the canvassing board of the state, and was afterward an outspoken opponent of the Southern policy of the Hayes administration. In 1881 Mr. Chandler was again a member of the New Hampshire legislature, and in April, 1882, President Arthur appointed him Secretary of the Navy, in which office he carried out many important measures, and introduced reforms the result of which has been the saving of millions of dollars to the government of the United States. He was first elected United States senator June 14, 1887, to fill the unexpired term of Austin F. Pike, and was re-elected June 18, 1889. Mr. Chandler is a worker rather than a talker, and in every public position that he has held he has been known by what he has accomplished and not by what he has said.

WILLIAM EATON CHANDLER.

WILLIAM BOURKE COCKRAN.

—

TAMMANY'S great orator, recently a member of Congress, an earnest worker, and a man of influence in the House, is comparatively new as a figure in national politics. He was born in Ireland, February 28, 1854, and was educated in his native country and in France, coming to America when seventeen years of age. Soon after his arrival in this country he became a teacher in a private academy, and was, later, principal of a public school in Westchester County, New York. Here he labored for some time. His natural abilities outside of those required in his avocation were recognized while he was still a teacher, and he participated in Democratic conventions, and became at length a recognized person of influence in the affairs of the party in New York City. His pre-eminent oratorical powers gave him prominence, and at the convention which nominated Grover Cleveland for the presidency, in 1892, Mr. Cockran's speech in opposition was admittedly the ablest effort of the occasion. He was elected a member of the Fifty-second Congress, and re-elected to the Fifty-third, taking an active part in the debates on national issues. Though an active participant in the councils of the close political organization to which he belongs, and counted, as a matter of course, its spokesman on great occasions, Mr. Cockran is not so thoroughly identified with it in character as are other leaders who might be named, and is apparently rather inclined to take an independent course and be influenced rather by his convictions than the dictates of a "machine." His political opinions are broad and liberal, and, when made public in a speech, have always immediate force, from the remarkable tact and force of their expression.

WILLIAM BOURKE COCKRAN.

JOSEPH COOK.

FOR searching philosophical analysis, for keen and merciless logic, for dogmatic assertion of eternal truth in the name of science, it is doubtful if Joseph Cook, of Boston, has an equal on the lecture platform or in the field of religious literature. He is probably the most aggressive, as he is certainly the most celebrated, defender of the orthodox faith of the present day. Mr. Cook was born in Ticonderoga, N. Y., January 26, 1838. He was educated at Yale and Harvard, and after studying four years at Andover he was granted a license, but declined all invitations to any settlement as pastor. He preached in Andover for two years and in Lynn, Mass., for one year, and in 1871 went to Europe, where he devoted himself to study and travel until near the close of 1873. Upon his return he became a lecturer on the relations of religion, science and current reform. His "Boston Monday lectures," in Tremont Temple, Boston, attracted general attention and were widely published, many of them being afterward delivered by Mr. Cook in the various cities of the United States. In 1880 he made a lecturing tour around the world, attracting large audiences and favorable criticisms everywhere. Mr. Cook's published works include "Biology," "Transcendentalism," "Orthodoxy," "Conscience," "Heredity," "Marriage," "Labor," "Socialism," "Occident," and "Orient." His greatest popularity arises from the fact that he attempts to show that science is in harmony with religion and the Bible. President McCosh, of Princeton College, said of Mr. Cook as a lecturer: "He lightens and thunders, throwing a vivid light on a topic by an expression of comparison, or striking a presumptuous error as by a bolt from heaven."

JOSEPH COOK.

RICHARD HARDING DAVIS.

NO man of the present day in the United States has fairly won a position in the literary field at a lesser age than has Richard Harding Davis. Though but just past his thirtieth year, he is recognized as one of the most brilliant of story-tellers of a certain class, and that class a good one. He was born in Philadelphia, April 10, 1864, and is the son of L. Clark Davis, editor of the "Philadelphia Ledger," and Rebecca Harding Davis, an authoress popular everywhere for her charming stories. With such parentage it is not at all surprising that the son should have the literary gift in a marked degree. He received a thorough education at Lehigh University and Johns Hopkins', and, almost immediately after leaving college, engaged in literary work. After writing a book, which was not long upon the market, and a magazine story or two, he began newspaper work in Philadelphia, serving successively on the "Record," the "Press," and the "Telegraph," and paying a visit for the latter to England. On his return from England, he secured a connection with the New York "Evening Sun," and on that paper began the series of "Van Bibber" sketches, by which he is best known. It was not by these that he became first known, however, but by the spirited story of "Gallegher." It is a noticeable thing in all that he has accomplished and is what is greatest in his promise for the future that Mr. Davis' work shows with each successive volume increased care and quality, while none of the vigor is lost. He has published three or four books of travel, which are, in their way, as creditable as his stories. He has a future of exceptional brightness, being young and having "gifts" which may develop into something very great.

RICHARD HARDING DAVIS.

FRANCIS MARION CRAWFORD.

—

WITH a masterly touch in the delineation of natural men and women—with a fascinating and artistic style in depicting dramatic scenes and situations, whether they have the picturesque setting of southern Continental conditions or the more sober hue of American life—F. Marion Crawford has won great popularity as a novelist. He is the son of an American sculptor, Thomas Crawford, and was born in Bagni di Lucca, Italy, August 2, 1854. He was educated partly in America, at Concord, N. H., partly in Italy, and partly in England, where he was a member of Trinity College, Cambridge. He afterward studied at Karlsruhe and Heidelberg, and from 1876 to 1878 studied Sanskrit at the University of Rome. In 1879 he went to India and was editor of a daily paper, the "Indian Herald," at Allahabad. Returning to America in 1881, he remained until 1883, and then went to Italy, where, with the exception of occasional visits to this and other countries, he has since resided, his home being near Sorrento. Mr. Crawford's writings are chiefly in the line of fiction, though he has done some work in critical philosophy and philology, and has contributed sketches of travel to periodicals. His first novel, "Mr. Isaacs," made him famous in the literary world, and his succeeding ones, which have followed one another in rapid succession, have been eagerly sought after and widely commented upon. He has been awarded a prize of one thousand francs by the French Academy as an acknowledgment of the merit of his novels, and especially two of them, "Zoroaster" and "Marzio's Crucifix," which were written in French as well as in English. His latest, "Katharine Lauderdale," is a realistic American story.

FRANCIS MARION CRAWFORD.

AMOS JAY CUMMINGS.

NOT all newspaper writers are "born to blush unseen," although the concealment of their identity, as a rule, prevents them from becoming widely known through their work. An editor who has scratched his way into Congress with a sharp-pointed pen, is Amos J. Cummings, representing the Eleventh congressional district of New York City. Mr. Cummings was born in Conkling, Broome County, N. Y., May 15, 1841. He was educated in a district school, and at the age of twelve years entered a printing office as an apprentice. He has set type in nearly every state in the Union. As a boy he was with Walker in the last invasion of Nicaragua, and during the Civil war was sergeant-major in the Twenty-sixth New Jersey Infantry, being officially mentioned for gallantry in the battle of Fredericksburg. Mr. Cummings has filled editorial positions on the New York "Tribune," under Horace Greeley; was managing editor at different times of the New York "Sun" and of the New York "Express," and was editor of the "Evening Sun" and president of the New York Press Club when elected to the Fiftieth Congress. He has served four terms in Congress, and has done valuable work as a member of the committee on merchant marine and fisheries, as chairman of the committee on library, and chairman of the committee on naval affairs. Mr. Cummings is a champion of organized labor, and carries a working card as a printer, being the only representative in the House who is a member in good standing of a labor union. While in Congress he has continued his work as a newspaper correspondent, and his letters are always full of interest. For many years he wrote for the New York "Sun," over the signature of "Ziska."

AMOS JAY CUMMINGS.

DONALD McDONALD DICKINSON.

PECULIAR abilities, coupled with natural sagacity and tact, are
essential qualifications of the successful organizer and leader in
politics. In this respect there are probably few men in the United
States better equipped than "Don" M. Dickinson, of Michigan, whose
valuable services to his party were recognized in so substantial a way
by President Cleveland in 1888. Mr. Dickinson was born in Port
Ontario, Oswego County, N. Y., January 7, 1847. After obtaining a
preliminary education in the public schools, he entered the University of
Michigan, where he was graduated in 1867. He then took up the
study of law, and was admitted to the bar in Michigan, eventually
settling in Detroit, where for many years he has pursued the practice
of his profession. Of rare legal acumen, he quickly won a foremost
place at the bar, and has continually added to his reputation by his
connection with important cases and the admirable manner in which he
conducts them. By his shrewdness and foresight, as well as by his
eloquence and magnetism, he became a power in the Democratic party
of the state, and finally of the nation. In 1876 he was chosen chairman of the Democratic State Committee of Michigan, in which position
he rendered valuable service. In 1880 he was chairman of the Michigan delegation in the National Democratic Convention, and since that
time has always taken an active and prominent part in national campaign work. In 1884 he became a member of the National Democratic Committee, representing Michigan, and distinguished himself for
clever management and wise counsel. President Cleveland appointed
him Postmaster-General of the United States, January 17, 1888, a post
which he creditably filled for one year.

DONALD McDONALD DICKINSON.

JOACHIM CRESPO.

THE most important international topic during the last administration of President Cleveland was the dispute between England and America involving the question of the correct boundary line between British Guiana and Venezuela. The latter government claimed that Great Britain was encroaching upon their territory. President Cleveland took the stand that the question involved the terms of the Monroe Doctrine, namely, that the United States considers any attempt by a European power, to extend their system to any portion of this hemisphere, as dangerous to the peace and safety of the nation. Gen. Joachim Crespo, President of the Republic of Venezuela, has the peculiar characteristics of one who would be a leader of men. It has been said of him that he is possessed of two attributes which seldom go hand in hand. He is a shrewd and conservative business man, rich in land and herds—a veritable cattle king of the South; but above all he is a brave and gallant soldier, a soldier whose iron nerve has endeared him to the hearts of his countrymen. His first act of bravery and patriotism was to head a revolutionary rising against the unconstitutional acts of President Palachio. That merciless despot was driven from the Presidency and General Crespo accepted the provisional head of the government. He immediately issued a pronunciamiento ordering a constitutional election. He was elected, and at once showed his affection for his country and loyalty to the people by adopting a new constitution, patterned as nearly after that of the United States as the different conditions of the country would permit. President Crespo was born in Barcelona, Venezuela, in 1845. The action of President Cleveland in the boundary question was heartily endorsed by every one.

JOACHIM CRESPO.

GEORGE R. DAVIS.

THE man upon whom rested the chief responsibility for the conduct of the World's Columbian Exposition of 1893 was Col. George R. Davis, of Chicago. There is that in the character of the man which speaks well for the wisdom of the National Commission in making him Director-General of that greatest of modern enterprises. Colonel Davis has clearness of judgment and a thorough knowledge of men, besides executive ability of a high order and a natural tact in the management of large and varied interests. He was born at Three Rivers, Palmer, Massachusetts, January 3, 1840, and after receiving his early education in the public schools, attended Williston Seminary, where he graduated in 1860. He studied law and was admitted to the bar, but upon the breaking out of the war he enlisted in the Eighth Massachusetts regiment, and soon rose to the rank of captain. In 1863 he resigned to organize a battery of light artillery, and at a still later period he was a major in the Third Rhode Island cavalry. After the war Colonel Davis became a resident of Chicago and took a leading part in the organization of the First regiment, Illinois National Guard, of which he was made commander. In 1876 he was nominated for Congress by the Republicans of his district, but was defeated. Two years later, however, he was elected, and served three successive terms. At the close of his congressional career he was elected treasurer of Cook County, and upon leaving that office became Director-General of the World's Fair. The story of his splendid work in that position is known to the world. To his individual efforts the success of the great exposition is largely due. He is now looked upon as a power in Western politics.

THOMAS McINTYRE COOLEY.

—

ADMIRED no less for his modest, gentle disposition and entire freedom from affectation than for the great intellectual force that made him a power on the bench, it is not strange that Judge Thomas M. Cooley has taken with him into his retirement the esteem and gratitude of the people. Judge Cooley was born in Attica, N. Y., January 6, 1824. He began the study of law in Palmyra, N. Y., in 1842, and removing to Michigan the next year was admitted to the bar at Adrian in January, 1846. For a time he edited the Adrian "Watch-Tower," a newspaper, and in 1857 was assigned to the work of compiling the general statutes of Michigan, which were published in two volumes. In 1858 he was appointed reporter of the Supreme court, which office he held for seven years. In 1859 he was made justice of the Supreme court of Michigan, becoming chief justice in 1868, and served until 1885, when he retired permanently from the bench. When the law for the regulation of interstate commerce went into effect Judge Cooley was made chairman of the Interstate Commerce Commission, a post which he resigned in 1893. He has held the professorship of constitutional and administrative law in the University of Michigan, and the chair of American history in the same college. He is the author of a number of legal works, digests and commentaries, that are much used in the profession, and has written a history of the governments of Michigan. Judge Cooley is regarded as one of the most eminent authorities on constitutional law in the country, and his decisions while on the bench were all marked by clear, convincing analysis and common sense; a great man intellectually, a remarkably gifted and honest American citizen.

THOMAS McINTYRE COOLEY.

HENRY LAURENS DAWES.

—

WHATEVER great ability, long experience, ripe judgment, accumulated public honors and a spotless private character can do to render any one an object of interest, respect and admiration, they have done for ex-Senator Henry L. Dawes, of Massachusetts. Mr. Dawes was born in Cummington, Mass., October 30, 1816, and graduated at Yale in 1839. After a brief experience as a teacher and as a journalist he was admitted to the bar in 1842, and served in the Legislature from 1848 to 1850, when he was elected to the State Senate. He was a member of the constitutional convention in 1853, and afterward attorney for the Western District of Massachusetts until 1857, when he was elected to Congress. By successive re-elections he continued a member of that body until 1873, and in 1875 he succeeded Charles Sumner in the United States Senate. There he remained until 1893, when he retired from public life. As Representative and Senator he was the author of many tariff measures, and it was through his efforts that the completion of the Washington Monument was undertaken. The entire system of Indian education, due to legislation, was created by Mr. Dawes. The severalty bill, the Sioux bill, and the bill making Indians subject to and protected by our criminal laws are among the important bills of his authorship. Another notable measure of his was the introduction of the Weather Bulletin in 1869, at the suggestion of Prof. Cleveland Abbe, for the purpose of collecting and comparing weather reports from all parts of the country. In fine, the legislative career of Mr. Dawes has been crowded with able and valuable service to the people of the United States, and is one of which any American might be proud.

HENRY LAURENS DAWES.
185

REGINALD DE KOVEN.

IT may perhaps be said that no musical composer in the United States has acquired prominence so rapidly as has Reginald De Koven. There were adventitious circumstances to assist him, but there was merit as well. He was born in Middletown, Conn., in 1859, and acquired his early education from his father, an Episcopal clergyman. At the age of eleven he was taken to Europe by his parents, and remained there about twelve years. He was educated at St. John's College, Oxford, taking his degree with honors, in 1879. He had shown musical ability and previous to taking his degree, had studied piano playing at Stuttgart, under Speidel, and after his university course, returned to Stuttgart for another year, studying under Dr. Lebert and Professor Pruckner. He then took a course with equally eminent teachers at Frankfort and at Florence, Italy. He came to Chicago in 1882. The musical ability in him manifested itself, and he wrote the words and music of the song "Marjorie Daw," which was successful, and the taste for reputation thus achieved seems to have led him on. Later, he wrote "The Begum." It was produced by the McCaull Opera Company, and was a marked success in the leading cities of the country. Since then his advancement in the musical world has been rapid. He has produced a number of operas ranking among the most popular on the stage to-day, some of which have proved equally popular abroad. More recently he has been engaged by "Harper's Weekly" to conduct the musical department of that journal. He writes of music as well as he composes it, and his studies abroad and practical experience in producing his own operas has given him a knowledge and grasp of the subjects upon which he writes.

REGINALD DE KOVEN.

ANNA ELIZABETH DICKINSON.

—

NOT merely as a brilliant public speaker, but as a playwright actress and philanthropist, Anna Elizabeth Dickinson has made her name familiar throughout the continent. She was born in Philadelphia, October 28, 1842. She attended the Friends' Free School in the city named, her parents belonging to that society. Her father died when she was but two years of age, leaving his family in straitened circumstances, and the child had few advantages of education, but she studied and read enthusiastically and developed a remarkable talent. Her first address was made at a Friends' meeting when she was but fifteen years old. After that she spoke frequently, generally on slavery and temperance. She became a teacher, but in 1861 was given a place in the United States Mint in Philadelphia, but was removed because of grave charges made against General McClellan in a public address. She then made a profession of lecturing, and soon gained an extended reputation. The receipts of one lecture delivered at Washington, in 1864, were over $1,000, which sum she donated to the Freedman's Relief Society. In 1876 Miss Dickinson decided to leave the platform for the stage, and made her debut in a play called "A Crown of Thorns," and written by herself. Its reception was not what she had hoped, and she next essayed "Hamlet" and other Shakespearian roles, but her fort was not as an actress, and she returned to the lecture field, where she was again most successful. She wrote three plays other than the one mentioned. She has not lectured since 1892, her failing health preventing her. She acquired a fortune in the lecture field, but has given away the bulk of it in all kinds of charities. Miss Dickinson has retired from active life.

ANNA ELIZABETH DICKINSON.

JOHN WARWICK DANIEL

AS distinctively the representative of old Virginia orators of the present day, Senator John W. Daniel occupies a conspicuous position. He was born in Lynchburgh, Campbell County, Va., September 5, 1842, and comes of a family distinguished in the law and statesmanship and in the conduct of the state's affairs. He received his early education in the schools of Lynchburgh, at Lynchburgh College, and at Dr. Harrison's university and school. He had a gift for languages, and at eighteen had a knowledge of Latin, Greek, French and German. He was but nineteen when the Civil war broke out, and entered the Confederate army at once. He was wounded at the first battle of Manassas in 1861, at Boonesboro in 1862 and at Antietam, and at the Battle of the Wilderness had his leg broken in a charge. He served with marked distinction through the war in the armies of northern Virginia, and at the time of the Battle of the Wilderness was on the staff of General Early. He studied law after the war, and entered immediately upon its practice. Later he wrote "Daniel on Attachments" and "Daniel on Negotiable Instruments," both of which books have become successes. He entered public life in 1869 and served two terms in the Virginia house of delegates. He was a member in the Virginia Senate from 1875 to 1881. He was that year beaten in the race for governor of Virginia, but was elected to Congress in 1885, and during his first session was elected to the United States Senate to succeed Senator Mahone, taking his seat in March, 1887, for the term expiring in March, 1893. In 1891 he was re-elected for the term expiring in 1899. The degree of LL. D. has been conferred upon him by Washington and Lee University and the University of Michigan.

JOHN WARWICK DANIEL
189

MARY LOWE DICKINSON.

A WRITER of marked ability, but perhaps more widely known in the educational field, Mary Lowe Dickinson has thousands of friends throughout the United States who recognize the quality and extent of what she has accomplished. She was born in Massachusetts, but, after her marriage, resided for some years abroad, and is now a resident of the city of New York. An early experience in life as a teacher led her to realize the need for a more practical education for girls and women, and she has sought to teach better systems of training. Her latest work of great importance was in Denver, Colo., where she held a full professorship in English literature. Such an estimate was placed on the value of her services, not only as an instructor, but as a social and moral influence, that her chair was one of the first to be fully endowed, and when ill-health obliged her to resign this position the chair was named for her, and she was made Emeritus Professor, and holds now its lectureship in English literature. She has been secretary of the Woman's Branch of the American Bible Society, national superintendent of the so-called department of higher education in the Woman's Christian Temperance Union and president of the Woman's National Indian Association. She conducted for six years a magazine devoted to the care of invalids, and held an associate editorship with Edward Everett Hale in his Magazine of Philanthropy. She is general secretary of the Order of King's Daughters and the editor of its magazine. Her principal literary works are "Among the Thorns," "The Amber Star," and "One Little Life," novels; and, in poetry, "The Divine Christ" and "Easter Poems." Her productions are characterized by exquisite refinement.

MARY LOWE DICKINSON.

NEAL DOW.

VIGOROUS and persistent warfare against the liquor traffic for more than half a century is the record that stands to the credit of that venerable reformer, Neal Dow, who recently celebrated the ninetieth anniversary of his birth at his pleasant home in Portland, Me. Mr. Dow was born in Portland, March 20, 1804. He was twice elected mayor of that city, in 1851 and 1854, and through his efforts the Maine liquor law, prohibiting under severe penalties the sale of intoxicating beverages, was passed in 1851. He was a member of the Maine Legislature in 1858-59. As colonel of the Thirteenth Maine volunteers, during the Civil war, he joined General Butler's expedition to New Orleans, and in April, 1862, was commissioned brigadier-general of volunteers and placed in command of the forts at the mouth of the Mississippi. Subsequently he was transferred to the district of Florida. He was twice wounded in the attack on Port Hudson, May 27, 1863, and was a prisoner of war for over eight months. He resigned his commission November 30, 1864. In 1857, and again in 1866 and 1873, Mr. Dow went to England at the invitation of the United Kingdom Temperance Alliance, and addressed crowded meetings in all the large cities. He spent many years in earnest endeavor to win the popular sanction for prohibitory legislation. In 1880 he was the candidate of the National Prohibition party for president of the United States, and received 10,305 votes. It was largely through his efforts that the prohibitory amendment to the constitution of Maine was adopted in 1884. In the ranks of reformers there is no more picturesque figure than Neal Dow, and in his green old age there is none held in greater reverence by an appreciative and admiring people.

NEAL DOW.

MARY KAVANAUGH OLDHAM EAGLE.

THE rare tact and ability shown by Mrs. K. O. Eagle in connection with the Woman's Congress of the Columbian Exposition was no more than was expected of her by those familiar with what she had already accomplished in the field of church work and as a social leader. She was born in Madison County, Kentucky. Her father, William K. Oldham, a leading stock-farmer in the Blue Grass region, and her mother, nee Kate Brown, of Brown's Cove, Va., were both of Revolutionary stock. The daughter's early education was conducted chiefly at home, after which she graduated from Mrs. Julia A. Lewis' famous school, Science Hill, Shelbyville, Ky. She became a member of the Baptist Church in 1874, and has been one of the notable workers for that organization since that time. In 1882 she became the wife of Hon. Jas. P. Eagle, of Arkansas, who was Speaker of the House in 1885 and who has since been twice elected governor of the state. Mrs. Eagle has been president of the Woman's Central Committee on Missions since 1882, and was the first president of the Woman's Mission Union, of Arkansas. In her husband's successful political career she has been an active factor. During his term as governor, the Executive Mansion was famous for the bounteous Southern hospitality shown there, and Mrs. Eagle has in all her husband's campaigns been a tactful worker. As a member of the Board of Lady Managers of the World's Columbian Exposition, and as chairman of the Committee on Congresses, her reputation became more than national. She was selected as editor of the papers read, and the splendid volumes lately issued bear evidence that her literary skill is equal to her ability in other directions.

MARY KAVANAUGH OLDHAM EAGLE
197

GEORGE FRANKLIN EDMUNDS.

FOR many years the man best known in the United States Senate as a fearless foe of political jobs and legislative intrigues was the veteran statesman from Vermont, George F. Edmunds. He was born February 1, 1828, in Richmond, Vt., but after becoming a lawyer removed to Burlington to practice his profession. From 1854 to 1859 he was a representative in the Legislature, serving three years as Speaker, and was elected to the State Senate in 1861, retiring at the end of the term. In March, 1866, he succeeded Solomon Foot as United States senator, and by successive re-elections was continued in that office until he resigned in 1891. Senator Edmunds was active in the Andrew Jackson impeachment, acted an influential part in the passage of the re-construction measures, and was the author of the act for the suppression of polygamy in Utah, known as the "Edmunds act." He was a member of the Electoral Commission of 1876, was president pro tem. of the Senate after Mr. Arthur became President, and member of many important committees. At the National Republican conventions of 1880 and 1884, held in Chicago, he received thirty-four and ninety-three votes, respectively, each on the first ballot, for the presidential nomination. As a legislator, Mr. Edmunds was noted for his legal acumen, his readiness in repartee, and his love of strictly parliamentary procedure. The passage of the Pacific railroad funding act was largely due to his influence and exertions, and he was a leader in many noted legislative movements during his twenty-five years in the Senate. He retired to private life two years before the completion of his last term, resuming the practice of his profession at Burlington, Vt. He carried with him the respect and admiration of the people.

GEORGE FRANKLIN EDMUNDS.

EDWARD EGGLESTON.

LITERATURE gained what the ministry lost when that ever-popular novelist and historian, Edward Eggleston, forced by failing health to abandon pastoral work, began writing for the press as a means of supporting his family. Mr. Eggleston was born in Vevay, Ind., December 10, 1837. He was prevented by delicate health from entering college, and his education was mainly self-acquired. In 1856 he spent four months in Minnesota, hoping to be benefited by the climate, and then returning to Indiana became a Methodist preacher, riding a four-weeks' circuit. In six months his health broke down, and he was compelled to return to Minnesota, where he was variously occupied until 1866. He then removed to Evanston, Ill., and for six months was associate-editor of the "Little Corporal," a children's paper. A year later he became editor of the "Sunday-School Teacher," in Chicago, and was active in Sunday-school work until 1870, when he went to New York as literary editor of the New York "Independent." He succeeded Theodore Tilton as superintending editor of that paper, but resigned in July, 1871, to become editor of "Hearth and Home," which position he held for more than a year. In that paper he first published, serially, his story of "The Hoosier Schoolmaster," depicting early life in Indiana. It became immensely popular, and has been translated into various foreign languages. It was followed by "End of the World," "Mystery of Metropolisville," "The Circuit Rider," "Roxy," "The Hoosier School Boy," and a number of other works. From 1874 until 1879 Mr. Eggleston was pastor of a Brooklyn church, but again failing health compelled him to retire, and he has since devoted himself to literature.

EDWARD EGGLESTON.
199

CHARLES WILLIAM ELIOT.

TO be the president . of Harvard College is, of course, about the highest honor that can come to any one of the great educators in the United States. It may be fairly said that at the present time it appertains to one who truly deserves such fortune. Charles William Eliot was born in Boston, Mass., March 20, 1834. He was fitted for college at the Boston Latin school, and was graduated at Harvard in 1853. In the following year he was appointed tutor in mathematics and studied chemistry. In 1858 he was made assistant professor of mathematics and chemistry, but in 1861 taught chemistry in the Lawrence scientific school. In 1863 he went to Europe and spent two years in the study of chemistry and in an examination of the systems of public instruction in France, Germany and England. On his return in 1865 he was appointed professor of analytical chemistry in the Massachusetts Institute of Technology. Mr. Eliot became president of Harvard University in 1869. As the result of his assumption of the direction of affairs, Harvard has assumed much of the style of the more famous English universities, adopting the elective system and making various changes in its curriculum. President Eliot has received the degree of LL. D. from Williams, Princeton and Yale, and is a member of a great number of learned societies of the country. He is a fluent and forceful speaker on public occasions, and is in great demand at all events where the dignity of the university would not be lowered by his presence. Besides "Chemistry Memoirs," written with Prof. Frank H. Storer, an "Essay on Educational Topics" he has published, in connection with Professor Storer, a "Manual of Inorganic Chemistry" and a "Manual of Qualitative Chemical Analysis."

CHARLES WILLIAM ELIOT.

STEPHEN BENTON ELKINS.

WELL-INFORMED, daring, shrewd, and typically American is Stephen B. Elkins, whose name in the public mind is somehow associated with New Mexico. It is known that there was New Mexico and that there was Stephen B. Elkins, and that because of him New Mexico, somehow, developed faster. He was born in Perry County, Ohio, September 26, 1841. His family removed to Missouri when he was but a child. He received an ordinary preliminary education and graduated from the Missouri University in 1860. He studied law, but as soon as the Civil war began entered the service as captain of the Seventy-seventh Missouri regiment. The war left him in New Mexico, where he studied law and was admitted to the bar, engaged at once, with a decided speculative instinct which is in him, in mining and stock-raising, and became rapidly a rich man. He became interested in politics, also, and was a member of the Territorial Legislature, United States district attorney, and then a delegate to Congress, a strong fighter for the admission of New Mexico as a state. As the leading representative of New Mexico he acquired national prominence and influence in party councils. He was a strong advocate of Blaine for the presidency. He was Secretary of War under Harrison, and is today an important factor in the politics of the Republican party. Of late Mr. Elkins has devoted attention rather to his various important business interests than to politics, but, young man as he is, and with a record in the political field such as he has already made, it is unlikely that his will not be a future voice in the direction of governmental affairs. He is not of the class of men who can retire early from active effort.

STEPHEN BENTON ELKINS.

WILLIAM CROWNINSHIELD ENDICOTT.

- - —

A TYPICAL living and forceful representative of what we call the "old New England families" is William C. Endicott. He is a direct descendant of Gov. John Endicott, the colonial ruler of Massachusetts, who died in Boston in 1665, after years of vigorous and often hasty-tempered action, and who was certainly a Puritan of the Puritans. He is a grandson of that Jacob Crowninshield who was prominent as a congressman, and who was appointed Secretary of the Navy by President Jefferson, but who died before entering upon the discharge of his duties. Of the same type as these men is the one who was Secretary of War during the first administration of President Cleveland. He was born in Salem, Mass., November 19, 1827. He graduated at Harvard in 1847, and after a law school course was admitted to the bar in 1850. He rapidly acquired a position as a young man of judgment and ability, and was elected a member of the Salem common council in 1852, five years later becoming city solicitor. He retired from that office in 1864 and resumed practice, but in 1873 was appointed to the bench of the Supreme court of Massachusetts. This office he held for ten years, resigning at the end of that time on account of ill health. He had remained something of a figure in politics. He was originally a Whig, but with the termination of that organization became a Democrat, and was, in 1884, an unsuccessful candidate for governor of Massachusetts. In 1885 he was appointed by President Cleveland Secretary of War and served out the term of office. He has not of late actively engaged in Democratic political affairs in his state, but is at all times a possibility with his party and a recognized leader in every important movement.

WILLIAM CROWNINSHIELD ENDICOTT.

WILLIAM MAXWELL EVARTS.

HAVING followed the profession of the law for more than fifty years, and during that period left an indelible impression upon it by his great legal learning and his high standing as a practitioner, William M. Evarts, of New York, has well earned the rest he is now enjoying. He was born in Boston, Mass., February 6, 1818; graduated at Yale in 1837, and admitted to the bar in New York in 1841. In 1851, while assistant district attorney in New York City, he successfully conducted the prosecution of the Cuban filibusters concerned in the Cleopatra expedition. His able and successful handling of other celebrated cases, some of them of a national character, soon earned him a wide reputation. In the Republican National Convention of 1860 he proposed the name of William H. Seward for the presidency. In 1868 President Johnson chose him as chief counsel in the impeachment trial, and from July 15, 1868, until the close of Johnson's administration he was Attorney-General of the United States. He acted as counsel for the United States before the tribunal of arbitration on the Alabama claims in 1872, and was senior counsel for Henry Ward Beecher in the famous trial of 1875. In 1877 he was advocate of the Republican party before the electoral commission, and during the administration of President Hayes was Secretary of State. In 1881 he went to Paris as delegate of the United States to the International Monetary Conference, and from 1885 to 1891 he was United States senator from New York. Many of his public addresses have already taken a place among the great orations of the century, notably his eulogy on Chief Justice Chase and his speech at the unveiling of Bartholdi's Statue of Liberty.

WILLIAM MAXWELL EVARTS.
207

JOHN VILLARS FARWELL.

WHAT energy, industry and perseverance will accomplish for a young man, when aided by good habits and a strict adherence to the highest rules of honor, is illustrated in the life of that successful merchant and moral educator, John V. Farwell, of Chicago. Mr. Farwell was born in Campbelltown, Steuben County, N. Y., July 29, 1825, and is the son of a farmer. He removed with his family to Illinois in 1838, settling in Ogle County, and in 1845 went to Chicago, without a dollar in his pocket, to look for work. His first employment was in the office of the city clerk. Afterward he was employed successively in the dry goods houses of Hamilton & White, Hamilton & Day and Wadsworth & Phelps, and acquired an interest in the latter firm in 1850. The name of the firm was changed in 1860 to Cooley, Farwell & Co., of which Marshall Field and L. Z. Leiter were subsequently members. In 1865 the firm became J. V. Farwell & Co., and so continued until 1891, when it was incorporated under its present name of The J. V. Farwell Company. Mr. Farwell has always taken a deep interest in religious matters. He was practically the founder of the Young Men's Christian Association in Chicago, which now owns one of the handsomest buildings in the city, and aided D. L. Moody, the evangelist, in the establishment of the Illinois State Mission, of which he was president for ten years. He has also served as chairman of the Chicago branch of the United States Christian Commission. In connection with others he formed a syndicate which built the Texas State House, and which was conceded for the work three million acres of land in that state. He is one of the recognized greatest business men of the great central city of the continent.

JOHN VILLARS FARWELL
209

EDGAR FAWCETT.

GATHERING much of the material for his novels from the lower strata of society, Edgar Fawcett has probably done as much as any other living writer to bring to the attention of thinking people the inconsistencies and weaknesses of the social system as it exists in this boasted nineteenth century. At the same time he has gained for himself a high reputation as a clever and realistic novelist, and as a poet. Mr. Fawcett was born in New York City, May 26, 1847. He was graduated at Columbia College in 1867, and has since devoted himself to literature, writing novels, poems, essays and magazine articles, many of which have attracted general attention and caused much discussion. His books include "Short Poems for Short People," "Purple and Fine Linen," "Ellen Story," "Poems of Fantasy and Passion," "A Hopeless Case," "A Gentleman of Leisure," "An Ambitious Woman," "Song and Story," "Tinkling Cymbals," "The Adventures of a Widow," "Rutherford," "The Bunting Ball," "The New King Arthur," "Social Silhouettes," "Romance and Revery," "The House at High Bridge," "Douglas Duane," "A Man's Will," "Olivia Delaplaine," "Divided Lives," "A Demoralizing Marriage," "Agnosticism and Other Essays," "Miriam Balestier," "Solarion," "The Evil that Men Do," "Fabian Dimitry," and "A Daughter of Silence." Mr. Fawcett has also been successful as a playwright. His stories are unique in style, cleverly planned and as cleverly worked out, full of picturesque descriptions, thrilling incidents and interesting situations, and often with a weird and fantastic thread running through them. His poems are artistic, and at times exceedingly felicitous in form and pregnant with deep and tender meanings.

EDGAR FAWCETT.

211

KATE FIELD.

VARIED accomplishments, kept constantly under the lash of persistent energy and hard work, have made Miss Kate Field one of the best known women in America. She lives in Washington, but would be equally at home in Chicago, New York, London, San Francisco, or Paris. Born in St. Louis and educated in Boston and Italy, she has since been all over the world, and is essentially cosmopolitan. After receiving a classical education Miss Field gave special attention to musical studies, and made several prolonged visits to Europe. During her stay abroad she became a correspondent of the New York "Tribune," the Philadelphia "Press," and the Chicago "Tribune," and also furnished sketches for periodicals. In 1874 she appeared as an actress at Booth's Theater, New York, and proved herself to be possessed of considerable dramatic talent. Later, however, she left the stage, and has since devoted herself to lecturing and to journalism, the two occupations in which she has achieved her greatest success. Among her published works are "Planchette's Diary," "Adelaide Ristori," "Mad on Purpose" (a comedy), "Pen Photographs from Charles Dickens' Readings," "Hap-Hazard," "Ten Days in Spain" and "History of Bell's Telephone." She founded "The National Review" several years ago, and is the founder and editor of "Kate Field's Washington," the only periodical in the world bearing a woman's name. Miss Field claims that whatever she may be is due to heredity, as her father, Joseph M. Field, was a brilliant and versatile man, and her mother, Eliza Lapsley Riddle, of Philadelphia, one of the most charming actresses of her day. At any rate, she has built a lasting monument for herself as a journalist, author, editor and orator.

KATE FIELD.

DAVID ROWLAND FRANCIS.

THE state of Missouri has had a long line of distinguished governors, but never one who so quickly gained a national reputation for broad statesmanship as David R. Francis. He is today one of the most popular Democrats of the country, and is destined to receive higher honors than any that have yet been bestowed upon him. Ex-Governor Francis was born in Richmond, Madison County, Ky., October 1, 1850, and at the age of sixteen went to St. Louis, where he graduated at the Washington University, in 1870. He entered mercantile life, and eventually became one of the leading grain merchants of the city, rising to the honorable position of president of the Merchants' Exchange, in 1883. He was a delegate to the National Democratic Convention in 1884, and his voice was heard in able advocacy of Cleveland and Hendricks, at Chicago. In 1885 he was nominated for mayor of St. Louis, and triumphantly elected over his Republican opponent, who, four years before, had received a majority of fourteen thousand votes. Mr. Francis became so popular as mayor that when he was nominated for governor in 1888, it is safe to say that no candidate for that office ever had a more enthusiastic following. He was elected and gave the state one of the ablest administrations it has ever had. A warm personal friend of President Cleveland, it is commonly believed in high political circles that Mr. Francis could have been a member of President Cleveland's Cabinet, had he so desired. The prediction is frequently and confidently made that at an early date he will represent Missouri in the United States Senate, and certainly, with his capabilities and popularity, there is nothing preposterous in placing the goal of his future advancement at even a higher altitude.

DAVID ROWLAND FRANCIS.
215

STEPHEN JOHNSON FIELD.

ONE of the most eminent of American jurists, and a member of a distinguished family, is the senior Associate Justice of the United States Supreme Court, Stephen Johnson Field. He was born in Haddam, Conn., November 4, 1816, and removed with his family in 1819 to Stockbridge, Mass. In 1829 he accompanied his sister to Asia Minor, her husband, Rev. Josiah Brewer, having undertaken an educational mission to the Greeks, and remained abroad two and a half years. He graduated at Williams College in 1837, after which he studied law, and was for seven years the partner of his brother, David Dudley Field. In 1848 he traveled extensively in Europe, and upon his return went to California, finally settling in Marysville in 1850, and was elected first alcalde of that city. He was a member of the second Legislature of California, and while serving on the judiciary committee framed the laws creating the judicial system of the state. He became a judge of the Supreme Court of California in 1857, and chief justice two years later. In 1863 he was appointed by President Lincoln Associate Justice of the United States Supreme Court, which position he still holds. He was a member of the electoral commission of 1876, and voted with the Democratic minority. In 1880 he was a candidate for the presidential nomination before the Democratic convention and received sixty-five votes. Williams College conferred upon him the degree of Doctor of Laws in 1866. In 1889 a vicious assault was made upon Justice Field in a California hotel by Judge Terry, a noted lawyer of that state, and the latter was killed by a United States marshal named Nagle, who had been deputed to protect Justice Field. Justice Field is still hale and vigorous.

STEPHEN JOHNSON FIELD.

217

JOHN FISKE.

A MONG the deep thinkers of the day John Fiske occupies a conspicuous place. He was born in Hartford, Conn., March 30, 1842. He received a thorough education, his father being a well-known editor, and graduated at Harvard, and afterward at the Harvard Law School, but did not engage in the practice of his nominal profession. He became, almost at once, a writer whose work was such as to attract attention from the thinking world. He wrote about this time an article on "Mr. Buckle's Fallacies," which appeared in the "National Quarterly Review," and which was, perhaps, the first of his contributions to the press to attract general attention. In 1869 he was appointed Lecturer of Philosophy in Harvard. Since 1881 he has been Lecturer on American History in the Washington University, St. Louis, Mo., and has been a most prolific writer, and one the character of whose works has attracted the attention of the great thinkers of the world. Among what Professor Fiske has written may be included "Tobacco and Alcohol," "Myths and Myth-makers," "Outlines of Cosmic Philosophy Based on the Doctrines of Evolution," "The Unseen World," "Darwinism" and Other Essays, "Excursions of an Evolutionist," "The Destiny of Man Viewed in the Light of His Origin," "The Idea of God as Affected by Modern Knowledge" and "The American Political Idea Viewed from the Standpoint of Universal History." Professor Fiske is now engaged upon a work of magnitude, to be entitled "The History of the American People." It may be said of him that he ranks high in this country among the small group who correspond to the great scientists abroad, such as Darwin, Huxley, Tyndall, and others of their class.

JOHN FISKE.
219

ROSWELL PETTABONE FLOWER.

SOME men overcome obstacles and achieve success by sheer persistency of will, aided by tact and good judgment. Of such is Roswell P. Flower, governor of New York, who began life as a poor boy, and by the most stubborn perseverance and determination gained both wealth and distinction. Governor Flower was born in Theresa, Jefferson County, N. Y., August 7, 1835, and is the descendant of an Englishman who emigrated to Hartford, Conn., in 1686. He lost his father when eight years old, and a few years later left school, to assist in the support of the family. At the age of fourteen he became a clerk in a store, but subsequently received a high-school education. After working in a brick yard and as a postoffice clerk, he was for ten years a jeweler, and learned that trade thoroughly, but eventually decided that it did not offer the rapid transit to fortune which his restless ambition craved. He then became a broker in New York City, and from that time his rise was rapid. Success attended his operations, and he soon became a prominent figure in Wall street. He also took an active interest in politics, with the result that in 1881 he became a member of Congress, having been elected as a Democrat over William W. Astor. In 1886 he was appointed one of the electric sub-way commissioners in New York City. In 1888 he was again elected to Congress, and was re-elected in 1890, serving on various important committees, including the committee on ways and means and the committee on the quadro-centennial celebration. In 1892 he was elected governor of New York. He was succeeded in office by Levi P. Morton. Governor Flower gave $50,000 for the erection of the St. Thomas Home in New York.

ROSWELL PETTABONE FLOWER.

JOSEPH BENSON FORAKER.

A STRIKING figure anywhere would be the brilliant and aggressive ex-governor of Ohio, but especially attractive of attention is he as the leader of the younger element of the Republican party in Ohio. He was born near Rainsborough in the state named, July 5, 1846, and worked on a farm in his boyhood. When sixteen years old he enlisted in the Eighty-ninth Ohio regiment and served in the Army of the Cumberland until the end of the war. He was made sergeant in 1862. After the war he spent two years at Wesleyan University and later entered Cornell, where he graduated in 1869. He was admitted to the bar the same year and practiced in Cincinnati. In 1879 he was elected judge of the Superior court in Cincinnati, subsequently resigning the office because of ill health. Meantime he had attained popularity with his party as a brilliant and capable leader and became the Republican candidate for governor in 1883, making a splendid canvass though not a successful one. In 1885 he was again a candidate and was this time elected. In 1887 he was again elected and became decidedly the head of the most vigorous and aggressive element of his party in Ohio. In 1889 he was defeated by James E. Campbell, the Democratic candidate, but remained a potent force in the councils of his party, and has been a prominent figure in its national conventions. Still young in years, with a national reputation and recognized as a man of great force, and one possessing the qualities of a natural leader of men, the future of the Ohio ex-governor is one of vast possibilities. In 1896 he was elected Senator to succeed Calvin S. Brice, and certainly few men are better fitted to wear the toga than Ex-Governor Foraker.

JOSEPH BENSON FORAKER
225

J. ELLEN HORTON FOSTER.

POSSIBLY no other woman, unless it may be Mrs. Lease, of Kansas, exercises the direct influence upon politics that Mrs. J. Ellen Foster, of Iowa, does. She is a striking figure in her field, even more so because she is not absolutely controlled by some ism, but thinks for herself and acts accordingly. She has been an important factor in more than one state election. She was born in Lowell, Mass., November 3, 1840, and is the daughter of Rev. Jotham Horton, a Methodist preacher. She was educated in Lima, N. Y., and moved to Clinton, Ia., where, in 1869, she became the wife of D. E. Foster, a lawyer. She studied law and was admitted to practice, engaged in a business at first alone, eventually joining with her husband. Eventually she engaged in the temperance movement, in which she soon became a prominent figure. As superintendent of the legislative department of the W. C. T. U., she acquired a national reputation. In 1887 she visited England, where she made a study of the temperance question, and where, in England, she addressed great audiences. In the United States she has always been independent as to what should be the best course to pursue in temperance movements as to making connection with any of the great political bodies. As a result she has not always been in the closest affiliation with her own organization, but has, none the less, become a power politically, and has, perhaps, done as effective work toward general temperance as any woman in the world, though the lines upon which she has worked have not been such as the leaders of the W. C. T. U. have always agreed upon. She has been broader, however, and has had the courage of her convictions. She is a remarkable woman.

J. ELLEN HORTON FOSTER.
227

MARSHALL FIELD.

O F the great merchant princes of America there is none who stands so close to the people, by reason of his being one of them, as Marshall Field, of Chicago. A man of slender build, of modest yet impressive demeanor, he carries his business responsibilities as gracefully as he does his years, never permitting them to affect in the slightest degree his kindly, sympathetic nature. The greatest merchant in the world was born in Conway, Mass., in 1835. His father was a farmer. He came to Chicago in 1856 and obtained employment in the wholesale dry-goods house of Cooley, Wadsworth & Co., afterward Cooley, Farwell & Co., and now the John V. Farwell Company. He was given an interest in the concern in 1860, but in 1865 both Mr. Field and L. Z. Leiter withdrew from the house to join Potter Palmer in organizing the firm of Field, Palmer & Leiter. When Mr. Palmer dropped out, in 1867, the firm became Field, Leiter & Co., and since Mr. Leiter's retirement in 1881 the house has been known by its present name of Marshall Field & Co. It is the greatest mercantile establishment in the world, having branches in Paris, Manchester, Yokohama and other foreign centers, and carrying on a business amounting to over forty million dollars a year. Marshall Field's rule is to never borrow, never give a note, never to speculate in stocks, and to buy for cash. His charity seems to be boundless, and is never ostentatious. His gifts have been bestowed with discretion and public spirit. He gave one million dollars to the Columbian Museum fund, was a large contributor to the Chicago University, and is a liberal patron of many public institutions of a charitable and educational character. His career has been marked by a strict business policy.

ALICE FRENCH.

NO author of the present generation has more thoroughly mastered the art of writing short stories than has Miss Alice French. Her pen name of "Octave Thanet" is associated in the minds of all readers of current literature with many clever achievements in this line, and her sparkling style and exquisite humor have placed her in the front rank of magazine contributors. Miss French was born in Andover, Mass., March 19, 1850, and on both sides of the house is descended from the Puritans. She was educated in New England and goes there every summer, although for many years her home has been in Davenport, Iowa. She began to write shortly after her graduation at Abbot Academy, Andover, but took the advice of the editors and waited several years before venturing into print. Then she sent "A Communist's Wife" to the Harper's, who declined it, and afterward sent it to the Lippincott's, who accepted it. Since that time she has always found a place for her productions. Among her stories that have been issued in book form may be mentioned "Knitters in the Sun," "Otto the Knight," "Expiation," "We All," and "Stories of a Western Town." She has also edited "The Best Letters of Lady Mary Montagu." Personally, Miss French is a sociable, chatty, and altogether womanly woman, as sparkling and vivacious in conversation as she is in her writings. She is interested in historical studies and the German philosophers, has a fad for collecting china, likes all outdoor sports, and prides herself on her cooking. Miss French spends her winters at Clover Bend, Ark., where she has a delightful and cosy retreat, and where the greater portion of her literary work is done. She has a wide circle of friends and admirers.

ALICE FRENCH
231

HAMLIN GARLAND.

AN ultra advocate of the realistic is Hamlin Garland, prominent among the western writers of the new school who are photographing the fervid life of the Mississippi valley, photographing it faithfully, with its bare spots and those more luxuriant. He has brains and the writer's gift, and above all he is earnest and persistent. He is in the field of literature in which he should properly be found He was born in 1860 in the La Crosse valley, Wisconsin, and lived the life of the usual Wisconsin boy of the time. A very good life for a boy, that was, too. When he was seven years of age his family moved to Iowa and there he grew to manhood. He learned the life of the prairies, how to ride a horse and herd cattle, how to do all a prairie farmer does, what the prairie farmer endures and what he enjoys, all of which shows in his stories. In 1883 he went to Dakota with the "boomers," and from there he went to Boston, where he taught private classes in English and American literature for some years. Of late he has devoted himself entirely to literature and the lecture platform. He has published six volumes of stories of western life, one volume of "Prairie Songs" and one volume of essays -- "Crumbling Idols." He makes his headquarters in Chicago, but his summer home is with his parents, in West Salem, Wis. Among his works "Main Traveled Roads" is easily the volume which has been most striking and has given him most prominence. Still a young man, Mr. Garland has a splendid literary future before him. If not as the greatest of western novelists he will at least retain prominence as the essayist and lecturer, for in each field he is strong. But where the maximum of his powers will most develop is still uncertain.

HAMLIN GARLAND.

233

HENRY GEORGE.

IN these days, when people have learned to accept as a matter of
course the existing laws and customs governing the organization of
society, and to conform to them without question, the social reformer
finds his task no easy one. Among the political economists of the
present day Henry George takes high rank as an advanced thinker,
and has a following that increases in numbers every year. Mr.
George was born in Philadelphia, September 2, 1839. In his boyhood
he went to sea as an apprentice on a sailing vessel, and in 1858 he
reached California, where he became a journalist, and where he eventually wrote his first two books, "Our Land and Land Policy," and
"Progress and Poverty." In 1880 he removed to New York, and has
since been chiefly known by his writings and addresses on economic
subjects. In these he traces the social evils of our time to the treat-
ment of land as subject to complete individual ownership, and con-
tends that while the secure possession of land should be accorded to
the individual it should be subject to the payment to the community
of land values proper, or economic rent. This theory, known as the
"Single Tax," aims at abolishing all taxes for raising revenue except
a tax on the value of land, irrespective of improvement. His later
books are: "Irish Land Question," "Social Problems," "Property in
Land," "Protection or Free Trade," "The Condition of Labor," and
"A Perplexed Philosopher." Mr. George has lectured extensively in
this country, Europe and Australia, and between 1887 and 1890 published "The Standard," a weekly single-tax paper. In 1886 he was
a candidate for the mayoralty of New York on a labor ticket, receiving sixty-eight thousand votes.

HENRY GEORGE.

PARKE GODWIN.

—

KEEN political foresight, combined with legal knowledge, literary ability and a remarkable intellectual grasp, has made the name of Parke Godwin familiar to the ears of all educated people in this country. As a writer on topics pertaining to governmental reforms, he is especially well known. Parke Godwin was born in Paterson, N. J., February 25, 1816. He was graduated at Princeton College in 1834, after which he studied law and was admitted to the bar in Kentucky, but did not practice. He married the eldest daughter of William Cullen Bryant, the poet-editor, and from 1837 until 1853, with the exception of one year, was connected with the New York "Evening Post." In 1843 he issued the "Pathfinder," a weekly paper, which was suspended after three months. He contributed many articles to the "Democratic Review," in which he advocated reforms that were subsequently introduced into the constitution and code of New York. He was also editor of "Putnam's Monthly," to which he contributed many literary and political articles, afterward published in book form under the title, "Political Essays." In 1865 he again became connected with the "Evening Post." During the administration of President Polk he was deputy collector of New York, but he subsequently joined the Republican party and supported it by his speeches and writings. He is the author of "Popular View of the Doctrines of Charles Fourier," "Constructive Democracy," "Vala, a Mythological Tale," "Cyclopaedia of Biography," "History of France," "Out of the Past," a volume of essays, and has also edited an edition of William Cullen Bryant's prose and poetical writings, in six volumes. Mr. Godwin's opinions are much sought on political and literary questions.

PARKE GODWIN.
235

ARTHUR PUE GORMAN.

ONE of the most outspoken of men, with apparently no conceal-ments or reserves, and with abilities that eminently fit him for the high position in which his party has placed him, Senator Arthur P. Gorman, of Maryland, is regarded as a model of candor and honesty in the upper branch of Congress, where for a number of years he has represented his state as a conservative Democrat. Senator Gorman was born in Howard County, Maryland, March 11, 1839. He received a public school education, and in 1852 became a page in the United States Senate, where he remained until 1866, at which time he was the Senate postmaster. On September 1 of that year he was appointed collector of internal revenue for the Fifth district of Maryland, which office he held until March, 1869. Three months later he was made a director in the Chesapeake and Ohio Canal Company, of which he became president in 1872. In November, 1869, he was elected to the Maryland Legislature as a Democrat, re-elected in 1871, and chosen Speaker of the House during the ensuing session. He was elected to the State Senate in 1875, and served four years. In 1880 he was chosen to represent the state in the United States Senate, succeeding William Pinkney Whyte, and was re-elected in 1886 and 1892. His term of service will expire in 1899. In the Senate, Mr. Gorman wields a powerful influence. He is eloquent and forcible in debate, and his remarks always receive the closest attention. When a compli-cated or momentous question is under discussion, it is usually the speech of Senator Gorman that clears the atmosphere like a thunder-shower at the close of a sultry day, pointing the way to a solution of the problem.

ARTHUR PUE GORMAN.
237

ELISHA GRAY.

LABORERS in the field of electrical science do not often rise to the position attained by Prof. Elisha Gray in the development of that science. His works have made an impression scarcely less important than that of any other whose name might be mentioned. Professor Gray was born at Barnesville, Belmont County, Ohio, August 2, 1835. At the age of twenty-one he went to Oberlin College, where he studied for five years. It was not until his thirtieth year that he first turned his attention to electrical mechanism, with which he soon became fascinated. His first invention of practical importance was that of the needle annunciator for hotels, which was invented in 1870 and perfected in 1872. This was followed by the electrical annunciator for elevators, and later by the private telegraph line printer, so well known to this day. From 1873 to 1875 his attention was largely absorbed in developing a system of electro-harmonic telegraphy for the transmission of sounds over telegraph wires. On February 14, 1876, he filed at Washington a caveat for "Art of transmitting vocal sounds telegraphically." But Prof. A. Graham Bell, though probably anticipated in point of time by the caveat of Professor Gray, was granted a broad patent for speaking telephones, March 8, 1876, and sixteen years of litigation failed to deprive him of the credit as the inventor. Professor Gray's latest invention is the telautograph, for the transmission of written language in fac-simile. He resides at Highland Park, near Chicago, and is one of the most affable and genial of men. In his profession he is universally esteemed, both as a man and as a scientist and inventor of the highest rank. The world owes him much for his valuable discoveries.

ELISHA GRAY.

GALUSHA AARON GROW.

RENOWNED as a fearless and patriotic statesman during a critical period of the country's history- modestly retiring at the end of that period, only to be taken up thirty years after and elected to Congress by an unprecedented majority such is the record of Galusha A. Grow, of Pennsylvania. Mr. Grow was born in Ashford (now Eastford), Windham County, Conn., August 31, 1824, but when ten years old removed with his family to Susquehanna County, Pennsylvania. He was graduated at Amherst in 1844, after which he studied law and practiced at Towanda until 1850, when his health failed and he became a farmer. In that year he declined a unanimous nomination for the Legislature, but was soon after elected to Congress as a Democrat and served for twelve successive years, although in the mean time severing his connection with the Democratic party on the repeal of the Missouri compromise bill. His period of service was distinguished by much important legislation. His first speech was delivered upon the Homestead bill, a measure which he continued to urge at every Congress for ten years, when he had at last the satisfaction of signing the law as Speaker of the House. He served as Speaker from July 4, 1861, until March 4, 1863, when, upon retiring, he was given a unanimous vote of thanks, a most unusual proceeding. Mr. Grow was a delegate to the National Republican conventions of 1864 and 1868. In 1871 he settled in Houston, Tex., as president of the International and Great Northern railroad, but returned to Pennsylvania in 1875, and in 1876 declined a mission to Russia. In 1894 he was elected Congressman-at-large to succeed William Lilly, deceased, receiving the astonishing plurality of 188,294 votes over his strongest opponent.

GALUSHA AARON GROW.

GERTRUDE ATHERTON.

TO be intensely natural, yet to impart to her creations a touch of
ideality which may often be invisible in real life, although existing in an imperfect medium, is one of the literary principles of that
delightful writer of California stories, Mrs. Gertrude Atherton. Of her
favorite field California before the American occupation· Mrs. Atherton
has made an exhaustive study, living in the old towns with the rem-
nants of the race of which she writes, and storing up knowledge of
their customs and traditions. She was born on Rincon Hill, San
Francisco, and was educated by her grandfather, Stephen Franklin, who
was a nephew of Benjamin Franklin. Her father was Thomas L.
Horn, one of the original Vigilance Committee. As a child she composed stories, and at fifteen she wrote a play which was acted by
schoolmates at St. Mary's Hall, Benicia, Cal. Her education was
completed at Sayre Institute, Lexington, Ky., and soon thereafter she
was married to George H. B. Atherton, of California. She continued
her persistent pursuit of knowledge, however, with an ambition to one
day take a place in American literature. Her first published story,
"The Randolphs of Redwoods," appeared in the San Francisco "Argo-
naut." But her best work is in her stories of old California, "The
Doomswoman" and the eleven shorter ones that have been collected
under the title, "Before the Gringo Came." Some of her stories have
appeared in "The London Graphic," "Blackwood's" and other English
periodicals, and the "London Speaker" recently referred to her as one
of the pioneers of the true American literature. Mrs. Atherton, who
now resides at Yonkers, N. Y., has in preparation a novel to be entitled, "Patience Sparhawk and Her Times."

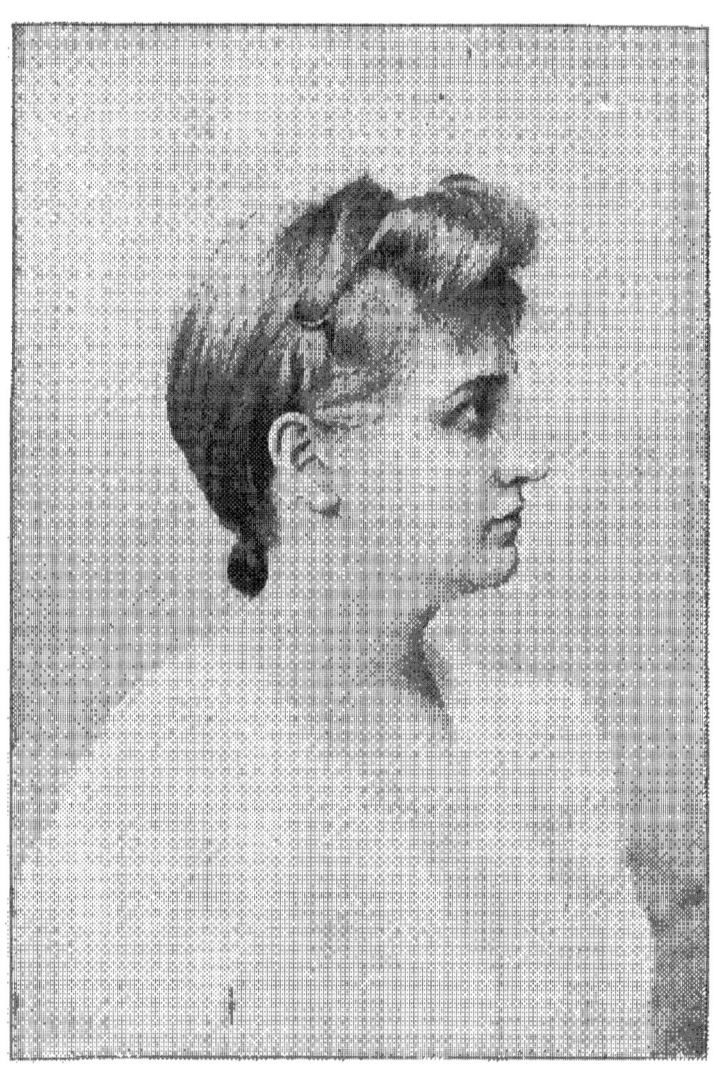

GERTRUDE ATHERTON.

HATTIE TYNG GRISWOLD.

READERS of current literature have for many years been familiar with the name of Mrs. Hattie Tyng Griswold, the talented author of many charming poems, stories and sketches. Mrs. Griswold, though known as a Western woman, is a native of Boston, Mass., where she was born January 26, 1842. Her father removed to Wisconsin while she was yet a child, and her life has been spent in that state. At the age of fifteen she began writing for the press, and a little later became a contributor to the New York "Home Journal," then edited by N. P. Willis, and to the Louisville "Courier-Journal," edited by George D. Prentice. These two men were literary lions in those days, and when they put the stamp of their approval on a production, there could be no question of its merit. She also wrote for the "Knickerbocker Magazine," and became quite a favorite of its editor, Charles G. Leland. In 1863 she was married to Eugene Sherwood Griswold, of Columbia, Wis., where she has continued to reside to the present time. Her pleasant home is the resort of many of the famous men and women of the day, for she has an extensive personal acquaintance with literary and other celebrities. Mrs. Griswold's first volume of collected poems was published in 1878, under the title of "Apple Blossoms." An edition of her later poems has been prepared for the press. In 1886 she published "Home Life of Great Authors," one of the most successful books of recent years. Among her works of fiction may be mentioned two stories for girls, "Waiting on Destiny" and "Lucile and Her Friends," and a novel entitled "Fencing with Shadows," which have added not a little to the author's reputation.

HATTIE TYNG GRISWOLD.
246

HORACE GRAY.

PRESIDENT ARTHUR made good appointments. The tact and sense of that typical man of the world made him, perhaps, a better judge of men than was more than one other of the presidents possibly surpassing him in genius. Not the least sensible and satisfactory among the appointments made by President Arthur was that of Horace Gray, of Massachusetts, to be associate justice of the Supreme Court of the United States. Horace Gray was born in Boston, Mass., March 24, 1828. He received a thorough preliminary education and was a graduate from Harvard in 1845, and from the Harvard Law School in 1849. He was admitted to the bar in 1851, and found himself at once in a field congenial to his special talents and inclinations. He was appointed reporter of the supreme judicial court of Massachusetts in 1854, and held that position until 1861, when he was appointed associate justice of the same court August 23, 1864. His remarkable legal ability was manifested in his position on this dignified bench, and in 1873 he was appointed chief justice of the court. In that position he became widely known because of his legal learning and the thoughtfulness and fairness of his decisions, and December 19, 1881, he was commissioned associate justice of the Supreme Court of the United States. He has filled the difficult position with all the ability and fairness that was expected of him, and is a distinguished member of the highest judicial tribunal of the world. He is one of the hardest working members of a body where hard work has been the rule for a long time, in fact from the beginning of the government, and his opinions are respected by his associates as highly as is his character by the country.

HORACE GRAY.
247

ARCHIBALD CLAVERING GUNTER.

THERE can certainly be no question of the popularity of a novel when the demand for it swells the first edition to more than sixty-one thousand copies. Such was the fate of "Mr. Barnes of New York," and of that later production from the same pen, "Mr. Potter of Texas." And yet the author had to turn publisher in order to get his books before the public. Archibald Clavering Gunter is an Englishman by birth, having been born in Liverpool October 25, 1847, but at the age of five years he was taken to California by his parents, and was there educated, taking the degree of Ph. B. in University College, San Francisco. From 1867 until 1874 he followed his profession of mining and civil engineering, and then became a stock broker in San Francisco, operating in mining stocks. In 1877 he went to New York, having fully decided to make literature his occupation in life. He had previously written two successful plays, and he now produced several others that were even more successful. His first novel, "Mr. Barnes of New York," was finished in 1885, and published in 1887. It had been refused by all the publishing houses to which he had submitted it, and he finally organized the Home Publishing Company and issued the novel himself. It was a great success, and has been printed in several languages. Mr. Gunter's own dramatization of the story had a remarkable run, and was immensely popular. His later novels, "Mr. Potter of Texas," "Miss Nobody of Nowhere," and others, have also been very successful. Combining energy and enterprise with marked literary ability, Mr. Gunter has accumulated a fortune from the products of his pen within a few years. His stories are full of dramatic force and interest.

ARCHIBALD CLAVERING GUNTER.
249

JOHN HABBERTON.

THE author of that interesting and clever book, "Helen's Babies," awoke one morning to find himself famous, and all because he had written something which, rather unexpectedly to him, struck the popular fancy. That work gave him a reputation which he has since sustained. John Habberton was born in Brooklyn, N. Y., February 24, 1842. He lived in Illinois from his eighth to his seventeenth year, then went to New York, learned to set type in the establishment of Harper & Brothers, and subsequently entered their counting-room. In 1862 he enlisted in the army as a private, rose to the rank of first lieutenant, and served through the war. He was again in the employ of the Harpers, from 1865 to 1872, when he went into business for himself and failed in six months. This led him to become a contributor to periodicals, and later to accept the post of literary editor of the "Christian Union," which he held from 1874 to 1877, when he resigned to take an editorial position on the New York "Herald." His first literary work was a series of sketches of western life. His "Helen's Babies," after being rejected by three publishers, was brought out by a Boston house in 1876, and has sold to the extent of about three hundred thousand copies in the United States. Eleven different English editions of it have appeared, besides several in the British colonies, and it has been translated into French, German and Italian. A few of Mr. Habberton's other works are "The Barton Experiment," "The Jericho Road," "The Scripture Club of Valley Rest," "Other People's Children," "The Crew of the Samuel Weller," "The Worst Boy in Town," "Who was Paul Grayson?" and "Brueton's Bayou." His style is simple and natural and devoid of affectation.

JOHN HABBERTON.

EDWARD EVERETT HALE

IN the ranks of the literary workers of America there is one figure
that deserves the distinguishing title of the "Grand Old Man," of
letters. Edward Everett Hale, D. D., is a survivor of that class of
writers and thinkers of which Emerson, Lowell and Parkman were
such conspicuous representatives. He was born in Boston, Mass.,
April 3, 1822. After graduating at Harvard, in 1839, he studied theology and became a Unitarian minister. He was pastor of the Church
of the Unity, of Worcester, Mass., from 1846 to 1856, since which
time he has been pastor of the South Congregational Church, Boston.
Dr. Hale has published a large number of books. The one that first
gave him international fame was "The Man Without a Country,"
which appeared in 1861. Prior to that he had produced "The
Rosary," in 1848, and "America," in 1856. Among his subsequent
works may be mentioned "His Level Best," and other stories, 1872,
"Ups and Downs," 1873; "Working-Men's Homes" and "In His
Name," 1874; "Philip Nolan's Friends," 1876; "Boys' Heroes," 1885;
"What is the American People," 1885. He edited a series of stories
of the war, sea, adventure, etc., from 1880 to 1885, and (conjointly
with Miss Hale) wrote "A Family Flight Through France, Germany,
etc.," in 1881. Mr. Hale has been a frequent contributor to periodicals, was editor of the "Christian Examiner," and the founder and
editor of that popular publication, "Old and New." He afterward
became editor of "Lend Me a Hand," and his work in the field of
literature shows the same vigor and freshness today that characterized
it thirty years ago. His stories are interesting and wholesome and
show the masterly skill of the scholar.

EDWARD EVERETT HALE.

MURAT HALSTEAD.

LONG recognized as one of the most powerful and influential exponents of Republican principles in the West, the veteran editor of the Cincinnati "Commercial-Gazette" is a striking figure in political journalism. Like the majority of Americans who have achieved distinction by the force of superior abilities, guided by indomitable energy and pluck, Murat Halstead began life as a poor country boy. Born in Paddy's Run, Butler County, Ohio, September 2, 1829, he spent the summers on his father's farm, and the winters in school until he was nineteen years old, and after teaching for a few months, entered Farmer's College, near Cincinnati, where he was graduated in 1851. While in college he had amused himself by contributing to the press, and finding that his articles were well received, and that he had a taste for such employment, he decided to adopt the profession of journalism. He became connected with the Cincinnati "Atlas," and then with the "Enquirer," and afterward established a Sunday newspaper in that city, of which he was editor. This enterprise was soon abandoned, and he obtained employment on the "Columbian and Great West," a weekly paper. He began work on the "Commercial," March 8, 1853, as a local reporter, and soon became news editor. In 1854 the "Commercial" was reorganized, and Mr. Halstead purchased an interest in the paper. In 1867 its control passed into his hands. He subsequently allied himself with the Republican party, which he has since supported. In 1890 Mr. Halstead edited a Republican campaign paper in New York, and President Harrison nominated him as Minister to Berlin, but the Senate refused to confirm the nomination. He is a stalwart figure in political journalism.

MURAT HALSTEAD.
255

JOHN MARSHALL HARLAN.

IN the administration of justice there is probably no man wearing the ermine today who has more thoroughly enlisted the confidence of the people than has John M. Harlan, associate justice of the United States Supreme Court. All his life Mr. Harlan has been of a judicial turn of mind. He was born in Boyle County, Kentucky, June 1, 1833, and was graduated at Center College, in that state, in 1850. After studying law at Transylvania University he practiced his profession at Frankfort, and in 1858 was elected county judge. He was afterward an unsuccessful Whig candidate for Congress, and was presidential elector on the Bell and Everett ticket. Removing to Louisville, he formed a law partnership with Hon. W. F. Bullock, and in 1861 entered the Union army as colonel of the Tenth Kentucky Infantry, serving in Gen. George H. Thomas' division. In 1863 he was elected attorney-general of Kentucky and filled the office until 1867. He was the Republican nominee for governor in 1871, and his name was presented by the Republican Convention of his state in 1875 for the vice-presidency of the United States. Judge Harlan was chairman of the Kentucky delegation to the Republican National Convention in 1876, and afterward declined a diplomatic position as a substitute for the attorney-generalship, to which, before he reached Washington, President Hayes intended to assign him. He served as a member of the Louisiana Commission, and on November 29, 1877, was commissioned an associate justice of the United States Supreme Court, as successor to David Davis. In his particular sphere Justice Harlan occupies a prominent place among the great men of America, and is justly honored for his eminent abilities and his pure life.

JOHN MARSHALL HARLAN.

WILLIAM RAINEY HARPER.

———

YOUNGER in years than the great majority of men who have gained reputations as scholars and educators, it is yet doubtful if there is a college professor in the United States who stands higher as a Hebraist and master of Biblical literature than William R. Harper, president of the University of Chicago. Born at New Concord, Ohio, July 26, 1856, President Harper is but thirty-eight years of age. After graduating at Muskingum College, and after three years of study at home, he took a two years' graduate course in Sanskrit, Greek and comparative philology at Yale under Professor Whitney, receiving the degree of Ph. D. In the same year he accepted the principalship of Masonic College, Macon, Tenn., and after teaching there for one year went to Denison University, Granville, Ohio, where he spent three years in teaching. From there he was called to the professorship of Hebrew and the cognate languages in the Baptist Union Theological Seminary at Morgan Park, Ill., near Chicago, where he began teaching Hebrew on the inductive method. In 1881 he organized a correspondence school of Hebrew, which later developed into The American Institute of Sacred Literature, now having its headquarters in Chicago. He also published "The Hebrew Student," the forerunner of the present "Hebraica," and "The Old and New Testament Student," now "The Biblical World." In 1886 he went to Yale as professor of Semitic languages and literature, afterward taking the chair of Biblical literature in English. In 1891 he became principal of the Chautauqua System, and in the same year was made president of the University of Chicago. President Harper is the author of several Hebrew, Greek and Latin text-books.

WILLIAM RAINEY HARPER.

FRANCIS BRET HARTE.

AS the founder of a distinct school of American literature, as well as for the truly artistic work that he has done in his chosen field, Bret Harte deserves the fame that he has won. He was born in Albany, N. Y., August 25, 1839, and received a common school education. After the death of his father he went with his mother to California in 1854, and, after unsuccessful ventures at teaching and mining, he became a compositor in a newspaper office at Sonora. In 1857 he went to San Francisco, and while setting type in the office of the "Golden Era" began writing anonymous sketches of his mining camp experiences. The result was that he was invited to join the corps of writers. Soon afterward he became associated in the management of the "Californian," a literary weekly, short-lived, but of interest as containing his "Condensed Novels." In July, 1868, the publication of "The Overland Monthly" was begun, with Mr. Harte as its organizer and editor. The second issue contained "The Luck of Roaring Camp," the first of those dialect character sketches of Western mining life of which he was the pioneer writer. It was followed by "The Outcasts of Poker Flat" and other stories, and the reputation of the author was established. In 1870 appeared his "Plain Language from Truthful James," popularly known as "The Heathen Chinee." His later novels and stories have all been exceedingly popular. He settled in New York in 1871, and became a regular contributor to magazines. In 1878 he was appointed United States Consul to Crefeld, Germany, whence he was transferred in 1880 to Glasgow, Scotland, and continued in that office until 1885. At present he is residing abroad, engaged in literary pursuits.

FRANCIS BRET HARTE.

JOSEPH ROSWELL HAWLEY.

QUITE an exceptional man in his generation, presenting in the very highest form the qualities that are calculated to shine both in the field and in the forum, Senator Joseph R. Hawley, of Connecticut, is one of the most distinguished of the soldier-statesmen of the Republic. He was born in Statesville, N. C., October 31, 1826, removed to Connecticut in 1837, was graduated at Hamilton College in 1847, and began the practice of law in Hartford in 1850. The first meeting for the organization of the Republican party in Connecticut was held in his office, at his call, February 4, 1856. One year later he abandoned law practice and became editor of the Hartford "Evening Press," the new distinctively Republican paper. He responded to the first call for troops in 1861, raising the first company of the First Connecticut volunteers, and is believed to have been the first volunteer in the state. Entering the service as a captain, he made a splendid war record and was mustered out in January, 1866, with the brevet of major-general. In April of that year he was elected governor of Connecticut, serving one year. In 1867, having consolidated the "Press" and the "Courant," he resumed editorial life, and more rigorously than ever entered the political contests following the war. He was always in demand as a speaker throughout the country, and was president of the National Republican convention in 1868. He served in the Forty-third and Forty-sixth Congresses, and in 1881, by the unanimous vote of his party, was chosen United States Senator, being re-elected in 1887, and again in 1893, for the term ending March 3, 1899. In the National convention of 1884 the Connecticut delegation unanimously voted for him for President in every ballot.

JOSEPH ROSWELL HAWLEY.
263

JULIAN HAWTHORNE.

INHERITING much of his distinguished father's talent, imaginative genius and graceful style of expression, Julian Hawthorne has established a reputation as a fluent and versatile writer. Mr. Hawthorne was born in Boston, Mass., June 22, 1846, was educated at Harvard, and studied civil engineering in the scientific school at Cambridge. In October, 1868, he went to Dresden to study, but the Franco-German war began while he was visiting at home in the summer of 1870, and he obtained employment as a hydrographic engineer under Gen. Geo. B. McClellan, in the department of docks, New York. In 1871 he began to write stories and sketches for magazines, and in 1872, deciding to devote himself to literature, went to England and then to Dresden, where he remained two years. While there he published his novels "Bressant" and "Idolatry." He settled in London in September, 1874, writing much for magazines, and for two years was a writer on the staff of the London "Spectator." In 1875 he published the sketches entitled "Saxon Studies" in the "Contemporary Review," and his novel "Garth," which was followed by novelettes and collections of stories entitled "The Laughing Mill," "Archibald Malmaison," "Ellice Quentin," "Prince Saroni's Wife," "Sebastian Strome," and the "Yellow Cap" fairy stories. He returned to New York in 1882, and published "Dust," "Noble Blood" and "Fortune's Fool;" also edited "Dr. Grimshaw's Secret," the posthumous romance of his father, Nathaniel Hawthorne, and wrote the biography of his father and mother. During the last dozen years he has made his home chiefly in this country, and has done some of his best work for American magazines and syndicates.

JULIAN HAWTHORNE

DAVID BREMNER HENDERSON.

RIPE experience and sound judgment are no less essential than intellectual strength and force of character in the man who would
be a leader of men. It is a combination of all these qualities that gives
David B. Henderson, of Iowa, his power and influence in the National
House of Representatives. Mr. Henderson was born at Old Deer,
Scotland, March 14, 1840. He was brought to the United States
when six years of age, settling first in Illinois, but removing in 1849
to Iowa, where he was educated in the public schools and at the
Upper Iowa University. He was reared on a farm until he was
twenty-one years of age, when the Civil war breaking out, he enlisted
as a private in the Twelfth Iowa regiment, in September, 1861. He
was soon after commissioned first lieutenant, and served with his regiment until the loss of a leg caused him to be discharged, February
16, 1863. In May of that year he was appointed commissioner of
the Board of Enrollment of the Third district of Iowa, serving as such
until June, 1864, when he re-entered the army as colonel of the Forty-
sixth Iowa regiment, and served until the close of hostilities. He was
collector of internal revenue for the Third district of Iowa from November, 1865, until June, 1869. In the mean time he had been admitted to
the bar, and in 1869 he became a member of the law firm of Shiras,
Van Duzee & Henderson. He was Assistant United States District
Attorney for about two years, resigning in 1871, and is now a member of the law firm of Henderson, Daniels & Kiesel, of Dubuque.
He was elected to the Forty-eighth Congress as a Republican, and has
since served continuously in that body, where he is distinctly one of
its leading forces.

DAVID BREMNER HENDERSON.

HILARY A. HERBERT.

AMONG the Southern men who have come into prominence by
reason of their sturdy integrity, great force of character and
superior accomplishments, is the Secretary of the Navy, Hilary A. Herbert. During an unusually long career in Congress he has distinguished himself in many ways, and especially by a thorough knowledge of the intricate affairs of the navy. Mr. Herbert is a native of
Laurensville, S. C., where he was born March 12, 1834, but while
he was yet a child his father removed to Greenville, Ala. He was
educated in the universities of Alabama and Virginia, studied law and
was admitted to the bar. Entering the confederate service as a captain, he was rapidly promoted until he became colonel of the Eighth
Alabama volunteers, and was disabled in the battle of the Wilderness,
May 6, 1864. He continued the practice of law at Greenville until
1872, when he removed to Montgomery, where he has since resided.
Colonel Herbert was first elected to the Forty-fifth Congress, and has
been re-elected seven times, so that he was, when appointed Secretary
of the Navy, about to enter upon his fifteenth continuous year in the
National House of Representatives. He is known as a profound
thinker, a forcible speaker in debate, and one of the few men in Congress who could be assigned to any kind of work with the assurance
that it would be accomplished promptly, intelligently and thoroughly.
He is particularly qualified to perform the duties of the high position
he now occupies, and he enjoys the confidence of the administration,
as well as the respect of all who have been associated with him in
his public life. His course in the cabinet has been such as to retain
for him the confidence of all parties.

HILARY A. HERBERT.
269

ABRAM STEVENS HEWITT.

IF there were to be selected from among all men a typical American, in the broadest sense of that term, the choice might justly fall upon Abram Stevens Hewitt. He is a cultivated man, and has such talent, such practical ability, and such force of character, that he has made a distinct mark in the world. He was born in Haverstraw, N. Y July 31, 1822. During his college course at Columbia he supported himself by teaching, and after his graduation, in 1842, remained in the college as acting professor of mathematics. He studied law and was admitted to the bar in 1855, but abandoned that profession to become associated with Peter Cooper in the iron business. In 1862 he went to England to learn the process of making gun barrel iron, and, at a heavy loss to his firm, furnished the United States Government with material during the war. The introduction of the Martins-Siemens or open hearth process for the manufacture of steel in this country is due to his judgment. The plan of the Cooper Union was devised by its own trustees, with Mr. Hewitt as their active head, and as secretary of this board he directed its financial and educational details. He was active in politics, but left Tammany, joined the Irving Hall society, and was one of the organizers of the County Democracy in 1879. He was elected to Congress in 1874 and served continuously, with the exception of one term, until 1886. In that year he was elected mayor of New York, defeating Henry George and Theodore Roosevelt. Columbia College gave him the degree of LL. D. in 1887. The firm of Cooper & Hewitt owns and controls the Trenton, Ringwood, Pequest and Durham iron works. Mr. Hewitt has a record to be proud of.

THOMAS WENTWORTH HIGGINSON.

THE prominent position which Thomas Wentworth Higginson has held in the ecclesiastical, literary and political world for more than a generation gives a special value and interest to his portrait and biography. Born in Cambridge, Mass., December 22, 1823, he was graduated at Harvard in 1841, and at the divinity school in 1847, becoming in the last-named year pastor of the First Congregational church in Newburyport, Mass. He resigned his pastorate in 1850 to become a candidate for Congress on the Free-soil ticket, but failed of election. From 1852 until 1858 he was pastor of a Free church in Worcester, Mass., after which he left the ministry to devote himself to literature, and became conspicuous as an anti-slavery agitator. In 1856 he aided in organizing parties of free-state emigrants to Kansas, and served as brigadier-general on Gov. J. H. Lane's staff in the free-state forces. Entering the Civil war as captain in 1862, he was soon made colonel of the Thirty-first South Carolina volunteers, the first regiment of freed slaves mustered into the National service. He took Jacksonville, Fla., was wounded at Wiltown Bluff, S. C., in August, 1863, and resigned from the army in 1864. From that year until 1878 Colonel Higginson dwelt in Newburyport, Mass., and then removed to Cambridge, Mass., where he has since resided, engaged in literary occupation. He was a member of the Massachusetts Legislature in 1880 and 1881. He has written extensively on educational and other topics for Harper's periodicals, the "Atlantic Monthly" and other magazines. His first publication was "Thalatto," a compilation of poetry. He is noted for his broad-minded liberality, his keen insight into human nature, and his general knowledge.

THOMAS WENTWORTH HIGGINSON.

GEORGE FRISBIE HOAR.

NOTED for his legal acumen, his broad statesmanship and his extended and diversified culture, Senator George F. Hoar, of Massachusetts, is regarded as one of the truly great men connected with the government at Washington. Born in Concord, Mass., August 29, 1826, he was graduated at Harvard in 1846, studied law and began the practice of his profession in Worcester. He was a member of the Massachusetts House of Representatives in 1852 and of the State Senate in 1857. He was elected as a Republican to four successive Congresses, serving from March 4, 1869, until March 3, 1877. He was elected United States senator to succeed George S. Boutwell, taking his seat March 5, 1877, and was re-elected in 1883, 1889 and 1895. His term of service will expire March 3, 1901. Senator Hoar was a delegate to the Republican National conventions of 1876, 1880, 1884 and 1888, presiding over the convention of 1880. He was one of the managers on the part of the House of Representatives of the Belknap impeachment trial in 1876, and was a member of the electoral commission in that year. From 1874 to 1880 he was an overseer of Harvard College, and in the latter year was regent of the Smithsonian Institution. He has been president, and is now vice-president, of the American Antiquarian Society, trustee of the Peabody Museum of Archaeology, trustee of Leicester Academy, and is a member of the Massachusetts Historical Society, the American Historical Society, the Historic-Genealogical Society and the Virginia Historical Society. The degree of LL. D. has been conferred upon him by William and Mary, Amherst, Yale and Harvard Colleges. Senator Hoar is a typical American statesman.

GEORGE FRISBIE HOAR.

MARY JANE HOLMES.

FOR stories of domestic life that are pure in tone and free from sensational incidents, without having an avowedly moral purpose, no living American author enjoys a wider popularity than Mrs. Mary J. Holmes. It may be added that no woman novelist, with the possible exception of Mrs. Harriet Beecher Stowe, has received so large profits from her copyrights. Mrs. Holmes, whose maiden name was Hawes, was born in Brookfield, Mass., and is described as a very precocious child, who studied grammar and arithmetic at the age of six, and taught school at thirteen. While yet a child she was possessed with an inspiration to write, and was only fifteen when articles from her pen began to appear in print. She was subsequently married to Daniel Holmes, a prominent lawyer and graduate of Yale, and lived for a period in Versailles, Ky., where she gained the knowledge of Southern life and Southern character portrayed in some of her stories. But she ultimately made Brockport, N. Y., her home, and there she and her husband now reside in a lovely place which they call "Brown Cottage." Mrs. Holmes' first book was "Tempest and Sunshine," and it has been followed by twenty-five or thirty others. That they are popular is proven by the fact that about two million copies have been sold, and that there is a continued demand for them. In addition to her novels she has written many articles and stories for papers, magazines and syndicates. Her long stories are usually printed serially in a periodical before appearing in book form, and as she never sells a copyright her revenues from her work are very large. Mrs. Holmes has traveled extensively in almost every part of the world. She is an untiring worker.

MARY JANE HOLMES.

HARRIET G. HOSMER.

THE name of no sculptor in the United States is more widely known than is that of Harriet Hosmer. The quality of her art has long been recognized and her work has at all times sustained a reputation early acquired. She was born in Watertown, Mass., October 9, 1830. Her father was a physician; she was left motherless and led largely an outdoor life. Her genius showed itself when she was but a mere child, much of her time being spent in a clay pit near her father's home where she amused herself by modeling horses, dogs, and other creatures. She was given a good education and took art lessons with her father, and later took a medical course in St. Louis, Mo. In 1851 she executed her first important work, an ideal head of "Hesper." In 1852 she went to Rome with her father and Charlotte Cushman and there became a pupil of Gibson. After two years of study she produced two busts, "Daphne" and "Medusa," which were exhibited in this country. Her success thenceforth was rapid and her rank in the art world fully recognized. Her first full-length figure, "Oenone," was produced in 1855. Then followed "Will o' the Wisp," "Puck," "Sleeping Fawn," "Waking Fawn," "Zenobia," a statue of Marie Sophia, queen of the Sicilies, Beatrice Cenci and other works as noted. Among these a bronze statue of Thomas H. Benton is in St. Louis, where Miss Hosmer spends much of her time. Among her patrons have been distinguished people abroad, including the Prince of Wales, and various great societies. She executed a statue of Queen Isabella for the Columbian Exposition. Miss Hosmer is a clever writer and has contributed valuable art studies to the magazines.

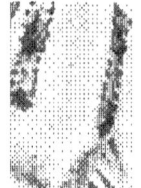

OLIVER OTIS HOWARD.

.

PRESENTING as he does a combination of the soldier and scholar in a degree that is unusual in this country, Gen. O. O. Howard, of the United States army, has both a military and a literary record. He was born in Leeds, Me., November 8, 1830, and was graduated at Bowdoin in 1850. In 1854 he graduated at West Point, becoming first-lieutenant, but resigned in 1861 to take command of the Third Maine regiment in the Civil war. For gallantry at Bull Run he was made brigadier-general of volunteers. He was twice wounded at the battle of Fair Oaks, losing his right arm June 1, 1862, but participated in many succeeding engagements, being again wounded at Pickett's Mill. In November, 1862, he became major-general of volunteers, and in March, 1865, was brevetted major-general for gallantry in various battles. General Howard was commissioner of the Freedman's Bureau from March, 1865, until July, 1874, when he was assigned to the command of the department of the Columbia. In 1877 he led the expedition against the Nez Perces Indians, and in 1878 the campaigns against the Brannocks and Piutes. He was commissioned major-general in 1886, and is now in command of the department of the Atlantic. He has contributed many articles to magazines, has published "Donald's School Days," "Chief Joseph, or the Nez Perces in Peace and War" and "Isabella of Castile," and is the author and translator of "Life of the Count De Gasparin." The degree of A. M. was conferred upon him by Bowdoin College, and that of LL. D. by Waterville, Shurtleff, and the Gettysburg Theological Seminary. He was made chevalier of the Legion of Honor by the French government in 1884.

OLIVER OTIS HOWARD.

VINNIE REAM HOXIE.

IN the realms of art America furnishes no greater name, perhaps, certainly not among women, than that of Vinnie Ream Hoxie, the famous sculptor, who enjoys the distinction of being the first woman who ever received an order from the United States Government for a statue. Mrs. Hoxie was born in Madison, Wis., September 23, 1846. A portion of her early life was spent in Washington, D. C., where her father held an office, but her family afterward lived in the West, and she was educated at Christian College, Missouri. During the war her family returned to Washington, where she was for a time employed in the postoffice department, but subsequently studied art, and soon devoted her whole attention to sculpture. Her work in this line was so successful that she made busts of General Grant, Reverdy Johnson, Albert Pike, John Sherman and Thaddeus Stevens, besides producing "The Indian Girl," a full-length figure cast in bronze, the marble "Miriam," etc. But her most important piece at this time was the statue of Abraham Lincoln, ordered by the Government and placed in the Capitol at Washington. Miss Ream spent three years abroad, and produced medallions of many eminent men. On her return, she modeled a bust of Lincoln for Cornell University, a life-size statue of "Sappho," "The Spirit of the Carnival," etc. Her later works include a statue of Admiral Farragut, which was cast in bronze from metal obtained from the flagship "Hartford," and placed in Farragut Square, Washington. She was married May 28, 1878, to Capt. Richard L. Hoxie, of the United States Corps of Engineers. Mrs. Hoxie does not allow her devotion to art to interfere with her family duties. She has a wide circle of friends and admirers.

VINNIE REAM HOXIE.

285

JOHN JAMES INGALLS.

THE student and writer in politics, has, in the man who so long represented Kansas in the United States Senate, proved a distinguished figure. John James Ingalls was born in Middletown, Mass., December 29, 1833. He graduated at Williams College in 1855, studied law and was admitted to the bar in 1857. He removed to Atchison, Kan., in 1858, and there engaged in the practice of his profession. He was a member of the Wyandotte convention in 1859, secretary of the territorial council in 1860, and of the State Senate in 1861, and was a member of the latter body in 1862. In the same year he was an unsuccessful candidate for lieutenant-governor of Kansas. After his defeat he accepted the editorship of the Atchison "Champion," which he retained for three years. At about this time he won almost national reputation by a series of brilliant magazine articles. He was again defeated for the lieutenant-governorship in 1864, but was elected to the United States Senate for the term beginning in 1873. This office he held by successive re-elections for three terms, and in 1887 was chosen president pro tempore of the Senate. He ranked among the ablest debaters in that body. He was defeated by the Populist party in Kansas when a candidate for re-election for a fourth term, but has remained a political factor of importance, delivering many addresses, contributing important articles to the reviews, and losing none of his prestige as one of the most brilliant of orators and writers. In the Senate his keen logic, his wonderful gift of sarcasm, and his political audacity made him especially dreaded by all opponents. He is not surpassed as a debater of the aggressive type and a master of scathing criticism.

JOHN JAMES INGALLS.
287

WILLIAM LYNE WILSON.

MANY a congressman who opposed with his voice and vote the so-called "Wilson bill" will cheerfully testify to the brilliant intellect and engaging personality of its author. Few men in the National House of Representatives were personally more popular than William L. Wilson, of West Virginia. Mr. Wilson entered Congress from the study of a college president. He was born in Jefferson County, Virginia, May 3, 1843, and was educated at the Charlestown Academy, Columbian College and the University of Virginia. During the Civil war he served in the Confederate army, and for several years after the war was a professor in Columbian College, but on the overthrow of the lawyer's test oath in West Virginia he resigned his chair and entered upon the practice of law in Charlestown, where he still resides. He has taken an active part in various political campaigns, and was permanent president of the National Democratic Convention, at Chicago, in 1892. He was elected president of the West Virginia University in 1882, but resigned during the following year to take his seat in the Forty-eighth Congress. Mr. Wilson was a member of Congress for twelve successive years. From the first he has advanced steadily to the front ranks, until now he is the Democratic leader on the floor, made so by force of character and ability, and against the preference of the Speaker. His hard work during the winter of 1894, in behalf of his favorite tariff measure, the "Wilson bill," so affected his health that for a time after the passage of the bill by Congress he was seriously ill and spent several months under a physician's care, traveling in Mexico. Upon the resignation of Mr. Bissell, from the office of Postmaster-General, Mr. Wilson was appointed his successor.

WILLIAM LYNE WILSON.
287

EDWARD KEMEYS.

BECAUSE of his taking the great wild animal life of this country at this time, and turning it into enduring marble or bronze and so illustrating its very pulse and spirit and personality, Mr. Edward Kemeys is a great man. He has done other things. He has made men's faces and forms and is a sculptor of note in such direction, but, after all, what is greatest about Mr. Kemeys is that he has recognized the interest and the importance in art of representing the wild animals, more particularly the carnivora, of the continent, and that he has seized upon that life while still existing, transforming it into something permanent. He is a naturalist, a history-maker, a sympathizer with nature as well as a sculptor, who has done this thing. A strong, rude poem is one of Mr. Kemeys' wild animals put into marble. He makes the great cats as they have lived in our wilds something to wonder over and to study and enjoy. He was born in Savannah, Ga., in January, 1843. He was at school in New York when the Civil war began, but entered the army at once and came out as a captain. After the war he farmed in Illinois, then was one of the Engineer Corps in Central Park, N. Y., then, somehow, got to modeling things in clay. He succeeded as a sculptor. He went West and studied the animals, shot and dissected the buffalo, shot and dissected mountain lions, saw all these animals playing or fighting and then, finally, came back eastward and began to make those figures of our wild beasts, just as they are, which have attracted the attention of the cultivated world. He is potent in a great field, one of those who are giving to American art a character of its own and what will compare favorably with the original productions of other nations.

EDWARD KEMEYS.

GEORGE KENNAN.

—

TO be an intelligent traveler and explorer, and to be able to graphically describe what one sees, is to be a useful contributor to the history and geography of the world. Such a person is George Kennan. He was born in Norwalk, Ohio, February 16, 1845, and obtained a high-school education by attending school during the day while working at night as a telegraph operator. In 1864 he was assistant chief operator in the telegraph office at Cincinnati, and in December of the same year went to Kamchatka, by way of Nicaragua, California and the North Pacific. As a leader of one of the Russo-American Telegraph Company's exploring parties in Northeastern Siberia, in 1865 and 1866, and as superintendent of construction for the middle district of the Siberian division from 1866 until 1868 he explored and located a route for the Russo-American telegraph line between the Okhotsk Sea and Behring Strait. In 1870 he went again to Russia to explore the mountains of the Eastern Caucasus, proceeded down the Volga River to the Caspian Sea, made extensive explorations on horseback in Daghestan and Chechnia, crossing the great range of the Caucasus three times in different places, and returned to America in 1871. In 1885 and 1886 he made a journey of fifteen thousand miles through Northern Russia and Siberia for the purpose of investigating the Russian exile system, visited all the convict prisons and mines, and explored the wildest part of the Russian Altai. On his return to the United States, Mr. Kennan published a series of magazine articles, afterward issued in book form, and lectured extensively on Siberia He is also the author of "Tent Life in Siberia and Adventures Among the Koraks and Other Tribes in Kamchatka and Northern Asia."

GEORGE KENNAN.

CHARLES KING.

WHOEVER has failed to read the delightful army stories of Capt. Charles King is not fully competent to discuss current literature. Captain King is a resident of Milwaukee, Wis. He was born in Albany, N. Y., October 12, 1844, being the only son of Gen. Rufus King, grandson of Charles King, LL. D., president of Columbia College, and great-grandson of Rufus King, of New York, who was twice Minister to England and twenty years United States senator. In 1845 Gen. Rufus King settled in Milwaukee, and in 1862 his son was sent by President Lincoln to West Point, where he became adjutant of the Corps of Cadets and was graduated in 1866. He served twice as instructor of tactics at West Point; was aide-de-camp to General Emory during the reconstruction days in New Orleans; commanded his troop of the Fifth regiment of cavalry during the Apache campaign, and was severely wounded in action at Sunset Pass. Captain King served through the Sioux and Nez Perces campaigns of 1876, and 1877 as adjutant of the Fifth cavalry. He was promoted to the rank of captain in 1879, and placed on the retired list because of wounds received in the line of duty. For ten years he was inspector and instructor of the Wisconsin National Guard and colonel of the Fourth Wisconsin infantry, and is now making a study of the European armies. He is best known as an author of military history and soldier stories. His novels, "The Colonel's Daughter," "Marion's Faith," "Captain Blake," "Between the Lines," "Dunraven Ranch" and others, have been widely read throughout the United States and abroad. While in the army Captain King was known as a gallant soldier. He is now regarded as an able teacher of military tactics.

CHARLES KING.
295

DANIEL SCOTT LAMONT.

HERE was probably no member of President Cleveland's Cabinet who possessed more influence with the executive than did the man who, within a few years, developed from a private secretary into that prominent official, the Secretary of War. During Mr. Cleveland's first administration Daniel S. Lamont was his confidential man, and at that time his imperturbable manner and chilling politeness gave White House visitors the impression that his chief characteristics were secretiveness and discretion. Mr. Lamont was born in Cortland County, New York, February 9, 1851, and was the only child of a country merchant. After completing an academic course he entered his father's store as a clerk, but soon abandoned that occupation to seek a political career. He was a delegate to Democratic State conventions before he was of age, and was a member of the New York Assembly in 1870, 1871 and 1875. He was afterward chief clerk in the New York State department under John Bigelow, and was confidential secretary to Samuel J. Tilden during the latter's term as governor of New York. From 1875 until 1883 Mr. Lamont was secretary of the Democratic State Committee of New York, and as such displayed a marvelous acquaintance with the details of state politics, as well as knowledge of public men and politicians. His ability to remember persons and call them by name was quite remarkable. He introduced into the management of the War Department a shrewdness and tact that was of more value than mere statesmanship. Mr. Lamont is a business man and a methodical one. He acquired a reputation for ability and sterling honesty, and without seeking it made many friends and admirers while in office.

DANIEL SCOTT LAMONT.

ISABELLA BEECHER HOOKER

WITH the blood of the Beechers in her, it is not surprising that the subject of this sketch should have shown force of character and become widely known. Isabella Beecher Hooker was born in Litchfield, Conn., February 22, 1822. She was the first child of the second wife of Dr. Beecher, and one of that wonderful family so justly recognized with the Fields, the Washburnes, the fighting McCooks and others as among the notable ones produced in this republic. She married John Hooker, of Hartford, Conn., in 1841. Mr. Hooker is a lawyer who has achieved a standing in his profession and has refused a seat on the supreme court bench of his native state. Soon after their marriage the couple moved to Hartford, Conn., where they have since resided. Mrs. Hooker has continued since her marriage her efforts in the direction of attaining woman suffrage. She is one of the best known living exponents of the claims of the women who want to vote. She has written much and well, and has talked much and well. She was one of the conspicuous figures in the Woman's Department of the World's Fair in 1893. At the golden wedding of Mr. and Mrs. Hooker occurred something phenomenal. The event took place August 5, 1891; Senator Joseph B. Hawley acted as master of ceremonies, and there was a demonstration such as Hartford has rarely seen; the judges of the supreme court of the state paid their respects in a body, and woman's movements were represented by distinguished representatives such as Susan B. Anthony and others. It was an event of note of the day. Such demonstration from such people could have come to no ordinary person. In a green old age Mrs. Hooker is still the center of an earnest circle of reformers.

ISABELLA BEECHER HOOKER.

WILFRID LAURIER.

BRILLIANT and magnetic, if not always logical, with unquestioned sincerity in his devotion to principle and with an enthusiasm that is infectious, Sir Wilfrid Laurier, the leader of the Liberal party in Canada, belongs to the dramatic school of statesmen. He was born in St. Lin, Quebec, November 20, 1841. He was educated at L'Assomption College, graduated in law at McGill University, and admitted to the bar in 1865. From 1871 to 1874 he was in the Quebec Assembly. He then entered the Dominion Parliament, and in 1877 was appointed Minister of Inland Revenue in the Mackenzie government, a position which he held until the resignation of the Ministry, in 1878. Since that year he has held no office, though he has continued to sit in Parliament. Upon the retirement of Edward Blake from the Liberal leadership, in 1887, M. Laurier, who had already been recognized as the head of the French-Canadian wing of the party, was unanimously chosen to succeed him. He has since been knighted for his services to the cause which he represents. He was violently outspoken in his denunciation of the execution of Louis Riel, and demanded the latter's exemption from punishment upon the ground of his nationality. Sir Wilfrid was at one time editor of "Le Defricheur," is an earnest advocate of temperance, and was a delegate to the Dominion Prohibitory Convention at Montreal in 1875. Impassioned and eloquent in debate and on the platform, Sir Wilfrid Laurier has an enthusiastic following, especially with the extreme wing of the Liberal party, and is respected for his marked ability even by his political opponents. His power over his French-Canadian followers is absolute and they are devoted to him, heart and soul.

WILFRID LAURIER.

VICTOR F. LAWSON.

IT has come to few men to reap greater profit from journalism than has Victor F. Lawson. He was born in Chicago, September 9, 1850. His father was a native of Norway, who came to the United States prior to 1840 and soon after settled in Chicago, where he accumulated a handsome estate, including the premises at 123 Fifth avenue, now occupied by the "Daily News." Mr. Lawson received his early education in the public schools, graduating in the high school in 1869, and later attending Phillips Academy in Massachusetts and Cambridge University. Returning to Chicago, he engaged in the business as manager of his father's estate and publisher of the "Skandinavian." In July, 1876, he purchased an interest in the "Daily News" and assumed the business management of that paper. The subsequent remarkable success of the "News" was due in no small degree to the industry, enterprise and capital which Mr. Lawson put into the concern. In March, 1881, Mr. Lawson and his partner, Melville E. Stone, began to issue a morning edition of the paper, which was called the "Morning News," later the "Record." Mr. Stone was soon afterward bought out by Mr. Lawson, but the successful career of the two newspapers continued, and is among the phenomena of journalistic triumphs of the time. The income from the papers is very great, and Mr. Lawson has become a rich man. He takes an active interest in public affairs and the general welfare of the community. Each summer thousands of poor children have a happier life because of his Fresh Air Sanitarium in Lincoln Park, and in various other ways has he manifested his regard for the obligations attaching to him, and which have resulted in so much good.

VICTOR F. LAWSON.

MARY ELIZABETH LEASE.

WHETHER or not one may agree with the views of the remarkable woman whose name has become familiar because of its
frequent appearance in the political news from Kansas, there will be
little inclination to deny her vigor and enthusiasm or her gift of express-
ive language. Mary Elizabeth Lease was born in Pennsylvania, September 11, 1853. Her parents were Joseph P. Clyens and Mary Elizabeth Murray Clyens. She was educated in the Allegheny, N. Y.,
convent school, and in the Young Ladies' Seminary at Ceres, N. Y.
She married Charles L. Lease in 1873, and has for some years been
a resident of Wichita, Kan. She visited Great Britain and Canada,
and, impressed with reform ideas, made a study of what she saw.
She took up the study of the law, and of recent years has been
actively engaged in politics. The political revolution in Kansas brought
her to the front, and she became prominent as a Populist leader,
attracting special attention by her bitter opposition to the re-election of
John J. Ingalls as United States senator, and later, in the last presidential campaign, by her Southern speaking tour in company with
General Weaver, the Populist candidate. She was appointed president of
the board of trustees of the charitable institutions of the state of Kansas and has held other places of official trust. Impulsive, ambitious
and eloquent, and living in a state where political experiments have
found their trial field, Mrs. Lease has acquired a reputation all her
own, and one fairly the result of her own intellect and courage. She
would, perhaps, have a better following were her views less radical
and her course less aggressive toward those she does not like in politics, but she has at least the courage of her convictions.

MARY ELIZABETH LEASE

CHARLES B. LEWIS.

GENERAL writers of wit, humor, pathos and descriptive narrative are by no means few in the American field of journalism, but none has gained a wider reputation in his particular line than Charles B. Lewis, better known by his pen-name of "M. Quad." Mr. Lewis was born in northern Ohio early in the forties, and, after receiving a common-school education, learned the printer's trade. Desiring to better his condition, and hearing of an opening in Maysville, Ky., he started for that place, and came very near losing his life in consequence. The steamboat on which he took passage on the Ohio river was blown to atoms by the explosion of its boiler, and for several months Mr. Lewis hovered between life and death in a Cincinnati hospital. When the war broke out he went to the front with the Seventh Michigan cavalry, and served with his regiment throughout the conflict. After being mustered out he went to Michigan and again took up the printer's trade. He was connected for a time with the Pontiac "Bill Poster," and then drifted to Lansing, where one winter he was engaged to act as legislative correspondent for the Detroit "Free Press." He subsequently went to Detroit and became a reporter for the "Free Press," continuing his connection with that paper for over twenty-five years. He made himself and his paper famous with his short stories and articles depicting the humorous and pathetic phases of city life. A few years ago he became connected with a New York paper, and since that time has resided in Brooklyn. He is now on the staff of the American Press Association. Mr. Lewis has written a number of novels that have been well received, but he is best known and most admired as a humorist.

CHARLES B. LEWIS.
307

SARA JANE LIPPINCOTT.

DESERVING to be remembered always as the pioneer in the present well-occupied field of magazines for children, Mrs. Sara J. Lippincott still occupies a place in the esteem of thousands of men and women who think of her only as "Grace Greenwood," the editor of the "Little Pilgrim," and the author of many entertaining books and short stories. Mrs. Lippincott is now living quietly in her pleasant home in Washington, D. C., and is still a great friend of the children. She was born in Pompey, Onondaga County, N. Y., September 23, 1823. Much of her childhood was passed in Rochester, N. Y., but in 1842 she removed with her father to New Brighton, Pa., and in 1853 married Leander K. Lippincott, of Philadelphia. She published occasional verses at an early age under her own name, and in 1844 her first prose publications appeared in the New York "Mirror," under the pen-name of "Grace Greenwood," which she has since retained. For a number of years she edited in Philadelphia the "Little Pilgrim," a high-class juvenile monthly magazine, which attained a wide popularity. She is also the author of many addresses and lectures, and has been largely connected with periodical literature as editor, contributor and newspaper correspondent. "Ariadne" is probably the best known of her poems. Among her books are "Greenwood Leaves," "History of My Pets," "Poems," "Recollections of My Childhood," "Haps and Mishaps of a Tour in Europe," "Merrie England," "Forest Tragedy and Other Tales," "Stories and Legends of Travel," "History for Children," "Stories from Famous Ballads," "Stories of Many Lands," "Stories and Sights in France and Italy," "Records of Five Years," and "New Life in New Lands."

SARA JANE LIPPINCOTT.

IDA LEWIS.

WHAT the story of Grace Darling is to Great Britain, that of Ida Lewis is to America. Ida Lewis was born in Newport, R. I., in 1841. Her father, Capt. Hosea Lewis, was keeper of the Lime Rock lighthouse in Newport harbor, and the daughter became in early life a skilled swimmer and oarswoman. She is now a lithe, active woman of fifty-two, and is still at the lighthouse and the work she did so many years ago. She has rescued sixteen persons from drowning, and was only a slight girl of seventeen when her first rescue was made, a very daring one, of the crew of a boat upset near the lighthouse in a storm. The next morning she rowed them over to Fort Adams, whence an attempt had been made to launch a boat but had been abandoned as hopeless. There was astonishment at the Fort when she arrived with those whom she had rescued. Many similar feats of bravery have followed. The United States Government recognized the heroism of Miss Lewis and bestowed upon her a gold medal of the first class, the first ever given to a woman. The Humane Society of Massachusetts has given her a silver medal, and the Life Saving Benevolent Society of New York has done the same. Her snug little home is filled with testimonials of recognition of her heroism. She is one of the happiest of women in her increasing age. Her soft, abundant hair is scarcely tinged with gray, and her bright eyes are full of contentment. She has suffered grave losses of friends and relations, but her cheeks have the hue that the sea air gives and she is sturdy and joyous and buoyant all the time. She breakfasts at six, has enough to occupy all her time, and is almost the ideal of a cheerful philosophical Christian.

IDA LEWIS.

HENRY CABOT LODGE.

THOUGH one of the youngest of the senators of the United States, Henry Cabot Lodge is by no means the least conspicuous. He was born in Boston, May 12, 1850, and is a member of one of the oldest New England families. He graduated from Harvard University in 1871. Three years later he graduated from the law school, and in 1875 received the degree of Ph. D. for his thesis on the Land law of the Anglo-Saxons. The quality of his acquirements and his natural talent were soon recognized, and he was appointed to the position of university lecturer on American history. At about the same time he accepted the position of editor of the "North American Review." He was elected to the Massachusetts legislature in 1880 and re-elected in 1881. He acquired rapidly a prominence in party councils, serving for two years as chairman of the Republican State Central Committee and appearing as a delegate in the Republican National Convention of 1880 and 1884. In 1884 he became a candidate for Congress and was defeated, but was successful in 1888. He served in the Fiftieth, Fifty-first and Fifty-second Congresses and was re-elected to the Fifty-third. In 1893, with the expiration of the senatorial term of Henry L. Dawes, Mr. Lodge was elected for the term expiring in 1899. Mr. Lodge has been an overseer of Harvard University since 1884 and is widely known as a man of letters. He is the author of a number of books, among which are "Life and Letters of George Cabot," a "Short History of English Colonies in America," a "Life of Daniel Webster," and "Studies in History." He is a man of wonderful ability, and although not a conspicuous partisan his voice is potent in the councils of his party.

HENRY CABOT LODGE.

MARY SIMMERSON CUNNINGHAM LOGAN.

CURRENT history affords no more striking example of how the wife of a great man may become identified with her husband's career, appearing as his best adviser in the gravest crisis of political and civil life, than has been furnished by the wife of the late Senator John A. Logan. Before her marriage Mrs. Logan was Mary Simmerson Cunningham, daughter of John M. Cunningham, of Missouri. She was born August 15, 1838, in Petersburg, Boone County, Mo., and was educated in the Convent of St. Vincent, in Kentucky. On leaving that institution she assisted her father, who had been elected sheriff and county clerk of Williamson County, Missouri, and appointed register of the land office at Shawneetown, Ill. While thus engaged she met John A. Logan, then prosecuting attorney, and was married to him November 27, 1855. During the years that her husband was winning fame on the battle-field she conducted the affairs of the homestead and the small farm attached, and lent all the aid possible to his advancement. When General Logan appeared in politics, after the war, she manifested an active interest in his political affairs, and greatly assisted him by her earnest, tactful work. At the time of his nomination for the vice-presidency with Mr. Blaine, it was she who restrained the impetuosity of her husband, who would have scorned the nomination, and prevented any differences between the leaders of the party. Mrs. Logan was one of the most gracious and popular hostesses during her husband's senatorial career. His death very nearly caused her own also, but recovering her health she became editor of the "Home Journal" of Washington, and is still a prominent factor in various public enterprises.

MARY SIMMERSON CUNNINGHAM LOGAN.

JAMES LONGSTREET.

THE man who was considered the hardest fighter in the Confederate service during the Civil war, and who was known in the army as "Old Pete," is now living quietly on a farm near Gainesville, Ga. Gen. James Longstreet was born in the Edgefield district, Hamburg, S. C., January 8, 1821. He removed with his mother to Alabama in 1831, and was appointed from that state to the United States Military Academy, where he graduated in 1842. After serving on garrison and frontier duty for several years, his regiment participated in the war with Mexico, where his conspicuous bravery won him repeated promotions, culminating in the rank of brevet major. He was severely wounded at the storming of Chapultepec. After the war he served as adjutant, captain and paymaster, chiefly on the Texas frontier, until 1861, when he resigned. In that year he was commissioned brigadier-general in the Confederate army, and after the first battle of Bull Run was promoted to major-general. His brilliant war record is well known. Early in 1864 he was wounded by the fire of his own troops in the battle of the Wilderness, and a year later was included in the surrender at Appomattox. He had the unbounded confidence of his soldiers, who were devoted to him. After the war he engaged in commercial business in New Orleans, and affiliated with the Republican party. He was appointed surveyor of customs of the port of New Orleans by President Grant; supervisor of internal revenue, postmaster at New Orleans and Minister to Turkey by President Hayes, and United States marshal for the district of Georgia by President Garfield. Gainesville, in the latter state, has since been his home.

JAMES LONGSTREET.
315

DALTON McCARTHY.

THE leader of a party which is but a skeleton army, Dalton McCarthy yet occupies an enviable position, so far as his standing in the eyes of the people of the Dominion of Canada is concerned. He is about fifty years of age at the present time, and was for many years a barrister of prominence in Barrie, Ontario. None in his profession occupied a higher standing at the bar. He moved to Toronto, where his success was continued. He became a queen's counsel, taking a lively interest in politics, and became eventually a member of the Dominion Parliament. He attached himself to the Conservatives and soon acquired prominence in its councils. The time came when certain differences of opinion between him and the leaders of the party became so marked that he separated from them, though his affiliations did not extend in the direction of the Liberals. He became the recognized head of what was known as the Equal Rights party, or league, something which may be explained to American readers as corresponding in a measure with the so-called "Mugwumps" of the United States, that is, those who form a middle party—a sort of balance-wheel. The party has never become dominant in Canada, but has always been respected alike by Conservatives and Liberals. At the recent election in Ontario it cut no figure, but is still an existent entity. Mr. McCarthy, aside from being a jurist of admitted great ability, is a fluent and ready debater and a forceful man in support of any measure which he may countenance in the Dominion Parliament. He is one of the strong and admirable figures in Canadian politics. His followers believe firmly in him and those who oppose his measures recognize his power.

DALTON McCARTHY.

ALEXANDER KELLY McCLURE

STERNLY opposed to machine power in party management, and official incompetency and dishonesty in public office, Alexander K. McClure, the able editor of the Philadelphia "Times," is widely known as a champion of pure politics. He was born in Sherman's Valley, Perry County, Pa., January 9, 1828, and at the age of fourteen was apprenticed to the tanner's trade. In 1846 he began the publication of a Whig paper, the "Sentinel," at Mifflin, Pa. He sold this paper in 1850, purchased an interest in the Chambersburg "Repository," became its editor, and made it one of the most noted anti-slavery journals in the state. In 1853 he was the Whig candidate for the position of auditor-general, being the youngest man ever nominated for a state office in Philadelphia. He was a member of the convention that organized the Republican party in 1855, and of the National Convention that nominated Fremont for the presidency in 1856. In the latter year he sold the "Repository," quitted journalism, and shortly thereafter was admitted to the bar. He served in the Legislature and State Senate from 1857 to 1860. In 1862 he repurchased the Chambersburg "Repository," but lost it in the burning of Chambersburg in 1864. In 1868 he settled in Philadelphia and practiced law. He supported Horace Greeley in the campaign of 1872, and was elected as an Independent Republican to the State Senate. In the following year he was an independent candidate for the mayoralty of Philadelphia, and was defeated by a small plurality. Deciding to return to journalism, he joined Frank McLaughlin in the establishment of the "Times," a daily newspaper, in 1873, and since its foundation he has been its editor-in-chief.

ALEXANDER KELLY McCLURE

ALEXANDER McD. McCOOK.

A GREAT family are those McCooks; they know something; they are cultivated and intellectual, but they will fight on every possible occasion. It is doubtful, if in the history of the United States any other single family in two generations has ever made such a fighting record as have these same McCooks. The Doones, of whom Blackmore tells us, were hardly comparable with the McCooks, though the latter have fought only for the right. There were and are two branches of the family, known in Ohio as the "fighting McCooks," which branches are known respectively as the "Dan tribe" and the "John tribe." They are simply a good American family who acquired an astonishing reputation during the Civil war. Gen. Alexander McCook is but one of the family—there were sixteen fighting McCooks in the Civil war, all officers, except one who was killed at Bull Run in the first fight, and they made records of note. Of course, such people go to West Point, when they can. Gen. Alexander McCook was born on a farm near New Lisbon, Columbiana County, Ohio, April 22, 1831. He entered the United States Military Academy at West Point, and graduated in the class of 1852. At the opening of the Civil war he was made colonel of the First Ohio regiment, and from that time his record was but improved with successive campaigns. He was made a major-general for distinguished services at the battle of Shiloh, was later in command of the army of the Cumberland, and, later still, of one of the trans-Mississippi departments. His appointment to the command of the department of the Colorado was but a just recognition of his service and ability. General McCook deserves the gratitude of the whole nation.

ALEXANDER McD. McCOOK.

WAYNE MacVEAGH.

MEASURES and movements designed to purify politics and establish governmental reforms have ever had a stanch advocate in Wayne MacVeagh, of Pennsylvania, who has found it easy to snap party ties in the interest of what he conceives to be a patriotic duty. That is why, after holding high public positions by the grace of the Republican party, he is now United States Ambassador to Italy by appointment of a Democratic President. Mr. MacVeagh was born in Phoenixville, Chester County, Pa., April 19, 1833. He was graduated at Yale in 1853, studied law, was admitted to the bar, and served as district attorney of Chester County from 1859 until 1864. He was captain of cavalry in 1862, when the invasion of Pennsylvania was threatened, and in 1863 was chairman of the Republican Central Committee of Pennsylvania. In 1870 he was appointed United States Minister to Turkey, returning the following year, and in 1872 became a member of the Pennsylvania Constitutional Convention. He was the chief member of the "MacVeagh Commission" that was sent to Louisiana in 1877 by President Hayes to represent him unofficially, and to endeavor to bring the conflicting parties in that state to an understanding. In 1881 he was appointed United States Attorney-General in the cabinet of President Garfield, but resigned on the accession of President Arthur, and resumed his law practice in Philadelphia. He was for several years chairman of the Civil Service Reform Association of that city, and also of the Indian Rights Association. In December, 1893, the embassy to Italy was offered by President Cleveland to Mr. MacVeagh, who accepted it, and soon after took up his residence in that country.

WAYNE MacVEAGH.
325

JOHN WILLIAM MACKAY.

THE most noted and perhaps the most romantic incident in the mining history of this country was the discovery, in 1872, of the famous Bonanza mines, with their fabulous deposits of silver and gold. The name most prominently connected with this discovery was that of John W. Mackay, who became widely known as the chief of the "Bonanza Kings." Mr. Mackay was born in Dublin, Ireland, November 28, 1831. He came with his parents to New York in 1840, where he was later apprenticed to the trade of ship building, but in 1849 he caught the gold fever and went to California, where he lived a miner's life for several years with varying fortunes. He acquired a technical and practical knowledge of mining, and in 1860 left California for Nevada, where, in 1872, he was among those who discovered the "Bonanza" mines on a ledge of rock in the Sierra Nevadas, under what is now Virginia City. The incident changed the face of the silver markets of the world. The mines were owned by John W. Mackay, James C. Flood, James G. Fair (afterward senator from Nevada) and William O'Brien, but Mr. Mackay's interest was double that of any of his partners. From one mine alone was taken $150,000,000 in silver and gold, and the active yield of all of them continued for several years, during which time Mr. Mackay personally superintended them. In 1878, with Flood and Fair, he founded the Bank of Nevada, with its headquarters in San Francisco, and in 1884, in partnership with James Gordon Bennett, he laid two cables across the Atlantic. In 1893 an attempt was made on Mr. Mackay's life by a crank in the Grand Palace Hotel, San Francisco. He received a serious pistol-shot wound, from which, however, he recovered.

JOHN WILLIAM MACKAY.
325

BRANDER MATTHEWS.

YOUNG man though he be, it is doubtful if among the writers and critics of the United States any one is more widely known than Brander Matthews. He was born in New Orleans, La., February 21, 1852, but his education was attained in the North. He graduated at Columbia College in 1871, and studied law in 1873, being admitted to the bar in the same year. Then, instead of practicing law, he promptly turned his attention to literature. He wrote plays, and later contributed freely to periodicals, using the pseudonym "Arthur Penn." He has been active in all things pertaining to the profession. He is one of the founders of the Authors' Club, and was prominent in organizing the American Copyright League and the Dunlap Society. Among his publications have been "The Theatres of Paris," "French Dramatists of the Nineteenth Century," "The Home Library," "The Last Meeting," "A Secret of the Sea," pen and ink essays on subjects of more or less importance, and several other works of equal quality. His plays include "Margery's Lovers," "This Picture and That," "A Gold Mine," and others of relative importance. He has edited various publications, such as the "Rhymster," "Poems of American Patriotism," "Sheridan's Comedies," "Ballads of a Book," and others of their class. He is a most industrious editor as well as writer. He, as a critic, is becoming daily more and more widely known and becoming so, to a great extent, because he is fair and just, giving credit where it is honestly due, whether the work to be criticised is the product of an unknown writer or a prominent author. It is not only his literary ability but his sense of justice which is giving him prominence.

BERTHA HONORE PALMER

EVENTS proved that no mistake was made in placing at the head of the Woman's Department of the World's Columbian Exposition so popular and capable a lady as Mrs. Potter Palmer. As president of the Board of Lady Managers she filled her position with such grace and dignity, such tact and intelligence, and such rare administrative ability as to excite the admiration of the world. Mrs. Palmer was born in Louisville, Ky., where her childhood and early girlhood were spent. Her father, H. H. Honore, was of French descent, and her mother belonged to one of the oldest and most aristocratic Southern families. She received her education in a convent near Baltimore, Md., and afterward removed with her family to Chicago, where her father became an extensive property owner. In 1871 she was married to Potter Palmer, one of Chicago's wealthiest citizens, and proprietor of the famous Palmer House. Mrs. Palmer has traveled much, and has a large acquaintance among distinguished people at home and abroad. Her mental acquirements and inherited grace and refinement have made her a leader in society, while her contributions to city and state charities are only surpassed by the good she privately does. During the World's Fair of 1893 she gained world-wide fame as president of the Board of Lady Managers, and it was universally conceded that a better selection for that responsible office could not have been made. Under her administration the Woman's Department attained proportions which formed one of the most remarkable developments of the Exposition. The Palmer residence on the Lake Shore Drive, Chicago, is one of the handsomest in a city noted for its beautiful homes. It is built in the style of an old feudal castle.

BERTHA HONORE PALMER.
331

JOSEPH MEDILL.

IN the forefront of American journalism stands a man whose fame is as inseparably associated with that of the Chicago "Tribune" as was Horace Greeley's with that of the New York "Tribune" a quarter of a century ago. Joseph Medill was born in New Brunswick, Canada, April 6, 1823. He removed with his parents to Stark County, Ohio, in 1831, and until he was twenty-one years of age worked on his father's farm. Subsequently he studied law, and began the practice of his profession at New Philadelphia, Ohio, in 1846. In 1849 he founded a Free-Soil Whig paper at Coshocton, Ohio, and thenceforth devoted himself to journalism. In 1852 he established the "Leader," a Free-Soil Whig paper, at Cleveland, and in 1854 was one of the organizers of the Republican party in Ohio. Shortly after this event he removed to Chicago, and in May, 1855, he and two partners purchased the Chicago "Tribune," which has ever since been conducted as a Republican journal. Mr. Medill was a member of the Illinois Constitutional Convention in 1870, when the organic law of Illinois was revised, and was the author of the minority representation and several other provisions of that law. In 1871 he was appointed by President Grant a member of the first United States Civil Service Commission, and in the following year was elected mayor of Chicago by an immense majority on the so-called "fire-proof" ticket. He spent a year in Europe in 1873-74, and upon his return purchased the controlling interest in the "Tribune," of which he became and now is editor-in-chief. Mr. Medill has a winter residence in Southern California, where he spends a portion of each year, but is still active and vigorous in the editorial management of his newspaper.

JOSEPH MEDILL

WILLIAM RALPH MEREDITH.

A STRIKING figure in the legislature of Canada's great Province of Ontario is William Ralph Meredith, leader of the opposition in that body. He was born in Westminster Township, Middlesex County, Ontario, March 31, 1840, graduated in 1859 at Toronto University, and later began the practice of law in London, Ontario, where he soon achieved a high standing. In 1888 he removed to Toronto, of which city he is now city solicitor, and became the head of one of the largest law firms there. In March, 1876, he was appointed a Queen's Counsel by the Ontario Government, and in October, 1880, he received a like honor from the Dominion Government. The degree of LL. D. was conferred upon him by the University of Toronto in May, 1889. Mr. Meredith has long been looked upon as one who will surely attain to a high position in the Canadian judiciary, but hitherto he has declined all overtures in that direction, doubtless, it is said, because of the position he occupies as leader of his party in the legislative assembly, and also because he looks to Ottawa as a larger field of political possibilities for him. In 1872 Mr. Meredith was elected to represent London in the Ontario Assembly. In 1878, on the elevation to the bench of the late Sir Matthews Crooks Cameron, he was unanimously chosen as that gentleman's successor in the leadership of the Conservatives in the legislature. He is a man of striking and agreeable personal appearance, a fluent speaker, and has, apparently, the full confidence of the political party to which he belongs and in the councils of which he leads. His position as leader of the opposition in Ontario gives him special prominence, because, as things are, he is in touch with the Ottawa Government.

WILLIAM RALPH MEREDITH.

WESLEY MERRITT.

A GOOD soldier with a good record is Gen. Wesley Merritt, of the United States army. He was born in New York City, June 16, 1836. He graduated at the United States Military Academy in 1860, was assigned to the dragoons and was promoted to be first lieutenant in 1861 and captain in 1862. He took part in Gen. Stoneman's raid toward Richmond in 1863, and was in command of the reserve cavalry brigade in the Pennsylvania campaign of the same year, being about this time commissioned brigadier-general of volunteers. For gallant conduct at Gettysburg he was brevetted major in the Regular army. He took part in various engagements in central Virginia in 1863-64, and was brevetted lieutenant-colonel and colonel in the Regular army and major-general of volunteers for gallantry in the battles of Yellow Tavern, Hawe's Shop and Winchester. He was brevetted brigadier-general and major-general in the Regular army for bravery at the battle of Five Forks, and later was commissioned major-general of volunteers. After the war he was employed chiefly on frontier duty until 1882, when he was placed in charge of the United States Military Academy at West Point. Here his strictness made him for a time almost unpopular with the cadets, but they learned to know his real quality and to regard him as a great head of a great school. In 1887 he was ordered to Fort Leavenworth, and in 1887 became brigadier-general. His career since the date named has been what was to be expected of such a man with such a record. He is one of the trusted generals of the army of the United States, and is at the present time commanding the department of Missouri, with headquarters at Chicago. He is a fine soldier.

WESLEY MERRITT.

CINCINNATUS HEINE MILLER.

—

RECOGNIZED by all who can read and understand, as a great poetic genius, Cincinnatus Heine (better known as Joaquin) Miller occupies an admitted position in American literature. Sir Edwin Arnold has declared Joaquin Miller one of the two American poets whose fame will endure. He was born in the Wabash district, in Indiana, November 10, 1841, and when thirteen years old immigrated . with his family to Oregon. Three years afterward the boy went alone to California, but returning later to Eugene, Ore., he became the editor of the Democratic "Register" in that town. In 1863 he opened a law office in Canyon City, Ore., and from 1866 to 1870 served as county judge of Grant County. It was at about this time that his first poems appeared, one collection, entitled "Joaquin et Al.," giving him the name by which he is best known. In 1871 he published, in London, "Songs of the Sierras" and "Pacific Poems." In 1873 appeared "Songs of the Sun Lands" and a prose volume entitled "Life Among the Modocs," "Unwritten History." His later works are the "Ship in the Desert," 1875; "The Danites in the Sierras," "The One Fair Woman," 1876; "Baroness of N. Y.," 1877; "Songs of Far Away Lands," 1878; "Songs of Italy," 1878; "Shadows of Shasta," 1881; "Memorie & Rime," 1884; "Forty-Nine, the Gold-Seeker of the Sierras," 1884, and he has since published other volumes, lately adding to his reputation by "The Building of the City Beautiful," appearing in 1893. A new edition of his works appeared in 1890 in response to the increasing appreciation of his undoubted genius. The poet lives on a height, near Oakland, Cal., overlooking the great ocean, of which he sings so well.

CINCINNATUS HEINE MILLER.

DARIUS OGDEN MILLS.

YEARS ago the "luck of D. O. Mills" became a proverb on the Pacific coast, but it was luck attended with a reputation for judgment, rapid decision, boldness and absolute integrity. Mr. Mills began at the very bottom of the ladder. Born in North Salem, Westchester County, N. Y., September 5, 1825, he was left without resources at the age of sixteen, and from a poorly paid clerk in New York City became, at twenty-two, cashier and one-third owner of a small bank in Buffalo. Two years later he went to California and established in Sacramento the gold bank of D. O. Mills & Co., which was immediately and conspicuously successful. He became largely interested in mines on the Comstock lode, forest lands and other property, and in 1864 founded the Bank of California, in San Francisco, of which he assumed the presidency. For years this bank had the highest credit in the financial centers both of Europe and Asia. Mr. Mills resigned and withdrew from the management of the concern in 1873, and two years later the bank was wrecked through disastrous speculations on the part of its president, William C. Ralston. Its failure created an excitement that convulsed the Pacific coast. Ralston committed suicide. Mr. Mills again became president, and in three years had firmly re-established the bank. He then left it, and gradually transferred his heavy investments to the East, where he erected the largest office building in New York, and finally returned to reside near his birthplace. Mr. Mills has made several munificent gifts to the state of California and the city of New York, and gave $75,000 to found the Mills professorship of moral and intellectual philosophy in the University of California.

DARIUS OGDEN MILLS.

ROGER QUARLES MILLS.

IT is high praise to say of any man that he is best liked where he
is best known. No better evidence of a man's popularity and
influence in his own community could be desired than the fact that he
has been chosen to represent that community continuously for a quarter of a century in the legislative halls of the country. Such has
been the lot of Roger Q. Mills, the junior senator from Texas. Senator Mills was born in Todd County, Kentucky, March 30, 1832.
After receiving a common-school education he removed to Palestine,
Tex., in 1849, where he studied law, supporting himself in the mean
time by serving as an assistant in the postoffice and in the offices of
the court clerk. In 1850 he was elected engrossing clerk of the
Texas House of Representatives, and in 1852, by a special act of the
Legislature—for he was still a minor—he was admitted to the bar.
He practiced his profession at Corsicana, and in 1859 was elected to
the Legislature. Subsequently he was colonel of the Tenth Texas
regiment in the Confederate service. In 1873 he was elected to Congress from the state at large as a Democrat, and served continuously
in that body until he resigned to accept the position of United States
senator, to which he was elected March 23, 1892. In 1876 Mr. Mills
opposed the creation of an electoral commission, and in 1887 canvassed
Texas against the adoption of the prohibition amendment to its constitution, which was defeated. He introduced into the House of Representatives in 1888 the bill that was known by his name, reducing the
duties on imports and extending the free list. Senator Mills is a man
of much quiet force, whose opinions in legislative matters have great
weight.

ROGER QUARLES MILLS

341

HARRIET STONE MONROE.

———

BROUGHT suddenly into prominence as the poet-laureate of the World's Columbian Exposition, Miss Harriet S. Monroe, of Chicago, passed safely through the ordeal of criticism thus invited and now occupies a secure place among American poets. A volume of her poems, published under the title of "Valeria, and Other Poems," has won from well known critics pronounced and cordial commendation. Miss Monroe was born in Chicago, December 23, 1860, her parents having moved to that city from central New York five years earlier. Her education was begun in the public schools, and continued in Dearborn Seminary, and at the age of sixteen she entered the Academy of the Visitation, at Georgetown, D. C., where she remained two years. While there she gave special attention to the study of composition, and to some extent indulged her inclination to write verses for her own amusement. After leaving school she engaged seriously in literary pursuits, but for some time was content to have no other audience than her immediate friends. "Valeria" was first printed for private circulation in 1891, but in the latter part of 1892 the work was enlarged and brought out by a Chicago publisher. By request of the committee on ceremonies of the World's Columbian Exposition, Miss Monroe wrote the "Opening Ode" for the dedication of the White City, which occurred October 21, 1892. Parts of the poem were read and parts of it sung by the great chorus on that memorable occasion. In prose Miss Monroe has done considerable journalistic work, chiefly in the line of art and literary criticisms, and has written a number of clever essays on the English poets. She is a graceful writer, and her essays, like her poems, are distinguished by simplicity and sincerity.

HARRIET STONE MONROE.
343

JUSTIN SMITH MORRILL

ONE of the truly great men in the United States Senate, who commands the closest attention whenever he addresses that body on
any of the important questions of the day, is the senior senator from
Vermont. Senator Morrill has passed his eighty-fourth birthday, and
for nearly forty years his voice has been heard in the legislative halls
of the national government. He was born in Strafford, Orange County,
Vt., April 14, 1810. He received a common-school and academic education and engaged in mercantile pursuits until 1848, when he turned
his attention to agriculture. He was elected to Congress in 1855 as
a Republican, and was five times re-elected, serving from December,
1855, until March 3, 1867. During the stirring times immediately pre-
ceding the Civil war he was looked upon as a leader in the House,
and his power and influence never waned thereafter. He was the
author of the "Morrill" tariff of 1861, and acted as chairman of the
committee of ways and means in 1864 and 1865. In 1867 he was
elected United States senator from Vermont, and has served continuously in that body from March 4 of that year until the present time.
His present term will expire in 1897. Senator Morrill is the author
of "Self-Consciousness of Noted Persons," published in 1886, a work
which is a most interesting addition to thoughtful and analytical literature. He is a fluent and graceful writer, as he is a forcible and eloquent speaker. In debate he has few equals in the Senate, and he
is especially strong on all questions affecting the tariff, which he has
made a special study during his public life, and which has been the
subject of some of his ablest oratorical efforts, delivered from the standpoint of a protectionist.

344

JUSTIN SMITH MORRILL.
345

JULIUS STERLING MORTON.

INTIMATELY associated with all the material growth of Nebraska during the last forty years, J. Sterling Morton stepped into President Cleveland's Cabinet fully equipped for the intelligent performance of the duties devolving upon him as Secretary of Agriculture. Mr. Morton was born in Adams, Jefferson County, N. Y., April 27, 1832, but at an early age removed with his parents to Michigan, and was graduated at Ann Arbor University. He subsequently graduated at the Union College of Law, New York, and after a brief editorial career with the Detroit "Free Press" and Chicago "Times," settled in Bellevue, Neb., in 1854. In the following year he started the Nebraska City "News," and was elected to the territorial legislature. He was re-elected in 1857, and in 1858 was appointed secretary of the territory to fill the vacancy caused by the death of Gov. Thomas B. Cuming, serving in that capacity until May, 1861. In 1860 he was nominated for Congress, and was given the certificate of election, but was unseated by contest. In 1866 he was again defeated as the Democratic candidate for the first state governorship of Nebraska. After a retirement of fifteen years from politics, he was a candidate for the governorship in 1880, 1884 and 1892, each time failing of election, and in 1893 President Cleveland appointed him Secretary of Agriculture. Mr. Morton has been the favorite candidate of his party several times for the United States Senate. He is a practical agriculturist and horticulturist, and has contributed largely to the best literature on those subjects. He is also the author of the Arbor Day legislation, which provides that one day in each year, April 22, be made a public holiday devoted to tree planting.

JULIUS STERLING MORTON.

JOHN SINGLETON MOSBY.

——— -

AFTER a career that reads more like a thrilling romance than a
record of actual facts, that once famous Southerner, Col. John S.
Mosby, is now engaged in the practice of law on the Pacific coast.
He was born in Powhattan County, Virginia, December 6, 1833.
While attending the University of Virginia, he shot and seriously
wounded a student, who assaulted him. He was fined and sentenced
to imprisonment, but was pardoned by the governor, and his fine was
remitted. Becoming a lawyer, he practiced at Bristol, Va., until the
beginning of hostilities in 1861, when he enlisted in the Confederate
cavalry, and soon became noted as a fighter. Acting as scout, he
guided General Stuart's force in a bold raid in the rear of Gen. George
B. McClellan's position on the Chickahominy, June 14, 1862. In January, 1863, he crossed the Rappahannock into northern Virginia, which
had been abandoned to the occupation of the National army, and
recruited a force of irregular cavalry, with which he harassed the Federal lines by cutting communications, destroying supply trains in the
rear of invading armies, and capturing many cavalry outposts. In
March, 1863, he routed a cavalry force much larger than his own,
and a month later defeated a detachment sent especially to capture him.
Once he was surrounded in the rear of Hooker's army, but cut his
way through the lines. He was several times wounded. The Confederate Congress placed his partisan rangers on the same footing as
the cavalry of the line. After the war Colonel Mosby settled at War-
renton, Va. He supported Grant in 1872, and Hayes in 1876, for
the presidency, and by the latter was appointed consul at Hong Kong,
where he remained six years.

JOHN SINGLETON MOSBY.

LOUISE CHANDLER MOULTON.

THE author of many exquisite sonnets, which not a few critics have placed at the head of their kind in America, the literary reputation of Louise Chandler Moulton rests upon her poetry, notwithstanding the excellence and wide range of her prose work. Born in Pomfret, Conn., April 5, 1835, she was educated at Mrs. Emma Willard's Seminary in Troy, N. Y., and began to contribute to periodicals under the name of "Ellen Louise" at the age of fifteen. She was only nineteen when she published her first book, "This, That and the Other," which was very successful, and after her marriage in 1855 to William U. Moulton, a publisher of Boston, she wrote "Juno Clifford," a novel, and contributed many articles and short stories to the magazines. In 1873 Roberts Brothers, of Boston, became her publishers, and have issued many volumes of her poetical and prose works, which have had a large sale. From 1870 to 1876 she was the Boston literary correspondent of the New York "Tribune," and for five years she wrote a weekly letter on bookish topics for the Boston "Sunday Herald." Mrs. Moulton's home is in Boston, but she spends her summers and autumns abroad, principally in London and Paris, and her society and literary letters from those cities are much sought after by American newspaper publishers. Since the death of Philip Bourke Marston, in 1887, she has edited two volumes of his verses, "Garden Secrets" and "A Last Harvest," with a preface and biographical sketch of the author. It has been said of Mrs. Moulton that she is in herself two phenomena—the dedicated and conscientious poet, and the poet whose wares are marketable and popular. She is especially happy in her stories for children.

LOUISE CHANDLER MOULTON.

OLIVER MOWATT.

STURDY man physically as well as mentally is the premier and attorney-general of the province of Ontario, Canada. Oliver Mowatt (now Sir Oliver) was born in Kingston, Upper Canada, July 22, 1820. He received a thorough education, adopted the law as his profession, and was called to the bar in 1842. He was appointed a queen's counsel in 1856, and a bencher of the Law Society for the province in the same year. He became a member of the Senate, and an LL. D. of Toronto University. From 1856 to 1859 he was a commissioner for consolidating the public general statutes of Canada and Upper Canada. He entered political life in 1858, as representative of South Ontario; was provincial secretary in the same year; postmaster-general in 1863-64; and from November, 1864, until October, 1872, was vice-chancellor of Upper Canada. His prominence in the Liberal party of the province grew rapidly, and his acuteness as a political leader was soon recognized after he had fairly entered the political field. He left the bench at the period last named to form a new administration in Ontario, and became premier and attorney-general for the province, and representative of North Oxford in the Legislature. He is the author of many important legislative measures in the provincial parliament, among which is the judicature bill, an act passed for the fusion of law and equity in the courts of Ontario. Time does not seem to tell upon him as upon most men. He is the same genial, alert, and politic director of affairs that he was long ago, and still apparently capable of guiding the destinies of his party successfully for a long time to come. He has been in power for twenty-two years and has just been again triumphant in a hard-fought campaign.

OLIVER MOWATT.
355

THOMAS NAST.

NO other caricaturist in the world ever gained such wide popularity as Thomas Nast, whose famous autograph and peculiar style of work have for years been familiar to millions of readers of pictorial literature. Mr. Nast was born in Landau, Bavaria, September 27, 1840, and was brought to the United States by his father in 1846. When a boy of fourteen he spent about six months in the drawing classes of Theodore Kaufmann, and then, with no other preparatory art instruction, he was engaged as a draughtsman on an illustrated paper. In 1860 he went to England as special artist for a New York weekly paper, thence to Italy, where he followed Garibaldi, making sketches for the leading illustrated papers of New York, London and Paris. Returning to New York he began, in July, 1862, drawing war sketches for "Harper's Weekly." His very first political carica-ture, an allegorical design that gave a powerful blow to the peace party, brought him into public notice and he immediately became popu-lar. Besides his work for "Harper's Weekly," by which he is best known, Mr. Nast has drawn for other periodicals, illustrated a number of books, issued "Nast's Illustrated Almanac" for several years, and executed many caricatures in water colors. Since 1873 he has spent much of his time lecturing in the principal cities of the United States, drawing caricatures and sketches on the stage with extreme rapidity by way of illustration. In his particular line, pictorial satire, Thomas Nast stands in the foremost rank, and his talent in that respect has been productive of some excellent results, such as the overthrow of the Tweed ring in New York City, and the arousing of popular sentiment against various iniquities, political and otherwise.

THOMAS NAST.

KNUTE NELSON.

STURDY, thrifty and loyal, with mental and physical capacities that
enable them to adapt themselves to any line of useful work, the
United States has no better citizens than those who come from the
land of the Vikings. Knute Nelson, ex-Governor of Minnesota, is
one of these. He was born in the parish of Voss, near the city
of Bergen, Norway, February 2, 1843. When three years of age
he lost his father, and in 1849 he came to the United States with
his mother, living in Chicago until the fall of 1850, and then in the
state of Wisconsin until the summer of 1871. In August of the latter year he removed to Alexandria, Minn., which city has since been
his home. Mr. Nelson is a graduate of the Albion, Wis., Academy.
He served in the Civil war as a private and non-commissioned officer,
and was wounded and taken prisoner at the siege of Port Hudson,
La. After the war he studied law, and in 1867 was admitted to the
bar of the Circuit court of Dane County. He was a member of the
Wisconsin Legislature in 1868 and 1869; was county attorney for Douglas County, Minnesota, from 1872 to 1874; was state senator in the
Minnesota Legislature from 1875 to 1878; was presidential elector on
the Republican ticket in 1880, and was a member of the board of
regents of the State University from February, 1882, to January, 1893.
He was elected to the Forty-eighth Congress from the Fifth district of
Minnesota, and was twice re-elected, his course in that body being
such as to greatly increase his popularity. In 1892 Mr. Nelson was
nominated by acclamation for governor of Minnesota, and elected. He
has made a reputation as a conscientious and common-sense politician,
and his influence is great among his own countrymen in the Northwest.

KNUTE NELSON.
357

RICHARD JAMES OGLESBY.

—

PERPETUALLY beaming with cordial good nature, and as full of humorous anecdote and apt illustration as that other son of Illinois, the immortal Lincoln, ex-Senator Oglesby is affectionately referred to by his political friends, as he once was by his soldiers, as "Uncle Dick." He was born in Oldham County, Kentucky, July 25, 1824. Left an orphan at the age of eight years, he removed to Decatur, Ill., in 1836, and learned the carpenter's trade, which, with farming and rope-making, occupied him until 1844. He had studied law in the mean time, and in 1845 was admitted to the bar. He participated in the Mexican war as first lieutenant in the Fourth Illinois regiment, and in 1847 resumed the practice of law in Decatur. In 1849 he went to California and engaged in mining until 1851, when he returned to Illinois. In 1860 he was elected to the State Senate, but resigned in the following year to accept the colonelcy of the Eighth Illinois Volunteer regiment. He commanded a brigade at the capture of Fort Henry and Fort Donelson, and for gallantry was made brigadier-general. Again distinguishing himself at Corinth, where he was severely wounded, he was promoted to the rank of major-general. He resigned in 1864, and in November of that year was elected governor of Illinois. He continued in that office until 1869, and was again elected in 1872. During the following year he was chosen United States senator, serving in that capacity until March 3, 1879. In 1884 he was again elected governor for a term of four years, and since 1888 has held no public office. General Oglesby takes a great interest in the affairs of the Grand Army of the Republic. He is one of the greatest sons of his great state.

RICHARD JAMES OGLESBY.

GEORGE WASHINGTON PECK.

GRADUATING from the printer's case to the editorial tripod, and there acquiring a national reputation as a humorist, George W. Peck found it a comparatively easy matter to make the rest of the journey to the honorable position of governor of Wisconsin. His early life was a continuous struggle for a competence. Born in Henderson, Jefferson County, N. Y., September 28, 1840, he was taken to Wisconsin in childhood by his parents. At the age of fifteen he was apprenticed to the printer's trade in the office of the Whitewater (Wis.) "Register," and afterward worked in various places as a journeyman printer. In 1860 he purchased on credit a half interest in the "Jefferson County Republican," at Jefferson, Wis., but sold out a year later. In 1863 he enlisted as a private in the Fourth Wisconsin Volunteer Cavalry, and for two and a half years served with his regiment in the south, being promoted to the rank of lieutenant. In the fall of 1866 he went to Ripon, Wis., and started a newspaper called the "Representative," which he conducted for about two years, and was then engaged as a writer for the La Crosse "Democrat," published by "Brick" Pomeroy. He subsequently became half owner of that paper and changed its name to the "Liberal Democrat." In 1874 he founded the "Sun" at La Crosse, removed it to Milwaukee in 1878, called it "Peck's Sun," and made it a great success. As a vehicle for his humorous musings it became very popular. Some of his collected articles have been published in book form, notably "Peck's Bad Boy." Mr. Peck was first mayor of Milwaukee and was subsequently elected governor of Wisconsin on the Democratic ticket in 1892. He enjoys the respect and confidence of the people.

GEORGE WASHINGTON PECK.

THOMAS WITHERELL PALMER.

O F the many hundreds who have enjoyed his hospitality, or even of the many thousands who have formed his acquaintance in a social, political, or business way, it would be difficult to find one who has anything but praise for ex-Senator Palmer, of Michigan. His genial disposition and sympathetic nature have given him a strong hold on a wide circle of friends, whose number was greatly increased during the World's Fair of 1893. Thomas W. Palmer was born in Detroit, January 25, 1830. After receiving an education he made a pedestrian tour in Spain, traveled in South America, and then engaged in mercantile life in Wisconsin. Subsequently he became a successful lumber merchant in Detroit, and interested himself in the politics of the state, serving as a member of the board of estimates and as a state senator in 1878. He was defeated for Congress in 1876, but was elected United States senator from Michigan for a term of six years from March 4, 1883. Upon the election of President Harrison, Senator Palmer was appointed Minister to Spain, but not finding the climate of that country agreeable he soon after resigned and returned to Detroit. In June, 1890, he was elected president of the National Commission having charge of the World's Columbian Exposition of 1893, a post which he filled most acceptably until after the close of the Exposition. Mr. Palmer impresses one as a man who thoroughly enjoys life, and is anxious that everybody about him should do the same. He is noted for his magnificent hospitality, his optimistic estimate of human character and motives, and his readiness to extend a helping hand to those who are striving to gain a foothold in the world. Naturally, he has a host of friends.

THOMAS WITHERELL PALMER.

ELLA WILKINSON PEATTIE.

JOURNALISTIC ability of the highest order, and a versatility and capacity for work that are amazing, must be accorded to that brilliant western writer, Mrs. Ella W. Peattie. She was born in Kalamazoo, Mich., January 15, 1862, and before she was ten years old was taken by her parents to Chicago, where she grew to womanhood, and where she was married in 1883 to Robert Burns Peattie, a well-known Chicago journalist. She was an omnivorous reader from childhood, and had written several short stories that attracted attention before she became regularly employed on the Chicago "Tribune" as a reporter. She afterward held a similar position on the "Morning News"—now the "Record"—and in 1888 removed with her husband to Omaha, since which time she has been one of the leading editorial writers of the Omaha "World-Herald." In addition to her editorial work, which has taken the widest possible range of subject, she publishes every week a signed article on topics of her own choosing. Her regular literary work has included many contributions to such juvenile publications as "St. Nicholas" and "Wide-Awake," and such leading periodicals as the "Century," "Harper's Weekly," "Cosmopolitan" and "Lippincotts'." While in Chicago, between the rush of newspaper work and home duties, she wrote "The Story of America," a child's history, which has passed through many editions, and "With Scrip and Staff," a remarkable story of the children's crusade in the year 1200. She also wrote "The Judge," a novel, which was awarded a prize by the Detroit "Free Press," and afterward published in book form. She is one of the founders of the Omaha Woman's Club, and frequently lectures on literary and economical topics.

ELIA WILKINSON PEATTIE
365

JOHN McAULEY PALMER.

WHETHER on a battle-field or in a political campaign, in a legal contest or legislative debate, Senator John M. Palmer, of Illinois, is known as a man of aggressive courage. He is a native of Eagle Creek, Scott County, Ky., where he was born September 13, 1817. He removed with his father to Madison County, Illinois, in 1831, completing his education in Alton (now Shurtleff) College, and in 1839 settled in Carlinville, where he was admitted to the bar. He was twice elected probate judge of Macoupin County; was a delegate to the State Constitutional Convention in 1847; served as county judge for forty years thereafter, and was a member of the State Senate from 1852 until 1856. In the latter year he was a delegate to the Republican National Convention in Philadelphia, and in 1860 was a presidential elector on the Republican ticket. He was elected a member of the Peace Conference in Washington in 1861, and in the same year he was made colonel of the Fourteenth Illinois infantry, participating in the Civil war. He was promoted to the rank of brigadier-general December 20, 1861, and for conspicuous gallantry at the battle of Stone River was commissioned major-general November 29, 1862. General Palmer was elected governor of Illinois in 1868, and held the office until 1873. He was afterward three times a candidate for the United States Senate as a Democrat, but failed of election, and in 1888 entered the race for the governorship of Illinois and was defeated. In 1890 he was elected United States senator by the Democratic members of the Legislature, and has since been dealing sledge-hammer blows at the opposition in Washington. His term will expire March 3, 1897. He is a man of great force.

JOHN McAULEY PALMER.

367

THOMAS COLLIER PLATT.

VERY few shrewder men, very few men more earnest in following a path once entered upon, and very few more sensible and adaptable have appeared in American politics than Thomas Collier Platt, of New York. He was born in Owego, N. Y., July 15, 1833. He received a thorough education and entered Yale College, but left in 1853, at the end of his sophomore year, because of failing health. He continued his studies, however, and in 1876 received the honorary degree of M. A. He engaged in business, and eventually became president of the Tioga, N. Y., National Bank, and later engaged in the lumber business in Michigan, becoming a business man of decided prominence and influence. In 1872 he was elected to Congress, and was re-elected in 1874, in the mean time becoming a most important factor in state politics. In January, 1881, he was chosen United States senator, to take the place of Francis Kernan. His occupancy of the seat was but a brief one. There came the famous fight over the distribution of patronage in New York, and then followed the simultaneous resignation of Roscoe Conklin and Thomas Platt, the two senators from New York. Mr. Platt became again a candidate for the seat, but was defeated. He then became secretary and director of the United States Express Company, and since 1880 has been its president. He has not, however, disappeared from politics. He became commissioner of quarantine of New York, when his strong hand was felt as it is felt now in the trend of New York politics. He was a member of the National Republican conventions in 1876, 1880 and 1884, and for years was a member of the Republican National Committee. Mr. Platt is recognized as a power in politics.

THOMAS COLLIER PLATT.

TERENCE VINCENT POWDERLY.

FOR fifteen years the guiding star, the ruling spirit, of the order of Knights of Labor, the greatest organization of workingmen ever successfully planned or held together by wise council and tactful management, Terence V. Powderly has earned a place among the great men of America. Mr. Powderly was born at Carbondale, Pa., January 22, 1849. At the age of seventeen he was apprenticed to learn the trade of machinist in the Delaware & Hudson railroad shops, and three years later he obtained work in the shops of the Delaware, Lackawanna & Western Railroad Company, at Scranton. His first connection with a labor organization was in 1871, when he joined the Machinists' and Blacksmiths' Union, of Scranton, and since 1874, when he became a member of Assembly 88, Knights of Labor, he has been active in promoting the objects for which that organization was created. He was elected Grand Worthy Foreman of the Knights of Labor by the second general assembly, which convened at St. Louis in 1879, and at the convention held in Chicago during September of the same year he was chosen Grand Master Workman of the order. He was annually re-elected to that office and served until the latter part of 1893, when he was superseded by J. R. Sovereign, of Iowa. Mr. Powderly was one of the founders of the "Labor Advocate," a regular contributor to the "Journal of United Labor," and has been three times elected mayor of Scranton. In 1882 he was nominated for lieutenant-governor of Pennsylvania by the Greenback-Labor party, but declined the nomination. He has lately devoted himself to the study of law, and will give the remainder of his life to the practice of that profession and to the cause of labor.

TERENCE VINCENT POWDERLY.

JOHN WESLEY POWELL

A VALUED contributor to the cause of science, and one whose writings are regarded as standard and exhaustive on the subjects whereof they treat, Maj. John W. Powell is well fitted for the directorship of the United States Geological Survey, a position he has filled for a number of years. He was born in Mount Morris, N. Y., March 24, 1834, and spent much of his early life in Ohio, Wisconsin and Illinois, during which time he made collections of geological and natural history specimens. At the beginning of hostilities in 1861, he enlisted as a private in the Twentieth Illinois Infantry, afterward becoming lieutenant-colonel of the Second Illinois Artillery, and although he lost an arm at the battle of Shiloh he continued in active service until the close of the war. He then became professor of geology and curator of the museum in the Illinois Wesleyan University and in the Illinois Normal University, and in 1868 organized a party for the exploration of the Grand Canyon of the Colorado. The success of the expedition led the general government to sanction the establishment of a topographical and geological survey, a department that has since assumed its present form and name. Major Powell, under the direction of the Smithsonian Institution, established a Bureau of Ethnology, of which he remained chief until 1881, when he was appointed director of the Geological Survey, and served for thirteen years. He has received honorary degrees from various colleges and universities, both in this country and in Europe, and is a member of many learned societies. He has written extensively on his favorite themes, and is the author of a number of standard works on geology and natural history. He resigned the directorship of the Geological Survey in 1894.

JOHN WESLEY POWELL
373

JOSEPH PULITZER.

ENERGY, enterprise and the ability to perceive and to supply on the shortest notice the wants of the reading public, must be considered as a part of the capital necessary in the building up of a great metropolitan newspaper. These requisites are possessed in an extraordinary degree by that successful journalist, Joseph Pulitzer, proprietor of the New York "World" and the St. Louis "Post-Dispatch." Mr. Pulitzer was born in Buda-Pesth, Hungary, April 10, 1847. He came to America in early youth, and settled in St. Louis, where he quickly acquired a knowledge of English, became interested in politics, and was elected to the Missouri Legislature in 1869, and to the state constitutional convention in 1874. He entered journalism at the age of twenty on the St. Louis "Westliche Post," a German Republican newspaper, at that time under the editorial control of Carl Schurz. Subsequently he became its managing editor, and obtained a proprietary interest. In 1878 he founded the St. Louis "Post-Dispatch," and still retains control of that journal. In 1883 he purchased the New York "World," which, after twenty-three years of existence under various managers, had achieved no permanent success, and at once greatly increased its circulation. He is at present its editor and sole proprietor. Mr. Pulitzer was elected to Congress in 1884, but resigned a few months after taking his seat on account of the pressure of journalistic duties. Indomitable pluck and perseverance, coupled with keen foresight and a faculty for keeping a little ahead of the times, have enabled Joseph Pulitzer, within a comparatively few years, to enroll his name among the greatest journalists of the period and to become recognized as the creator of one of the most successful newspapers in the world.

JOSEPH PULITZER.

GEORGE MORTIMER PULLMAN.

FOR many years there has been no name so inseparably associated with progress in railway equipment as that of George M. Pullman. The sleeping cars invented by him, and bearing his name, are known all over the world. Mr. Pullman was born in Chautauqua County, New York, March 3, 1831, and began to support himself at the age of fourteen. At twenty-two he successfully undertook a contract for moving warehouses and other buildings along the line of the Erie canal, then being widened by the state. In 1859 he removed to Chicago and engaged extensively in the then novel occupation of raising entire blocks of brick and stone buildings. In the same year he began experimenting with the idea of inventing a sleeping-car for railway travel, and in 1865 the first car, built on the now well-known model, was completed, and named "Pioneer." The fleet has grown from one car to many hundred and its working force from half a dozen men to fifteen thousand. The cars are operated on nearly a hundred roads and over a mileage equivalent to five times the circumference of the globe. The Pullman Palace Car Company, of which Mr. Pullman is president, was organized in 1867, and from the first has regularly paid its quarterly dividends. Mr. Pullman designed and established the vestibuled trains, now so popular. In 1880 he founded, near Chicago, the industrial town of Pullman, where the numerous employes of the company reside with their families. Architecturally, the town is picturesque, and according to mortality statistics it is one of the most healthful places in the world. Mr. Pullman is addicted to no affectations; is plain in his address, thoroughly business-like in his habits and without ostentation in his liberal gifts to charity.

GEORGE MORTIMER PULLMAN.

JULIAN RALPH.

JULIAN RALPH, who, having made a brilliant record in journalism, is now making one as striking in literature, was born in New York City, May 27, 1853, his father being an English physician who came to this country early in the century. Mr. Ralph received his schooling in public and private schools and was forced by family reverses to shift for himself at fourteen, when he became a printer's apprentice. At eighteen he was local editor of the Red Bank, N. J., "Standard," and started a newspaper of his own, the "Leader," in the same town. That failed and he became editor of the Webster, Mass., "Times" during a broken period of eighteen months. At twenty he was a reporter on the "Daily Graphic" in New York, and at twenty-one went on the New York "Sun," on the staff of which journal he has been ever since. A series of humorous dialect sketches, entitled "The German Barber," first called public attention to his work, and of late years he has written many papers of travel and adventure for "Harper's," "The Century," and "Scribner's." Fiction he did not attempt until 1894, when he began to exploit his knowledge of the swarming poor of his native city in a series of short stories. His books are "On Canada's Frontier," "Our Great West," and "Chicago and the Fair." He was married in 1876 to Miss M. Isabella Mount, of Middletown, N. J., and is the father of five children. Mr. Ralph is perhaps one of the most notable exponents of the fact that a newspaper training rather fits than unfits a writer for purely literary work. A brilliant group of newspaper men have lately graduated with deserved honors in the literary field, but among them none is more prominent than the subject of this sketch.

JULIAN RALPH
379

OPIE READ.

RANKING high among American humorists and delineators of Southern character, Opie Read has firmly established himself in the good graces of the reading public. Born in Nashville, Tenn., December 22, 1852, Mr. Read received his education in a private school and at Neophogen College, Gallatin. He learned the printer's trade, which he followed for a livelihood for some years, and in 1873 became a newspaper reporter and general writer, associated with the "Patriot," of Franklin, Ky. He afterward had charge of the city department of the Little Rock (Ark.) "Gazette," and it was during this connection that he began writing those inimitable short stories and sketches of Southern life that subsequently made him famous. In 1882 he founded the "Arkansaw Traveler," at Little Rock, and the paper became so popular that in 1887, with a view to increasing the scope of the publication, it was decided to remove the plant to Chicago, from which city the paper was thereafter issued. In 1891 he withdrew from the "Arkansaw Traveler" for the purpose of devoting his whole time to regular literary work, and has published a number of novels that have added greatly to his reputation. He is the author of "A Kentucky Colonel," "Emmett Bonlore," "The Colossus," "A Tennessee Judge," "Len Gansett," and other novels, besides innumerable short stories. Recently he has achieved success on the platform by giving public readings from his own works. Like most large men, for Opie Read is a giant in stature, he is generous and warm-hearted to a degree. His conversation abounds with humorous anecdote and keen flashes of wit, and in the rooms of the Chicago Press Club, his favorite lounging place, he is especially popular.

OPIE READ.

WHITELAW REID.

THOUGH cast in a different mold, it may be said that the present editor of the New York "Tribune" is in some respects as great a man as his eminent predecessor, the sage of Chappaqua. Whitelaw Reid was born in Xenia, Ohio, October 27, 1837. He was graduated at Miami University in 1856, and in the following year took editorial charge of the Xenia "News." When the war broke out he went to Washington as the correspondent of the Cincinnati "Gazette," subsequently accompanying the Union army on its march south, and his descriptions of battles were valuable contributions to the record of the war. In 1865 he was invited by Horace Greeley to take an editorial position on the staff of the New York "Tribune," and upon the death of Mr. Greeley he succeeded to the ownership and management of that paper. Extremely earnest in his political views, Mr. Reid, since he became a resident of New York, has exercised a powerful influence in local, state and national campaigns, and upon the accession of President Harrison in 1889 he was appointed United States Minister to Paris. In 1892, when Mr. Harrison was a candidate for re-election, Mr. Reid received the nomination for vice-president, and suffered the common fate of Republican candidates in that year. He is the author of a number of books relating to the history of Ohio during the war, to the condition of the South after the war, and upon subjects of a political and journalistic character. He is regent of the New York State University, and a member of many social, political and scientific organizations. Under his able management the "Tribune" has become a great power in political circles and the representative Republican organ in the East.

WHITELAW REID.

GEORGE GRAHAM VEST.

A NATURAL orator, a man of intense feeling, generous impulses and marked ability, George G. Vest, United States senator from Missouri, has become well known, not alone in the state he represents, but throughout the country. He has been a conspicuous Democratic figure in the Senate for years. He was born in Frankfort, Ky., December 6, 1830. He attended the high school of B. B. Sayre, in Franklin, for ten years, and in 1846 entered Centre College, at Danville, in the same state, graduating in 1848. He studied law and removed to Georgetown, Mo., to engage in its practice. In 1856 he removed from Georgetown to Booneville. In 1861 he was elected to the Legislature, but soon entered the Confederate army, and later became a member of the Confederate Congress, in which body he served two years. At the close of the war he resumed the practice of the law in Sedalia, Mo., forming a partnership with Judge John F. Phillips. Mr. Vest from this date incidentally took part in the political canvasses of the Democratic party, and so became widely and favorably known throughout the state. In 1877 he removed from Sedalia to Kansas City, intending to engage in his profession there, but was elected to the United States Senate as a Democrat, in place of James H. Shields, Democrat, who had been elected to fill the place made vacant by the death of Louis V. Bogy. Mr. Vest was re-elected in 1885, and again in 1890. In the Senate he has served on the important standing committees, and has shown the possession of statesmanlike qualities, while his gifts as a speaker and his qualities of personal popularity have added to his strength in that body. In his own state there has been no candidate opposed to him on the occasion of his renominations.

GEORGE GRAHAM VEST.
387

JOHN ROGERS.

IN elevating the artistic taste of the masses, there can be no doubt that the well known "Rogers Groups" of statuary have had a large share. John Rogers, the sculptor, was born in Salem, Mass., and educated in the Boston high school. While working in a machine shop at Manchester, N. H., his attention was first drawn to sculpture, and he began to model in clay in his leisure hours. In 1858 he visited Europe, and upon his return, in 1859, he went to Chicago, where he modeled, for a charity fair, "The Checker Players," a group in clay, which attracted much attention. He produced also some other groups, but "The Slave Auction," which was exhibited in New York in 1860, first brought him to the notice of the general public. This was the forerunner of the celebrated war series of statuettes, which included, among others, "The Picket Guard," "One More Shot," "Taking the Oath and Drawing Rations," "Union Refugees," "Wounded Scout," and "Council of War." His works on social subjects, most of which have been produced since the war, include "Coming to the Parson," "Checkers up at the Farm," "The Charity Patient," "Fetching the Doctor," and "Going for the Cows." His groups in illustration of passages in the poets, particularly Shakespeare, have also been very popular, but he has been most successful in illustrating every-day life in its humorous and pathetic aspects. His equestrian statue of Gen. John F. Reynolds, which stands before the city hall in Philadelphia, was completed in 1883, and in 1887 he exhibited "Ichabod Crane and the Headless Horseman," a bronze group. A collection of Mr. Rogers' works was exhibited at the World's Columbian Exposition in 1893.

JOHN ROGERS.

ANNA KATHARINE GREEN ROHLFS.

BY far the most astonishing thing about that widely-read novel, "The Leavenworth Case," and the later productions from the same pen, is that they were written by a woman. The book in question is now used in Yale College as a text book to show the fallacy of circumstantial evidence, and is the subject of comments by learned lawyers, to whom it appeals by its mastery of legal points. Anna Katharine Green, which is the author's maiden name, and the one by which she is known throughout the world, inherits her legal turn of mind. She is the daughter of a lawyer, and was born in Brooklyn, N. Y., November 11, 1846. While she was yet a child the family removed to Buffalo, and there her education was conducted until she was old enough to enter Ripley Female College, at Poultney, Vt. In her childhood she composed innumerable poems and stories, and soon after her graduation she wrote her first novel, "The Leavenworth Case," which at once attracted the attention of the literary world, and was afterward dramatized. Her success brought eager invitations from publishers to furnish them stories, and other novels followed, including "A Strange Disappearance," "The Sword of Damocles," "Hand and Ring," "X. Y. Z.," "The Mill Mystery," "7 to 12," "Behind Closed Doors," "The Forsaken Inn," "A Matter of Millions," "Cynthia Wakeham's Money," and "The Old Stone House." Her poetical works are embraced in a volume entitled "The Defense of the Bride, and Other Poems," and "Risifi's Daughter," a drama. In November, 1884, she was married to Charles Rohlfs, of Brooklyn, N. Y. Her stories are all ingenious in plot and full of dramatic interest, and they have been published abroad in various languages.

ANNA KATHERINE GREEN ROHLFS.

WILLIAM STARKE ROSECRANS.

CHIEFLY as a great military leader, but in no small degree as a diplomat and as a promoter of large enterprises, Gen. William S. Rosecrans has won enduring fame. He was born in Kingston, Ohio, September 6, 1819, and was graduated at the United States Military Academy in 1842, entering the corps of engineers. In 1854, after attaining the rank of first lieutenant, he resigned to establish himself in Cincinnati as an architect and civil engineer. In 1855 he took charge of the Cannel Coal Company, of West Virginia, becoming also, in 1856, president of the Coal River Navigation Company, and in 1857 he organized the Preston Coal Oil Company. At the beginning of the Civil war he volunteered as aide to General McClellan, then commanding the Department of the Ohio, and later succeeded McClellan in the command of that department. In 1862 he was made commander of the Department of the Columbia, and conducted a campaign remarkable for brilliant movements and heavy fighting. After the war General Rosecrans went to California, and was offered the Democratic nomination for governor of that state, but declined it. He was appointed Minister to Mexico, July 27, 1868, and held that office until June 26, 1869, when he returned to the United States and declined the Democratic nomination for Governor of Ohio. He was subsequently for a number of years connected with important railway and mining projects in California and Mexico, and in 1876 he declined the Democratic nomination for Congress from Nevada. In 1881 he was elected to Congress from California, serving until March, 1885, and in June of the latter year he was appointed register of the United States Treasury by President Cleveland.

WILLIAM STARKE ROSECRANS.
393

WILLIAM EUSTIS RUSSELL

TO be governor of Massachusetts is, as it has been since the beginning of the republic, an honor to any man. Doubly great is it when the man who becomes governor has but lately attained manhood. This honor came to William Eustis Russell, who was born in Cambridge, Mass., January 6, 1857. He received the ordinary common-school education, but was widely popular, and when he was but twenty-five years of age was elected alderman and showed such marked ability that he was re-elected without opposition. In 1885 he became a candidate for mayor of Cambridge and was re-elected for three terms. He abandoned politics and went into business, but was called into the field again by the clamor of his party as the most available man in all Massachusetts for the Democratic party. He was made candidate for governor, but was defeated by a vote of twenty-eight thousand. He was again nominated in the succeeding year and was again defeated, but this time by only six thousand seven hundred and seventy-five votes. In 1890 he was again nominated and elected by nearly nine thousand plurality. He was re-elected at the end of his term and retained his place until the Republican upheaval in Massachusetts. He is one of the shrewdest and most careful of the young men in politics, for he is not yet forty years of age. His extraordinary success in such a state, at such an age, and under such circumstances, made him a prominent figure, and he has become, to an extent, conspicuous as a possible Democratic candidate for vice-president of the United States. He is one of the possible great factors in directing the affairs, not merely of his own state, but of the nation. It is already the political fancy to talk of him as presidential a possibility.

WILLIAM EUSTIS RUSSELL
393

PATRICK JOHN RYAN.

REMARKABLY eloquent, vigorous and impressive, with a depth of learning and force of character that make him a power in his particular sphere, Archbishop Ryan, of Philadelphia, has fairly won the ecclesiastical honors that have come to him. He was born in Cloneyharp, near Thurles, Ireland, February 20, 1831, receiving his education at Thurles and Dublin, and afterward entering Carlow College to prepare himself for the American mission. In 1853 he was ordained deacon, and during the same year he set out for St. Louis, Mo., where he finished his ecclesiastical studies in Carondelet Seminary, and was raised to the priesthood in 1854. Father Ryan became vicar-general February 15, 1872, was elected coadjutor archbishop of St. Louis and consecrated under the title of Bishop of Tricomia April 14. Owing to the age of Archbishop Kenrick, most of the work of governing the diocese devolved upon him, but he was equal to the emergency and his administration was energetic and successful. Bishop Ryan was one of the prelates selected in 1883 to represent the interests of the Roman Catholics of the United States in Rome. He was nominated archbishop of Philadelphia June 8, 1884. During that year he was present at the third plenary council of Baltimore, at which the opening discourse, "The Church in Her Councils," was pronounced by him. In 1887 he again went to Rome on business connected with the plan of establishing a Catholic university in Washington. As a pulpit orator, Archbishop Ryan has few equals in the ranks of American clergymen. Some of his lectures have been published, among the most popular of them being "What Catholics Do Not Believe," and "Some of the Causes of Modern Religious Skepticism."

PATRICK JOHN RYAN.
395

EDGAR SALTUS.

WIELDING English with the precision of the finished scholar, and displaying consummate skill in the handling of every subject that he undertakes to discuss, Edgar Saltus is unquestionably a master of the art literary. Moreover, he possesses the rare faculty of compelling interest in his subject by the very charm of his style. Mr. Saltus was born in New York City June 8, 1858. His early education was received at St. Paul's school, Concord, N. H., after which he went abroad and studied at the Sorbonne, Paris, and in Heidelberg and Munich, Germany. After his return he entered the Columbia College Law School, where he was graduated in 1880. His earliest literary efforts were in poetry, some of which gave evidence of the talent and artistic ability then in process of development, but his philosophical bent led him early into prose writing and to the revelation of thoughts and theories that at once attracted attention to his work. His first book was "Balzac," a biography published in Boston in 1884. He next devoted himself to the presentation of the pessimistic philosophy, a history of which he published in 1885 under the title of "The Philosophy of Disenchantment." This was followed by an analytical exposition, entitled "The Anatomy of Negation," which was first published in London in 1886, and in New York in 1887. Mr. Saltus is also the author of "Mr. Incoul's Misadventure," "The Truth About Tristrem Varick," "Eden," "Imperial Purple," "Mary Magdalene," and other works. In all his writings there is evinced a rare delicacy of touch, a felicitous blending of light and shadow, that give one the impression imparted by a series of artistically-drawn pictures, and stamp the writer as a word-painter of strong individuality.

EDGAR SALTUS.
397

JOHN McALLISTER SCHOFIELD.

IN noting the famous military men of today—those who have continued their connection with the army, whether confronted by grim-
visaged war or white-winged peace--one naturally turns to John M.
Schofield, the present commander of the army. General Schofield was
born in Chautauqua, N. Y., September 29, 1831. He graduated at
West Point in 1853, and two years later attained the rank of first
lieutenant. He then became professor of natural philosophy in the
West Point Academy, and later, while on leave of absence, was professor of physics, in Washington University, St. Louis. Being in St.
Louis at the time of the breaking out of the war, in 1861, his first
active service in the great contest was as chief of staff to General
Lyon, who was killed at Springfield, Mo. He was appointed major-
general of volunteers in 1862, and in 1864 commanded the Army of
the Ohio, forming the left wing of Sherman's army in the Atlanta
campaign, where he distinguished himself for bravery and good gener-
alship. General Schofield succeeded Edwin M. Stanton as Secretary of
War June 2, 1868, and remained in that office until the close of
Johnson's administration, and under Grant, until March 12, 1869, when
he was appointed major-general in the United States army and ordered
to the Department of the Missouri. He was president of the board
that adopted the present tactics for the army in 1870, went on a special mission to the Hawaiian Islands in 1873, and was president of
the board of inquiry on the case of Fitz-John Porter in 1878. Upon
the death of General Sherman, in 1888, he was placed in command
of the army, but under existing laws he was retired in 1895, being
succeeded by General Miles.

JOHN McALLISTER SCHOFIELD.

ALBERT SHAW.

A LBERT SHAW, now editor and publisher of the American "Review of Reviews," ranks very fairly among the great young men of the United States. He was born in Butler County, Ohio, July 23, 1857, and is, therefore, just thirty-seven years old. He was fitted for college privately, and went to Iowa in 1875, where he graduated in 1879 at Iowa College (Grinnell). His tastes were strongly for public questions and for writing, and he entered local Iowa newspaperdom, continuing his reading in economics and political science. Afterward he went for advanced study to the Johns Hopkins University (Baltimore), where in 1884 he took the degree of Ph. D. on completion of work in political economy, constitutional law and history, etc. Meanwhile he had accepted an editorial position on the Minneapolis "Morning Tribune." He was one of the founders of the American Economic Association ten years ago, and has contributed important monographic volumes to its publications, and also to those of the series of publications in history and politics of the Johns Hopkins University. In 1887 he went to Europe for a vacation of a year and a half, and traveled extensively, among other things making a special study of municipal government. On his return he was offered numerous university professorships, but decided to remain in journalism, but accepted lectureships at the Johns Hopkins, Cornell, University of Wisconsin, etc. After another year as editor of the Minneapolis "Tribune," he went to New York, at the opening of 1891, and established the American "Review of Reviews." He continues to edit that periodical, of which he is also the chief owner. He was married in 1893 to Mrs. Bessie Bacon, of Reading, Pa.

ALBERT SHAW.

GEORGE SHIRAS.

FOR a place in which to awake and find one's self famous, there is nothing to compare with the Supreme Court of the United States. A seat upon that bench brings to the occupant, necessarily, the attention of sixty millions of people, yet it does not follow that, before his elevation, a Supreme Court justice has been more than locally known. The jurist is not advertised as is the politician, nor is a Supreme Court appointment attained as the result of a definite struggle for that great distinction. It has been the subject of much comment that not the most famous men have secured the prominent life position, but it has been the subject of comment quite as much that the appointment of men comparatively unknown to the country at large has resulted well. George Shiras, Jr., was born in Pittsburg, Pa., January 26, 1832. He received a very thorough preliminary education, and later entered Yale College, graduating from that institution in 1853. He attended the Yale Law School in 1854, and was admitted to the Pennsylvania bar in 1856. He soon acquired a high standing, especially for his knowledge of corporation law as well as for his general scholarship. He received the degree of LL. D. from Yale University in 1883, and in 1888 was one of the Pennsylvania presidential electors. Upon the death of the associate justice of Brooklyn, in 1892, Mr. Shiras was appointed to the vacant place on the Supreme bench, and took the oath of office October 10 of the same year. His marked ability has been still further manifested in the position he now occupies. He is looked upon by his countrymen at large as one of the eminently safe men upon the bench, one who will be affected by no personal inclination but be ever strictly judicial.

GEORGE SHIRAS.

405

DANIEL EDGAR SICKLES.

PROMINENT among the men who have served their country faithfully in times of peace and fearlessly during the more trying period of war is Gen. Daniel E. Sickles. He was born in New York City October 20, 1823, and began life as a printer, but afterward studied law and was admitted to the bar in 1844. He became a member of the State Legislature in 1847, corporation counsel of the city of New York in 1853, and the same year secretary of the American legation in London. Two years later he was sent to the State Senate, and in 1857 was elected to Congress and re-elected in 1859. During his first Congressional term, discovering a guilty intimacy between his wife and Philip Barton Key, United States Attorney for the District of Columbia, he shot Key in the street February 27, 1859. He was indicted for murder, but acquitted. In 1861 he raised the Excelsior Brigade and entered the service as colonel, soon acquiring the rank of brigadier-general and later that of major-general. He was conspicuous for gallantry in many battles, and at Gettysburg lost a leg. In 1865 he was sent on a confidential mission to the South American republics, and in 1866 he joined the Regular army as colonel of the Forty-second Infantry. He was placed on the retired list in 1869, with the full rank of major-general, and one month later President Grant appointed him minister to Spain, a post which he filled until 1873. He became chairman of the New York Civil Service Commission in 1888, sheriff of Kings County in 1890, and was elected to the Fifty-third Congress as a Democrat. He is a sturdy and prominent figure in all movements, and, as some one has said, quoting the old phrase, "A man, every inch of him."

JERRY SIMPSON.

READERS whose impressions of the Medicine Lodge statesman have been derived from the ridicule of his political opponents, who dubbed him "Sockless Simpson" on account of a remark made in one of his campaign speeches, will be surprised to know that he is a rather good-looking, well-dressed man, with scarcely a suggestion of rural simplicity in his appearance or manner. Congressman Simpson, of Kansas, was born in the province of New Brunswick March 31, 1842, but his parents removed to Oneida County, N. Y., when he was six years of age. At the age of fourteen he began life as a sailor, which pursuit he followed for twenty-three years on the Great Lakes. During the early part of the Civil War he served for a time in Company A, Twelfth Illinois Infantry, but failing health compelled him to leave the service. In 1878 he drifted to Kansas, and is now living six miles from Medicine Lodge, Barber County, where he is engaged in farming and stock raising. Mr. Simpson was a Republican originally, casting his first vote for the second election of Abraham Lincoln, but during the past twelve years has voted and affiliated with the Greenback and Union Labor parties. He twice ran for the Kansas Legislature on the Independent ticket in Barber County, but was defeated both times by a small plurality. He was nominated for the Fifty-second Congress by the People's party and elected by the aid of the Democrats, who indorsed his nomination, and was re-elected to the Fifty-third Congress as a Farmers' Alliance candidate. Mr. Simpson is an earnest advocate of reforms for the benefit of the farmer and working classes, and is a member of the committees on Agriculture and Territories.

JERRY SIMPSON.

FRANCIS HOPKINSON SMITH.

FEW men can truthfully say that they have achieved success and reputation in three different professions. Yet that distinction has been gained by F. Hopkinson Smith, the artist author whose clever work is familiar to all lovers of art and readers of magazine literature. Mr. Smith was born in Baltimore, Md., October 23, 1838. He received a thorough education and became a civil engineer, which profession he followed with success for a number of years. During that time he built a large number of public works, many of them under contract with the United States Government. These include the Race Rock, lighthouse off New London Harbor, in Long Island Sound, and the Block Island breakwater. Mr. Smith is well known as an artist, and has produced some very effective work in water-colors and charcoal. Among his water-colors are "In the Darkling Wood," "Peggotty on the Harlem," "Under the Towers, Brooklyn Bridge," "In the North Woods," and "A January Thaw." He has been occupied also in book and magazine illustration, and in late years has become deservedly popular as an author. In addition to numerous contributions to periodicals, embracing stories, sketches of travel, studies of characters and customs, and art reviews, he has published in book form "Well-worn Roads," "Old Lines in New Black and White," "A Book of the Tile Club," and "Colonel Carter of Cartersville." He is a member of various art associations, and from 1875 until 1878 was treasurer of the American Water-Color Society. Mr. Smith has traveled extensively in foreign lands and written many charming magazine articles descriptive of his tours and observations, all illustrated by himself. He is also a humorist and a delightful entertainer.

FRANCIS HOPKINSON SMITH.
409

AINSWORTH RAND SPOFFORD.

VERY well known throughout the United States is the name of the present librarian of Congress, a man who has done well in the difficult post he has occupied for more than a generation. He was born in New Hampshire in 1825, but moved at a comparatively early age to Cincinnati, engaging there as a bookseller and publisher. He acquired a standing rapidly and became eventually editor of the "Daily Commercial." In 1861 he was made assistant librarian of Congress, and in 1865 was nominated to his present place. The position he occupies is in some respects the most important of its kind in the world. There is growing up under his supervision what will possibly be the greatest library the world possesses. His record for more than a quarter of a century has demonstrated him to be the man for so great a place. There is now being erected in Washington a gigantic structure adapted to hold a collection of books beyond all precedent. Upon his thoughtfulness and energy and his good sense and policy must depend in the immediate future, and probably as long as he may live, the degree of success and completeness of this enormous library which one of the greatest of nations is establishing. He has done many good things for the country. Largely through his efforts the great collection of books in the National Library has been made what it is, a collection which will soon contain a million books. To him is to be attributed the reform in the manner of issuing copyrights and the simple yet efficient manner under which that important branch of the business of the government is now conducted. He deserves the wide reputation he has achieved for discriminating judgment and high literary taste.

AINSWORTH RAND SPOFFORD.

HOKE SMITH.

ONE of the men who have been recently placed in conspicuous positions before the public, and who have demonstrated their fitness for the responsible places assigned to them, is Hoke Smith, Secretary of the Interior in President Cleveland's cabinet. Mr. Smith is a comparatively new man in national politics. He is a lawyer and an editor from Atlanta, Ga., born in Newton, N. C., September 2, 1855. In years he is the youngest member of the cabinet, representing that young element of the South that has come to the front in public affairs since the war. His father was Prof. H. H. Smith, a distinguished educator of New Hampshire, who came from Revolutionary stock. Hoke Smith was admitted to the bar in Atlanta in 1873, before he was of age, and became a popular railroad lawyer, not by appearing in the interests of the corporations, but by opposing their claims. He built up a large and remunerative practice. In 1887 he organized and became president of the Atlanta "Journal," now a leading afternoon paper of the South. At that time Henry W. Grady, of the Atlanta "Constitution," was an advocate of protection. Mr. Smith championed the principle of a low tariff. When Mr. Cleveland was defeated in 1888 Mr. Smith did not waver, but predicted the downfall of protection. He married the youngest daughter of Gen. T. R. R. Cobb and niece of the late Howell Cobb, and is closely related, by his own family as well as through his wife, to many of the leading families throughout the Southern states. Mr. Smith is persistent in carrying out his plans and in the performance of whatever work may be intrusted to him, giving little heed to the criticisms and vehement protests which his course sometimes provokes.

HOKE SMITH

EMMA DOROTHY ELIZA NEVITTE SOUTHWORTH.

MANY mothers, and even grandmothers, of today can remember with what pleasurable emotions they pored over the captivating novels of Mrs. E. D. E. N. Southworth when they were girls. Not a few of them have continued to read her works ever since, and even now wait impatiently for each new story from her pen; for, notwithstanding her advanced age, Mrs. Southworth is still writing. She was born in Washington, D. C., in the house and room once occupied by General Washington, December 26, 1819. She was graduated in 1835 and in 1840 she married Frederick H. Southworth, of Utica, N. Y. Four years later, thrown upon her own resources, she became a school teacher in Washington, and while so occupied began to write stories, the first of which, "The Irish Refugee," appeared in the Baltimore "Saturday Visitor." Subsequently she became a regular contributor to the "National Era," in the columns of which paper appeared her first novel, "Retribution." It was issued in book form in 1849, and the author at once attained such popularity that for years some of the leading publishers competed sharply for her stories. With unusual rapidity she wrote her succeeding stories, issuing sometimes three in a year. She has published about sixty volumes, and continues to be one of the most prolific of living writers. Many of her stories were first published serially in the New York "Ledger." They display strong dramatic power, and the majority have been translated into French, German and Spanish, and re-published in London, Paris, Leipsic, Madrid and Montreal. For twenty-three years Mrs. Southworth resided in a beautiful villa on the Potomac Heights, near Washington, but in 1876 she removed to Yonkers, N. Y.

EMMA DOROTHY ELIZA NEVITTE SOUTHWORTH.

GOLDWIN SMITH

HIS prominent connection with the Liberal movement in Canada and his championship of the United States Government have made the name of Goldwin Smith quite as popular on this side of the Dominion border as it is in Toronto, where he resides. This eminent author and scholar was born in Reading, Berkshire, England, August 13, 1823. He was educated at Eton and Oxford, and was afterward associated with the reorganization of the latter university, in which he was regius professor of modern history from 1858 to 1866. During the Civil War in America he wrote "Does the Bible Sanction American Slavery?" "On the Morality of the Emancipation Proclamation," and other pamphlets that influenced public opinion, so that when he visited this country in 1864, to deliver a series of lectures, he received an enthusiastic welcome and the degree of LL. D. from Brown University. Returning to the United States in 1868, Mr. Smith was appointed professor of English and Constitutional History in Cornell University, and resided at Ithaca until 1871, when he removed to Toronto. He has been prominent in educational affairs there, edited the "Canadian Monthly" for two years, founded the "Nation" in 1874, the "Bystander" in 1880, and the Toronto "Week" in 1884. He has written much for English reviews, and among his publications in book form the most popular in this country are "The Civil War in America," "Experience of the American Commonwealth," and "The Relations Between America and England." Mr. Smith advocates the consolidation of Canada and the United States, which he regards as the manifest destiny of the countries, and is heartily in the movement for commercial union between the two countries.

GOLDWIN SMITH.

HARRIET PRESCOTT SPOFFORD.

LUXURIANT in expression and intense in feeling, with descriptions and fancies glittering with sensuous delights and every variety of splendor, the stories of Harriet Prescott Spofford would be charming if their only merit was their artistic coloring. Mrs. Spofford began writing when very young. She was born in Calais, Me., April 3, 1835, but in her youth was taken by her parents to Newburyport, Mass., which city has ever since been her home. At the age of seventeen she was graduated at the Pinkerton Academy at Derry, N. H. While in school at Newburyport her prize essay on Hamlet attracted the attention of Thomas Wentworth Higginson, who became her friend and counselor. Her father, Joseph N. Prescott, suffered a stroke of paralysis which permanently disabled him, and her mother also became a confirmed invalid, so that she felt the need of making her talents available, and began to contribute to the Boston story papers. In 1859 her sparkling story of Parisian life, entitled "In a Cellar," appeared in the "Atlantic Monthly," and gave her a reputation. The editor of the magazine, James Russell Lowell, had hesitated to publish the story until satisfied that it was not a French translation. From that day she was a welcome contributor both of prose and poetry to the chief periodicals of the country. In 1865 she was married to Richard S. Spofford, a lawyer of Boston. Among Mrs. Spofford's published works may be mentioned "Sir Rohan's Ghost," "The Amber Gods, and Other Stories," "Azarian," "New England Legends," "The Thief in the Night," "Art Decoration Applied to Furniture," "Marquis of Carabas," "Poems," "Hester Stanley at St. Mark's," "The Servant Girl Question," and "Ballads about Authors."

HARRIET PRESCOTT SPOFFORD.

CLAUS SPRECKELS.

THE founder of and principal factor in building up the sugar-refining industry on the Pacific coast has become so well known through his enterprise and success that his name is familiar throughout all countries where sugar is dealt in as an article of commerce. Claus Spreckels was born in Lamstedt, Kingdom of Hanover, in July, 1828, and came to America in 1848, arriving at Charleston, S. C., where he began business as a clerk in a grocery store. Within two years he owned the store, and soon developed a wholesale trade and became an importer. In 1855 he removed his business to New York City, and in 1856 again transferred it to San Francisco, where he bought out his brother Bernard, who was engaged in the grocery trade. The Albany Brewery was started by him in San Francisco in 1857, and the venture proved so successful that he disposed of his grocery house and continued as a brewer until 1863. In that year he sold the brewery, and, with others, founded the Bay Sugar Refinery. For the purpose of acquiring a complete knowledge of the sugar business he went to Europe to master the process of manufacturing beet-root sugar, actually entering the great refinery at Magdeburg as a workman. Returning to San Francisco he built another and larger refinery, and in 1867 organized the present great corporation of the California Sugar Refinery, of which he is president and principal owner. This company refines fifty million pounds of sugar every year. Mr. Spreckels is also extensively engaged in sugar-planting in the Sandwich Islands, where he obtained a grant of forty thousand acres of cane land, and is cultivating sugar cane on an enormous scale. Pluck, perseverance, and natural business ability are the causes of his success.

CLAUS SPRECKELS.

AUGUSTUS ST. GAUDENS.

AUGUSTUS ST. GAUDENS, the sculptor whose design for a World's Fair medal failed to meet the approval of Secretary Carlisle and the Senate, is a New Yorker in everything but the actual accident of birth. He was born in 1848, of Irish and French parentage, and when but a mere child was brought by his parents to New York City. Their son showed his talent at a very early age. The first money he ever had he spent for a box of colors. Work to him was a necessity. At thirteen he had to leave school and was apprenticed to a cameo cutter. He spent his days at the bench and his evenings at the Cooper Union art schools. Within three years he had a reputation as one of the best cameo cutters in the city. At nineteen, having saved some money, he went to Paris to perfect his knowledge of cameo cutting. But he had an ambition to be an artist in a larger way and entered the studio of Jouffroy, the sculptor, where he worked with an energy that made him a favorite with his master. The war with Germany interrupted his studies and he went to Rome, where he opened his first studio. There he modeled a Hiawatha which ex-Governor Morgan, of New York, admired and had cut in marble. Then his success began. He made a bust of William M. Evarts, and after that orders fairly flowed in upon him. The Farragut statue in Madison Square, New York City, was his first great public commission. The critics at once pronounced it a masterpiece, as they did his Lincoln, his Pilgrim, and his Sherman. Even the rejected medal is admitted to be admirable from an artistic point of view, and is considered by those competent to pronounce judgment, a worthy example of his skill.

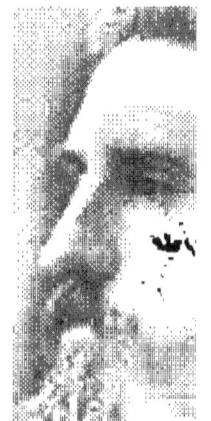

CHARLES WARREN STODDARD.

IT is scarcely an extravagance to say that there is nothing more charming in modern literature than the sketches and poems that have from time to time emanated from the pen of Charles Warren Stoddard. As one turns the pages of "South Sea Idyls," for example, the pulsing joys of the tropics come over him, and he feels all the bewildering charms of the free and careless life known only to the dweller under those summer skies. Mr. Stoddard was born in Rochester, N. Y., August 7, 1843, and was educated in New York City and California, to which state he removed with his father in 1855. In 1864 he went to the Hawaiian Islands, where he has since passed much of his time, and as traveling correspondent of the San Francisco "Chronicle" from 1873 to 1878 he visited many of the islands in the South Seas, Europe, Asia, Africa and the Pacific slope from Alaska to Mexico. His keen observation, his poetical temperament and his remarkable powers of description have enabled him to write most entertainingly of what he has seen. Mr. Stoddard began to write poetry at an early age, was for a short time an actor, has occasionally lectured, and has contributed to many of the leading magazines. In 1885 he became professor of English literature in Notre Dame University at South Bend, Ind., remaining in that position about a year. He revisited Europe in 1889, and upon his return took the chair of English Literature in the Catholic University of America at Washington, D. C., which post he still retains. His latest work, "Hawaiian Life, or Lazy Letters from Low Latitudes," has but recently been published, and is a masterpiece of descriptive writing. He is an earnest student equally of the books of nature and of those written by man.

CHARLES WARREN STODDARD.

· FRANCIS RICHARD STOCKTON.

QUAINT humor and droll philosophy, mingled with bits of tender sentiment, all strung on the thread of a prankish imagination, make up the stories that come to us from the clever author of that tantalizing fragment, "The Lady or the Tiger?" Mr. Stockton is an author of such marked individuality that there is none with whom to compare him. He was born in Philadelphia April 5, 1834. After receiving an education he became an engraver and draughtsman, and in 1866 invented a double graver. But soon thereafter he abandoned that occupation for journalism, toward which he had a natural leaning. After being connected with the "Post," in Philadelphia, and "Hearth and Home," in New York, he joined the editorial staff of "Scribner's Monthly," where he had an opportunity of developing the literary talent that had already made itself manifest. Upon the establishment of "St. Nicholas," in the autumn of 1873, he became its assistant editor. His earliest writings were fantastic stories for children, written under the name of Frank R. Stockton, which he has since retained. Later he attained a wide reputation for his short stories for older people, among them being the "Rudder Grange" sketches, "A Transferred Ghost," "The Spectral Mortgage," "A Tale of Negative Gravity," and "The Remarkable Wreck of the 'Thomas Hyke.'" But it was that little conundrum of three magazine pages, "The Lady or the Tiger?" that set everybody talking and made the author famous. His novels are "The Late Mrs. Null," "The Casting Away of Mrs. Lecks and Mrs. Aleshine," "The Dusantes" and "The Hundredth Man." Mr. Stockton's humorous view is broad, but his writings will outlive a thousand laughs.

FRANCIS RICHARD STOCKTON.

JOHN PIERCE ST. JOHN.

COMPARATIVELY few people are familiar with the early life of the man who is chiefly remembered as a former governor of Kansas, and as a subsequent leader of the Prohibition party, of which he was once the candidate for the presidency of the United States. Yet John P. St. John has had a checkered career. He was born in Franklin County, Indiana, February 25, 1833. In his early years he was employed on his father's farm, and was a clerk in a grocer's store. In 1853 he went to California, where he worked in various capacities, and made voyages to South America, Mexico, Central America and the Sandwich Islands. He also served in wars with the Indians in California and Oregon. In 1860 he removed to Charleston, Ill., to continue the study of law, which he had begun in his miner's cabin. Early in 1862 he enlisted as a private in the Sixty-eighth Illinois Volunteer regiment, and before the close of the war was lieutenant-colonel of the One Hundred and Forty-third regiment. After the war he resumed the practice of law at Charleston, but subsequently removed to Independence, Mo., where he practiced successfully for four years and gained a reputation as a political orator. He removed to Olathe, Kan., in 1869, served in the State Senate in 1873 and 1874, and was elected governor of Kansas as a Republican in 1878. He held that office until 1882, when he was defeated as a candidate for a third term. In 1884 he was the candidate of the Prohibition party for the presidency, and received 151,809 votes. He is still an active Prohibitionist, dividing his time between lecturing on temperance and the practice of his profession. He stands as an example of unswerving devotion to a noble principle.

JOHN PIERCE ST. JOHN.
431

RICHARD HENRY STODDARD.

--

FEW men are better known in what may be called the old New York literary group than Richard Henry Stoddard. He was born in Hingham, Mass., in July, 1825. When he was ten years of age his family removed to New York, in which city he learned the trade of an iron molder. The literary instinct was strong within him, though, and as early as 1848 he began contributing to the newspapers and periodicals of the day. He soon acquired a recognized place in the American literary world of the time, a place he has retained. He has produced a number of works, among them being included "Adventures in Fairyland," "Town and Country," "The Story of Little Red Riding Hood," "The Children in the Wood," "Putnam the Brave," "Memoir of Edgar Allan Poe," the "Bric-a-Brac," and "Sans Souci Series" of compilations and a number of volumes relating to English literature. If fault is to be found with Mr. Stoddard's work in the consideration of literary matters, it must be on the basis that he is not always in touch with the new schools of literature and has come to have creeds as to book-making; but it is admitted of him by all that he is an able essayist and critic, and that by his capable selections he has aided not a little in popularizing the best class of work in the United States. He has done much newspaper work, and is still a regular and vigorous writer for the daily press, being at the present time the literary reviewer on the New York "Mail and Express." He represents a school now passing away, which was a good one, which was conservative but which did much toward making American literature what it is. It was, at least, always a clean school and one tending to promote decent thought and action.

RICHARD HENRY STODDARD.

ADOLPH HEINRICH JOSEPH SUTRO.

AMONG the names most worthy of inscription upon the tablets of honored perpetually in America is the name associated in the public mind with one of the greatest engineering feats of the century—Adolph Sutro. This distinguished man was born in Aix-la-Chapelle, Rhenish, Prussia, April 29, 1830. He came to America in 1850, and went at once to California to engage in mining operations, for which his studies had fitted him. He visited Nevada in 1860, and after a careful inspection of the mining region there, planned the now famous Sutro tunnel through the heart of the mountain where lay the Comstock lode. Having interested capitalists in the project, he obtained a charter from the Nevada Legislature February 4, 1865, and the authorization of Congress July 25, 1866. Mining companies agreed to pay toll of two dollars for each ton of ore from the time when the tunnel should reach and benefit their mines. The work was begun October 19, 1869, and before the close of 1871 four vertical shafts were opened along the line of the tunnel, one of which was 552 feet deep. The distance from the mouth of the tunnel to the Savage mine, where, at a depth of sixteen hundred and fifty feet from the surface, it formed the first connection with the Comstock lode, is twenty thousand feet. Lateral tunnels connect it with the mines on either side of the main bore. In 1879 the great tunnel was finished and its projector became a millionaire many times over. Mr. Sutro has devoted a part of his fortune to the establishment of a fine library and art gallery in San Francisco, where he resides, and his gifts to public charities have been many and munificent. In his lovely home at Sutro Heights he has collected many souvenirs of his tours throughout the world.

ADOLPH HEINRICH JOSEPH SUTRO.

ADA CELESTE SWEET.

IN certain fields of effort probably no other woman in the country has accomplished so much as Ada C. Sweet, of Chicago. Not only has she become known as one of the most sincere and intelligent workers in the interest of reforms and humanitarianism, but she has demonstrated to the world that in the management of a difficult public office a woman's tact and judgment may at least equal those of a man. Miss Sweet is the daughter of Gen. Benjamin J. Sweet, a lawyer and distinguished officer in the Civil War, and was born at Stockbridge, Wis., February 23, 1853. At the age of sixteen she became assistant to her father, who was at that time United States Agent for paying pensions in Chicago, and afterward first deputy commissioner of internal revenue at Washington, remaining with him until his death, January 1, 1874. Shortly thereafter President Grant appointed her United States Agent for paying pensions at Chicago. In the conduct of this office, which employed a large clerical force and disbursed millions of dollars annually, Miss Sweet made a remarkable record, effecting many reforms and reducing the work to a system which was promptly adopted by the government in the reorganization of all the other pension agencies in the country. She resigned the office October 1, 1885, to engage in business on her own account, and, after visiting Europe, was for two years the literary editor of the Chicago "Tribune." Since 1888 she has pursued the vocation of United States Claims Attorney, finding time, however, to do much literary and philanthropical work, and to labor for governmental reforms, besides meeting all social obligations. Among other benefactions she founded the ambulance system in connection with the Chicago police department.

ADA CELESTE SWEET.

THOMAS De WITT TALMAGE.

COMBINING in an extraordinary degree the advantages of profound learning, the physical and mental qualifications of an orator, a deep religious sense and a pleasing manner, the Rev. T. De Witt Talmage is popular alike in the pulpit and on the platform. He was born in Bound Brook, N. J., January 7, 1832, and educated at the University of the City of New York. After graduating at the New Brunswick Theological Seminary in 1856, he was ordained pastor of the Reformed Dutch Church in Belleville, N. J. He had charge of the church in Syracuse, N. Y., from 1859 to 1862, and of one in Philadelphia from 1862 to 1869. During the war he was chaplain of a Pennsylvania regiment. In 1869 he became pastor of the Central Presbyterian Church in Brooklyn, N. Y., which post he still holds His congregation, in 1870, built the now famous Brooklyn Tabernacle, which was destroyed by fire in 1872, but at once rebuilt on a grander scale. It is the largest Protestant church in the country. The sermons of Dr. Talmage are published weekly in nearly six hundred religious and secular journals in this country and in Europe, being translated into various languages. He has at different times edited "The Christian at Work" in New York, "The Advance" of Chicago, and "Frank Leslie's Sunday Magazine," and has published a number of books. He received the degree of A. M. from the University of the City of New York in 1862, and that of D. D. from the University of Tennessee in 1884. Dr. Talmage has made a number of successful lecturing tours in the United States, always attracting large audiences wherever he appears, and has also traveled and lectured in Europe.

THOMAS DEWITT TALMAGE.

NICKOLA TESLA.

— -

A YOUNG Servian became an American and accomplished wonders. Born in Servia between thirty and forty years ago, Nickola Tesla is a Slav of Slavs, with the racial characteristics strongly stamped in look, speech and action, but he has developed the same genius which has marked the highest class of American students and inventors. His father was an eloquent clergyman in the Greek church, but to his mother may probably be traced the secret of his inventive genius, for she made looms and churns for the pastoral household while her husband preached. Tesla's electrical work started when, as a boy, in the Polytechnic school at Gratz, he first saw a direct-current Gramme machine and was told that a commuter was a vital and necessary feature in all such apparatus. He was interested. He persevered in mathematics and mechanical studies and mastered incidentally half a dozen languages, and at last became assistant in the Government Telegraph Engineering Department at Buda-Pesth. He drifted westward and made his way to Paris; he then made his way across the Atlantic to work in one of the Edison shops and to enter upon a new stage of development. He evinced a marvelous comprehension and ingenuity and soon won the admiration of the great inventor. He worked as arduously as did Edison himself, but worked on new lines, lines so divergent from those of the master that separation was wise. Tesla had become a genius of the electrical world by himself, supported by Edison. The pupil has made marvelous discoveries and is known throughout the civilized world because of what he has accomplished in his field. He has a future of vast promise and bids fair to rival his illustrious master.

NICKOLA TESLA.
439

MARY VIRGINIA TERHUNE

PROMINENT in the literature of domestic economy, as well as in the field of fiction, the name of "Marion Harland" is in very truth a household word in the United States. The lady who has made this pen-name famous is Mrs. Mary Virginia Terhune. She was born in Amelia County, Virginia, December 31, 1831. At the age of fourteen she began to contribute to a weekly paper in Richmond, and when in her sixteenth year sent to a magazine a sketch entitled "Marrying through Prudential Motives," which was reprinted in England, translated for a French journal, retranslated into English for a London magazine, and then reproduced in its altered form in this country. In 1856 she married Rev. Edward Payson Terhune, who is now pastor of a Brooklyn church. She has been a constant contributor of tales, sketches and essays to magazines, edited a monthly called "Babyhood" for two years, besides conducting special departments in "Wide-Awake" and "St. Nicholas," and in 1888 established a magazine called the "Home-Maker." Her first novel was "Alone: A Tale of Southern Life and Manners," issued under the pen-name of "Marion Harland," and has been followed by about twenty others, all of which have attained great popularity. She has also published a number of volumes on domestic economy, cookery, and various topics connected with home management, whereby she has become known to thousands of women throughout the civilized world, and is recognized as a high authority on all subjects associated with housekeeping. Mrs. Terhune has resided in New York since 1884, is a member of Sorosis and several other organizations of a literary and philanthropical character, and has lectured before various societies on her favorite themes.

MARY VIRGINIA TERHUNE
441

CELIA LAIGHTON THAXTER.

MANY people will be interested to know that they are in a great measure indebted to the late James Russell Lowell for the pleasure they have derived from reading the exquisite poems of Celia Thaxter, for it was he who discovered her genius. Mrs. Thaxter never sought admittance to the field of literature, but Mr. Lowell, while editor of the "Atlantic Monthly," happened to see some verses which she had written for her own amusement, and, without saying anything to her about it, christened them "Landlocked," and published them in the "Atlantic." Mrs. Thaxter was born in Portsmouth, N. H., June 29, 1835. When she was four years old her father, Thomas B. Laighton, took his family to the Isles of Shoals to live. The childhood of herself and two brothers was passed at White Island, where her father kept the lighthouse, which is described by her in her book, "Among the Isles of Shoals." During her later life she has continued to spend all her summers among those islands. In 1851 she was married to Levi Lincoln Thaxter, of Watertown, Mass., who died in 1884. After the publication of her first verses in the "Atlantic Monthly," she had many calls for her work, and at last, persuaded by the urgent wishes of her friends, John G. Whittier, James T. Fields and others, she issued her first volume of poems in 1871, and later the prose work "Among the Isles of Shoals." Her other books are: "Driftweed," "Poems for Children," and "Cruise of the Mystery, and Other Poems." Among the finest of her single poems may be mentioned "Courage," "Kittery Church-yard," "The Spaniards' Graves," "The Watch of Boon Island," "The Sandpiper," "A Tryst," and "The Song Sparrow." She is a most fastidious writer.

CELIA LAIGHTON THAXTER.
445

THEODORE RUGGLES TIMBY.

THE famous inventor, Theodore Ruggles Timby, was born in Dover, N. Y., April 5, 1822. His remarkable cast of mind was manifested at an early age, and, when only fourteen years old, he made a practical working model of a floating dry-dock. The circular form of Castle William in New York harbor suggested to him the idea of a revolving plan for defensive works, and in 1841 he submitted to the government the design of a revolving battery to be constructed of iron, the first practical suggestion for the use of iron in military defensive works. His first official record was made in 1843. He then sent a model of his turret to China, and in 1856 submitted his plans personally to Napoleon III. Later he patented a broad claim for a revolving tower for defensive and offensive warfare on land or water. The builders of the Monitor paid him a royalty of $5,000 for each turret constructed by them. Among the modifications of his revolving battery are the cordon of revolving towers across a channel, the mole and tower system, the subterraneous system, the tower and shield system, and the hemispheroidal system, together with the plan of firing heavy guns by electricity now in universal use. In 1888 Mr. Timby had a bill introduced in Congress to provide for the construction of a sixty-inch refracting telescope. As early as 1856 he had become deeply interested in the solution of the laws of solar light and heat, and is now engaged on an exhaustive paper, the result of his researches and conclusions. He has received the honorary degrees of M. A. S. D., and LL. D. In 1890 the Legislature of the state of New York passed a resolution asking Congress to give to Mr. Timby national recognition.

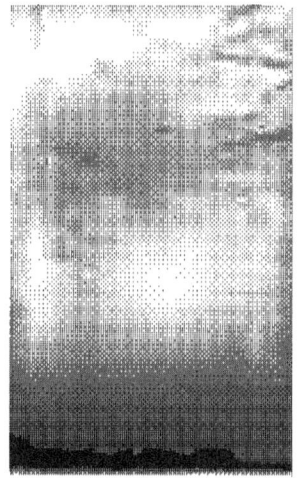

THEODORE RUGGLES TIMBY.

BLANCHE DILLAYE.

TO have acquired, while still a young woman, prominence in one of the most difficult of arts, and to be accepted in some respects as an authority in a field where far more men than women are in competition, is certainly sufficient cause for a just pride, and this is what Miss Blanche Dillaye has accomplished. She was born in Syracuse, N. Y., her parents being Hon. Stephen D. Dillaye, a widely known writer on economic subjects, and Charlotte B. Malcolm Dillaye, and was educated at Miss Bonney's and Miss Dillaye's school (now known as the Ogontz College) for young ladies. In the school, as had been the case from early childhood, Miss Dillaye evinced a talent for drawing, and she was finally allowed a year of study to develop herself in the art. She went abroad, but her final work came in connection with the Philadelphia Academy of Fine Arts. She became a teacher in a young ladies' school and still pursued her art studies. Her fondness was for black and white, and she was attracted toward etching as a specialty. Masters in this branch aided her and found an apt pupil. She is the author of many notable etchings, and has even more than a national reputation. Her work has been exhibited successfully in England and in the Paris Salon, and she has occupied many official positions in connection with art matters. At the Columbian Exposition she represented the state of Pennsylvania in the judgment of etchings, and during the exposition's progress a paper on her art was read by her before the Congress of Women, which attracted wide attention. She is an artist of great gifts in the special field she has selected, a field rapidly attaining greater prominence in the American world of art.

BLANCHE DILLAYE.

GEORGE ALFRED TOWNSEND.

—·

K NOWN to the world as a war correspondent, historian, novelist, lecturer, and the most prolific writer for the newspaper press in America, George Alfred Townsend ("Gath") has had a remarkable career. He is the son of a Methodist minister, and was born in Georgetown, Del., January 30, 1841. He was educated mainly in Philadelphia, and immediately after leaving school, in 1860, became city editor of "Forney's Press." In 1862 he was war correspondent for the New York "Herald," describing for that journal "McClellan's and Pope's campaigns. Later in the year he went to Europe, where he wrote for English and American magazines until June, 1864, when he returned and furnished for the New York "World" graphic descriptions of the closing battles and incidents of the war. He edited the New York "Citizen" for a time, then went to Europe to report the Austro-Prussian war, and afterward lectured, and wrote constantly for several years. His engagements with the Chicago "Tribune," Cincinnati "Enquirer," Boston "Globe" and other leading journals have made him famous as a political and descriptive writer and interviewer. He has used the pen-name "Gath" for twenty-six years. In addition to his other work he has published twenty books, several of them American historical novels. In 1885 Mr. Townsend founded a settlement and "literary factory," called Gapland, on South Mountain battle-field, fifty-eight miles from Washington. He spends his winters in Washington. In 1892 he made his sixth visit to Europe to study the haunts of Columbus and gather material for his novel, "Columbus in Love," which has since been published. Necessarily Mr. Townsend has a wide acquaintance with public men.

GEORGE ALFRED TOWNSEND.

JOHN TOWNSEND TROWBRIDGE

DESERVEDLY one of the most popular writers for the young in this country is J. T. Trowbridge. That clever critic, John Burroughs, once said of him: "He knows the heart of the boy and the heart of the man, and has laid them both open in his books." Mr. Trowbridge was born in Ogden, N. Y., September 8, 1827. He was educated in the common schools, and after teaching and working on a farm for one year in Illinois he settled in New York City, where he wrote for the journals and magazines. He went to Boston about 1848, and was subsequently connected with various newspapers and magazines in that city. From 1870 to 1873 he was managing editor of "Our Young Folks." He was one of the original contributors to the "Atlantic Monthly," in which magazine were published his poems, "The Vagabonds," "At Sea," and "The Pewee," and the popular short story, "Coupon-Bonds." His "Neighbor Jackwood" is the pioneer of novels of real life in New England, just as "The Vagabonds" is the first specimen, and one of the best, of the school of poetry since made popular by Bret Harte and others. Mr. Trowbridge has led an active literary life, and is still writing in the same happy vein that delighted us so much when "Cudjo's Cave" was fresh from the press. Among his best stories, besides those mentioned are: "Neighbors' Wives," "Farnell's Folly," "The Drummer Boy," "Martin Merrivale," "Father Brighthopes," "The Fortunes of Toby Trafford." "The Three Scouts," "The Silver Medal," "Bound in Honor," "The Jolly Rover," "The Tinkham Brothers' "Tide-Mill," etc. Mr. Trowbridge portrays human nature through his sympathy and hearty affiliation with it, not through mere intellectual acuteness.

JOHN TOWNSEND TROWBRIDGE

WILLIAM FREEMAN VILAS.

PLACED in a conspicuous position before the nation as chairman of the Democratic National Convention that nominated Grover Cleveland to the presidency in 1884, William F. Vilas leaped into public prominence at a bound. Prior to that time he had been merely a successful lawyer in Wisconsin, scarcely known outside of his own state. Senator Vilas was born at Chelsea, Vt., July 9, 1840. The family removed to Madison, Wis., in 1851, and he graduated from the Wisconsin State University in 1858, afterward receiving a legal education in the law school at Albany, N. Y. At the outbreak of the Civil War he entered the Union army and rapidly rose to the rank of colonel, distinguishing himself for bravery in many engagements. After the war he devoted himself to the practice of his profession in Wisconsin. He was a member of the State Legislature in 1884-85, and it was while occupying this position that he was a delegate to the Democratic National Convention held in Chicago, and was made chairman of that body. He was a revelation to the leaders of the party, who at once recognized in him a bright and able representative of that new Democracy which the party orators were preaching at that time. As a result of this recognition Colonel Vilas was appointed postmaster-general in President Cleveland's cabinet March 5, 1885, and served until January 16, 1888, when he became Secretary of the Interior, remaining such until the end of Cleveland's administration. He received the unanimous nomination of the Democratic legislative caucus for United States senator from Wisconsin in January, 1891, and was elected to succeed John C. Spooner, Republican. He is a speaker of remarkable clearness and brilliancy.

WILLIAM FREEMAN VILAS.

DANIEL WOOLSEY VOORHEES.

FEW living men in America can point to a longer or more active political career than that which the "Tall Sycamore of the Wabash" is now rounding out in the United States Senate. Daniel W. Voorhees was born in Butler County, Ohio, September 26, 1827, but was taken to Indiana in infancy by his parents. He was graduated at Asbury University and first practiced law at Covington, Ind., where he was an unsuccessful Democratic candidate for Congress in 1856. In 1858 he was appointed United States District Attorney for Indiana, and in 1861 he was elected to Congress, in which body he served until February 23, 1866, when his seat was contested successfully by Henry D. Washburn. He again sat in the National House of Representatives from 1869 until 1873, and upon the death of Oliver P. Morton was appointed to fill his seat in the United States Senate, serving from November 12, 1877, until 1879, when he was elected for a full term. He was re-elected in 1885 and 1891, and is today one of the leaders in the Senate. Senator Voorhees has achieved a wide reputation as an orator and legislator. His tall, commanding figure and intellectual stature early won for him the name of the "Tall Sycamore of the Wabash." His eloquence in debate and on the stump is liberally embellished with flashes of wit, humorous illustrations and sarcastic hits that always insure the close attention of his audience, and enable him to send his arguments home. He has advanced views on the silver question and is enthusiastic in all he undertakes. He is warm-hearted and earnest, and there is a great personal magnetism about the man which commands staunch friends. Senator Voorhees resides at Terre Haute, Ind.

DANIEL WOOLSEY VOORHEES

JOHN GRIMES WALKER.

TO have made a good record in the American Navy at any time since the "Constitution" fought its battles or Paul Jones sailed the seas, has been a distinction for any man. The American Navy has never lacked its ready heroes, though, and the Civil war brought them out in abundance. Among those ranking well is John Grimes Walker. He was born in Hillsborough, N. H., in 1835. He graduated at the United States Naval Academy in 1856 and was made a master in 1858. With the beginning of the war he served for a time on the "Connecticut" patrolling the Atlantic coast, and then in the "Winona," in the western blockading squadron. He was made a lieutenant-commander in 1862, and had command of the "Baron de Kalb" iron clad operating on the Mississippi river. He was in the command co-operating with Sherman, was in both attacks on Haines' Bluff, in the Yazoo river expedition, and in various other enterprises, including command of the naval battery, which bombarded Vicksburg in the rear, and was highly commended by Admiral Porter for the part he took in various affairs. It was here, in fact, that he showed the strength and intelligence that was in him and what sort of a sensible fighting naval officer he was. He was recklessly brave in all times of action, but never allowed his daring to affect his judgment as to what was best to do at any moment. He commanded the steamer "Saco" in the North Atlantic blockade in 1864 and the "Shawmut" in 1865. He was made commander in 1866, and for a time served at the Naval Academy at Annapolis. His course of promotion has been rapid, and he ranks deservedly among the sturdy and highly considered naval officers of the world today.

JOHN GRIMES WALKER
457

ELIZABETH STUART PHELPS WARD.

STRIKING originality and a peculiar aptness for mingling the seen and the unseen elements in life have had much to do with making the author of "The Gates Ajar" so popular with a large class of readers. Elizabeth Stuart Phelps –the name by which she is known to the world—was born in Boston, Mass., August 31, 1844. Her father was Rev. Austin Phelps, professor of sacred rhetoric in Andover Theological Seminary, who, in 1848, removed his family from Boston to Andover. The daughter received a thorough education, and began to write for the press at the age of thirteen. Her mother, Mrs. Elizabeth Stuart Phelps, was an author of note, and after her death, in 1852, Miss Phelps, who had been christened with another name, took her mother's name in full. Much of her life has been devoted to benevolent work in Andover, to the advancement of women, and to temperance and kindred reforms. In 1876 she delivered a course of lectures before the students of Boston University. Her published works include "Ellen's Idol," "Up Hill," "The Tiny Series," "The Gypsy Series," "Mercy Gliddon's Work," "I Don't Know How," "The Gates Ajar," "Men, Women, and Ghosts," "The Silent Partner," "Hedged In," "The Story of Avis," "My Cousin and I," "Old Maid's Paradise," "Sealed Orders," "Jack the Fisherman," "The Master of the Magicians," and many others, besides numerous sketches, stories and poems for magazines. In October, 1888, she was married to Rev. Herbert D. Ward. Her most popular book is "The Gates Ajar," which reached its twentieth edition within a year after its publication. All her works are marked by elevated spirit and profound thoughtfulness.

ELIZABETH STUART PHELPS WARD.

CHARLES DUDLEY WARNER.

DOWERED with a photographic power of reproducing what he sees, a humor which plays gently around whatever topic it touches, and a style distinctive in the possession of certain qualities as irresistible as they are delightful, Charles Dudley Warner occupies a high place in American literature. He was born in Plainfield, Mass., September 12, 1829, and graduated at Hamilton College in 1851. His recollections of his youth are embodied in that popular book, "Being a Boy." While in college he contributed to the "Knickerbocker" and "Putnam's Magazine," and did other literary work. He then studied law, and practiced in Chicago from 1856 to 1860, when he returned to the East, obtained control of the "Press," an evening paper of Hartford, Conn., consolidated it with the "Courant" in 1867, and during the following two years gained a reputation by a series of foreign letters to that journal, written from abroad. Subsequently he traveled extensively in Europe, and upon his return in 1884 became co-editor of "Harper's Magazine." His most important work in connection with that monthly was a series of papers beginning with "Studies in the South," followed by "Mexican Papers" and "Studies in the Great West." Mr. Warner has written and lectured much on educational and social science topics. He was an ardent Abolitionist during the anti-slavery agitation. His career as an author began in 1870, and among the best of his books are "My Summer in a Garden," with an introduction by Henry Ward Beecher; "Saunterings" and "Back-Log Studies." He also published, in conjunction with Samuel L. Clemens, "The Gilded Age." His other works include contributions to the magazines on social, artistic and literary topics.

CHARLES DUDLEY WARNER.

KATHLEEN BLAKE WATKINS.

CERTAINLY no other woman on this continent, and possibly no
man below the rank of editor-in-chief, exercises so direct an
influence upon the prestige and circulation of a newspaper as does
Mrs. Kathleen Blake Watkins, of the Toronto "Mail." By her brilliant work Mrs. Watkins has made a splendid reputation for that journal and for herself. She is a native of Ireland, born in Castle Bla-
keny in May, 1863, and educated in Dublin and Belgium. She was
married at the age of sixteen, and came to this country in 1884.
Shortly thereafter she entered upon a journalistic career in Canada,
where, with the exception of extended visits to the United States and
abroad, she has since resided. A remarkable feature of her work is
that she conducts successfully two entirely separate and distinct departments of the newspaper she represents, being special traveling correspondent and editor of the page devoted to the "Woman's Kingdom."
This latter department is one of the most striking and attractive on
any journal in the world, and has gained a large and steadily growing
constituency. Mrs. Watkins has published a series of popular sketches
on "Dickensland," being the result of explorations in every portion of
London made famous by the great English novelist. Her letters from
the World's Columbian Exposition in 1893 were remarkable for their
brilliancy and literary merit, and she has since been induced to issue
in book form a resume of the exposition. Mrs. Watkins is best
known by her pen-name of "Kit," over which she has done the greater
portion of her work. She has recently ventured into the field of fiction, and there is no doubt that should she turn her attention to that
class of literature her success would be great.

KATHLEEN BLAKE WATKINS.

JAMES B. WEAVER.

CREDIT should be given to the man whose loyalty to his convictions and devotion to a theory have twice prompted him to become the standard-bearer of a small following, and thus take upon himself the brunt of inevitable defeat. General Weaver, of Iowa, has made himself famous as a leader of forlorn hopes. He became the Greenback candidate for the presidency in 1880, and conducted a vigorous campaign against the two large parties that were engaged in a struggle for supremacy. In 1892 he accepted the nomination of the People's party and again made a brave fight, receiving over a million votes for president. James B. Weaver was born in Dayton, Ohio, June 12, 1833, and graduated at the law school of the Cincinnati College in 1854. He served with distinction in the Union army during the Civil war, attaining the rank of brigadier-general through gallant conduct in various engagements, and at the conclusion of hostilities he began the practice of law in Iowa. He was elected district attorney of the Second Judicial district of that state, and filled the position of revenue assessor, besides that of editor of the "Iowa Tribune," issued at Des Moines. He was elected to Congress in 1878, and again in 1884, and was re-elected in 1886. General Weaver is a plain, unassuming man of the people, impatient of the buncombe and claptrap employed by the professional politician, sternly honest and uncompromising, even though he may be mistaken, in his views on questions of national policy, and too broadly patriotic to submit to the restraint of party lines, or party dictation. With him consistency is almost a fault. Believing firmly in the cause he advocates, General Weaver is a noble example of unswerving devotion to principles.

JAMES B. WEAVER.

JAMES ABBOTT McNEILL WHISTLER.

TO be recognized throughout the English-speaking world as a great painter, a brilliant man, intellectually, and one with the love for light abundantly developed, is the fortune appertaining to the famous American artist who makes his home in London, with Paris as an occasional playground. James Abbott McNeill Whistler was born in 1834, and, after receiving the ordinary school education, was appointed to a cadetship in the United States Military Academy at West Point. He did not remain in the army, but, impelled by his artistic instincts, studied drawing later in Paris, and finally in 1863 settled in London. Since that time his career has been equally brilliant and eccentric. He holds decidedly original views concerning his art, and it would probably be denied of him as little as of any one in the world that he has the courage of his convictions. His views of art may be iconoclastic, but he at least believes in them, and is as ready to fight for them and over them as a tigress over her young. The collisions with conservatives, which have resulted from time to time, have aided largely in making Mr. Whistler renowned. His aggressiveness has partly made his fame, but he is a great artist—that is admitted everywhere. His experiments with colors in search of novel effects have produced magnificent results. His paintings are telling, and indicate a daring and knowing genius. His etching attracted more attention than any other work of the class at the Columbian Exposition in Chicago, and, as for his queer fantasies, the story of the peacock room has gone around the world. He is a remarkable man, undoubtedly a great artistic genius, and as undoubtedly one of the most deliciously belligerent of human beings.

JAMES ABBOTT McNEILL WHISTLER.
469

EDWARD DOUGLAS WHITE.

———

WELL versed in all that pertains to the theory and practice of law, with a judicial mind and a valuable experience on the supreme bench of his own state, Edward Douglas White is not likely to disappoint the expectations of his friends as associate justice of the United States Supreme Court. Mr. White was born in Lafourche parish, Louisiana, November 3, 1845. He was educated at Mount St. Mary's, near Emmitsburg, Md., at the Jesuit College in New Orleans, and at Georgetown College, District of Columbia. During the Civil war he served in the Confederate army, and in December, 1868, was licensed by the Supreme court of Louisiana to practice law. He soon gained a reputation as an accomplished lawyer and as a public speaker of much force and influence. In 1874 he was elected state senator, and served in that capacity until 1878, when he became judge of the Louisiana Supreme court. In 1888 he was elected United States senator as a Democrat to succeed James B. Eustis, taking his seat the following year. President Cleveland appointed him associate justice of the Supreme Court of the United States in February, 1894, to fill the vacancy caused by the death of Hon. Samuel Blatchford. Justice White's legal training and practice has been principally under the code of Louisiana, which is an adaptation of the French code, and which is derived from the Roman law rather than from the common law of England, which lies at the basis of the law practice and judicial decisions of all states except Louisiana. It is believed that the business of the Supreme court will be facilitated by the acquisition of a judge who is also familiar with the French and Roman systems of law. Mr. White is a scholar in more than the legal sense of the word.

EDWARD DOUGLAS WHITE.

FRANCES ELIZABETH WILLARD.

IT is doubtful if there is another woman in the United States who has accomplished more for the cause of reform and education than Miss Frances E. Willard. She was born in Churchville, N. Y., September 28, 1839, and graduated at Northwestern Female College, Evanston, Ill., in 1859. She became professor of natural science there in 1862, and was principal of Genesee Wesleyan Seminary in 1866-67. The following two years she spent in foreign travel and study. From 1871 to 1874 she was professor of aesthetics in Northwestern University and dean of the Woman's College, where she developed her system of self-government which has been adopted by other educators. Miss Willard left her profession in 1874 to identify herself with the Woman's Christian Temperance Union, serving as corresponding secretary of the national organization until 1879, when she became its president. She organized the Home Protection movement, and sent an appeal from nearly two hundred thousand people to the Legislature of Illinois, asking for the temperance ballot for women. On the death of her brother, Oliver A. Willard, in 1879, she succeeded him in his position on the Chicago "Evening Post." In 1886 she accepted the leadership of the White Cross movement in her own unions, and obtained enactments in many states for the protection of women. In 1888 she was made president of the American branch of the International Council of Women and of the World's Christian Temperance Union. She visited England twice in 1892, and was at the head of the women's committee of temperance meetings at the World's Fair in 1893. She has published nine volumes in addition to numerous magazine articles, and is editor-in-chief of the "Union Signal."

FRANCES ELIZABETH WILLARD.

WILLIAM COLLINS WHITNEY.

A CULTIVATED gentleman in politics, a man with millions behind him, a man with intellect as well—that is, perhaps, a fair, off-hand description of William Collins Whitney. He was born in Conway, Mass., July 15, 1841. He received a thorough preliminary education, and graduated from Yale in 1863 and from the Harvard Law School in 1865. He was admitted to the bar and began his practice in the city of New York, winning a reputable place in his profession. He became interested in politics, and in 1871 became identified with the Young Men's Democratic Club and later acquired a prominence almost beyond his years by the active part he took in the famous fight upon the Tweed ring. He was made inspector of public schools in 1872 and then ran as a candidate for district attorney under the auspices of the reformed Democracy, and was defeated. He took part in the Tilden campaign, and in 1875 was appointed corporation counsel in New York. During Mr. Whitney's term of office he saved New York City millions of dollars by his wise opposition to various claims brought by the ringsters against the city. He became a prominent figure in the better group of New York City Democracy, and with the election of Mr. Cleveland to the presidency, attained national prominence, being made Secretary of the Navy and fulfilling the duties of that most responsible position with energy, ability and tact. He has not lost since an iota of the eminence he had attained. He stands prominent among the great men of his party when future contingencies are considered, more particularly since his strength is so great among the better men of the city which is his party's stronghold, where he is recognized as a man of marked ability and a politician above reproach.

WILLIAM COLLINS WHITNEY.
473

ELLA WHEELER WILCOX.

—

IN these days of verse makers, when there are so many aspirants
for recognition in the realms of poesy, the young poet who gains
the especial attention and approval of the reading public must be more
than ordinarily gifted. No poetess of today has established herself
more securely in the hearts of the American people than Mrs. Ella
Wheeler Wilcox, who appeals more directly to the emotions of her
readers than almost any other writer of verse now before the public.
Mrs. Wilcox was born in Johnstown Centre, Wis., and her home
from early childhood was near Madison, the capital of the state. At
the early age of eight years she first displayed her poetical and literary
talent, and at fourteen she began writing for the newspapers. In a
very short time her work attracted attention, and when only seventeen
years old she was receiving pay for her verses and stories. Since
that time her star has been steadily in the ascendant. Her early
reputation was made under the name of Ella Wheeler, which was
changed in 1884 by her marriage to Robert M. Wilcox, of Meriden,
Conn. Since 1887 she has resided in New York City, where her
husband is engaged in a manufacturing business. Her published books
now in print are: "Poems of Passion," "Poems of Pleasure," "Mau-
rine," "The Beautiful Land of Nod," "An Erring Woman's Love,"
"Men, Women and Emotions," "How Salvator Won, and Other Rec-
itations," and "The Song of a Sandwich." Although her early education was only such as could be obtained at the district school, supplemented by three months in the Wisconsin State University, Mrs.
Wilcox enjoys the advantages of a higher education, acquired by studying the hearts of the people.

ELLA WHEELER WILCOX.

STEPHEN VAN CULEN WHITE.

A MOST sagacious financier, whose daring as a speculator is guided by an intelligence of such an order that the combination amounts to genius, Stephen V. White is one of the most prominent figures in the financial center of this country. He was born in Chatham County, North Carolina, August 1, 1831. His father, being a Quaker, was opposed to slavery, and after the famous Nat Turner insurrection removed with his family to Illinois, where he engaged in farming. Stephen was at that time but six weeks old, and he was reared in the wilderness. He was graduated at Knox College in 1854, studied law in St. Louis with B. Gratz Brown and John A. Kasson, and after his admission to the bar in 1856 began practicing in Des Moines. He attained high rank as a lawyer, but in 1865 he removed to New York and engaged in banking. In 1882 he organized the now well-known banking firm of S. V. White & Co. As a banker Mr. White has been noted for his large and bold operations in the interest of the Delaware, Lackawanna & Western railroad. Indeed, his operations have been such as could only have been conducted by a man possessed of phenomenal prescience, the power of cool calculation and supreme confidence in his own convictions. In 1891 his firm failed and his fortune was swept away, but in little more than a year he had canceled his obligations, which he was bound only by honor to pay, and was again in his old place in the New York Stock Exchange. Mr. White was elected to Congress from Brooklyn in 1886. He has long been a trustee of Plymouth church, is an expert astronomer, and has received the honorary degree of LL. D. from Knox College.

STEPHEN VAN CULEN WHITE.
477

AUGUSTA J. EVANS WILSON.

WITH a national reputation very firmly established, the author of "Beulah" has of late years chosen to do very little in the field of literature. It is not necessary that she should do more than she has already accomplished to fix her popular status. She was born near Columbus, Ga., in 1836. Her family removed to Texas, and afterward to Mobile, Ala., where in 1868 she became the wife of L. M. Wilson, and where she has since lived in a fine country home. The name of Augusta J. Evans had at that time already become famous. Her first novel, "Inez, a Tale of Alamo," was only moderately successful, but her second book, published in 1859, achieved a success which was almost instantaneous. It has passed through many editions and is still one of the popular novels. The Civil war put a check to her literary work, and for years there was a cessation of effort in the field for which she was so well equipped. Her next book, "Macaria," was printed on coarse brown paper, copyrighted by the Confederate States of America, and dedicated to the brave soldiers of the Southern army. It was printed in Charleston, S. C., published by a bookseller in Richmond, Va., was seized and destroyed by federal officers and was subsequently reprinted in the North, meeting with a very large sale. After the war she went to New York City and published her famous "St. Elmo," which was most successful. Her later works include "Vashti," "Infelice," and "At the Mercy of Tiberius." She is wealthy, and has chosen to live in retirement of late, and her absence from the literary field has been a source of regret to a great host of readers, since there is none who fills exactly her place in the broad field of literature.

AUGUSTA J. EVANS WILSON.

GEORGE HARDIN YENOWINE.

IF some thoughtful, knowing man, acquainted with all necessary circumstances, were to consider what one man has done most in the last fifteen years for the future of the city of Milwaukee, on Lake Michigan, he might say that the name he would select would be that of George Hardin Yenowine. Mr. Yenowine was born near Louisville, Ky., September 6, 1858. The son was to be educated as a doctor. The father engaged on the Confederate side in the Civil war, and the result was a decided disturbance in the Yenowine family program, but the blood was there still. The boy had to stay at home, and took up manfully the hard work on an impoverished farm. He was full of ambition, though, had ideas, and he made a little hand-press while still on the farm and tried to do printing with it; then became correspondent for the Louisville newspapers, and did such good work on the country news that he finally got a place on the Louisville "Evening Journal." Then came the usual newspaper man's life. In 1879 Mr. Yenowine moved to Milwaukee, where for six years he was city editor of the Milwaukee "Sentinel," and then editor of the "Evening Wisconsin." He next founded a newspaper of his own, which is widely known. He has been a factor in making Milwaukee what Milwaukee is today, a factor probably not recognized as it should be. Mr. Yenowine has prospered; he has bought his old Kentucky home, which has become a summering place for him. He is a very energetic business man and a journalist of ability. The fact that he is both Northern and Southern in thought makes him stronger, makes him what he is in all his views and all his enterprises, a broad and forceful American.

GEORGE HARDIN YENOWINE.

ROBERT CHARLES WINTHROP.

CHIEFLY associated in the popular mind today as the favorite orator of great historical anniversaries, Robert C. Winthrop rests secure upon his reputation as a statesman achieved before the middle of the nineteenth century. Mr. Winthrop was born in Boston May 12, 1809; graduated at Harvard in 1828, studied law with Daniel Webster, and served as a Henry Clay Whig in the Massachusetts Legislature from 1834 to 1840. During the next ten years he was in Congress, being Speaker of the House from 1847 to 1849, and distinguished himself as a ready debater and an accomplished parliamentarian. A series of impressive speeches on public questions delivered by him in Congress are still consulted as authorities. In 1850 he was appointed by the governor of Massachusetts to Daniel Webster's seat in the Senate, when the latter became Secretary of State. A year later he retired from active political life, and devoted himself to literary, historical and philanthropical occupations. He was president of the Boston Provident Association for twenty-five years, of the Massachusetts Historical Society for thirty years, and has held many other posts of dignity and usefulness. His "Washington monument" speeches of 1848 and 1885, his Boston Centennial address of 1876, his great Yorktown oration, and many others of his public speeches, are noted for their fervid eloquence, patriotism and scholarship. There is a portrait of Mr. Winthrop in the Capitol at Washington, presented by the citizens of Massachusetts, and another in the hall of the Massachusetts Historical Society. From the outset he has been at the head of George Peabody's trust for Southern education. His works are "Life and Letters of John Winthrop" and "Washington, Bowdoin and Franklin."

ROBERT CHARLES WINTHROP.

485

FELIX ADLER.

IT is safe to say that the science of moral philosophy has had no
more earnest and careful student than the scholarly founder of the
religious organization known as the Society for Ethical Culture. Prof.
Felix Adler is the son of a Jewish rabbi, and was born in Alzey,
Germany, August 13, 1851. At the age of five years he was brought
to the United States, where he passed through the New York public
school and Columbia grammar school, and graduated at Columbia College in 1870. He then went abroad to study at Berlin and Heidelberg, obtaining the degree of Ph. D. in 1872. Returning to America
he was appointed in 1874 professor of Oriental languages in Cornell
University, a post which he filled until 1876, when he gave it up to
establish in New York City the Society for Ethical Culture. This
religious but unsectarian society, which is addressed regularly on Sundays by its founder, has flourished from the beginning, and celebrated
its eighteenth anniversary in May, 1894. Its philanthropic work is
widely known and copied. Professor Adler established the first kinder-
garten for poor children in America, and was the first to introduce the
district nursing system, which has since been so generally adopted.
Earnest and persistent in his labor for tenement-house reform, he did
valuable service as a member of the tenement-house commission. It
was he who established the pioneer school of manual training, the
Workingmen's School in New York, where five hundred children of
the poor are educated according to the most improved methods. In
1890 he established the "International Journal of Ethics," which is
widely read at home and abroad. He has published "Creed and
Deed," a collection of lectures, and "Moral Education of Children."

FELIX ADLER.
486

JAMES GORDON BENNETT.

— —

BORN to editorial purple, James Gordon Bennett has at least shown that he has inherited many of the qualities of his famous father who gained the purple for him. It was a severe test of the stuff in a young man to succeed to such a property as the "New York Herald," to inherit the income of a prince and at the same time have imposed upon him the duties of a worker. Mr. Bennett has demonstrated that he possesses taste for each separate sphere; that he can spend as prodigally and his critics would say with just about the degree of reason of the average prince has been made clear enough, while he has not shirked the duty of managing his great property himself, managing it arbitrarily and completely, and taking the good and bad consequences; that he has the journalistic instinct is assured, that he has allowed it to develop only in certain channels is as well apparent. Born in 1841, and therefore a man still comparatively young, he is widely known upon two continents for his lavish mode of life, and his daring ventures upon lines never adopted before and requiring great expenditures with results but a matter of speculation. He is a forceful character. It was a bold thing to send Stanley into the heart of Africa to find Livingstone, and the enterprise succeeded. It was as startling an undertaking to fit out a North Pole expedition, and the enterprise failed. The European newspaper enterprises of Mr. Bennett have had equally varying fortunes. With his newspaper and his wealth, he might have become an impressive political factor in the United States. He prefers Paris or a yacht. He is a notable American, but he has not earned the title of a great one. Yet he has vigor and is a force in journalism.

JAMES GORDON BENNETT.

CALVIN S. BRICE

ALTHOUGH a young man, Calvin S. Brice, lawyer, railroad projector and political leader, has a proud record. Though business reasons keep him in New York, he is by birth an Ohio man; was born in Denmark, Ohio, September 17, 1845. He is the son of William Kirkpatrick Brice, from an old Maryland and Pennsylvania family, and a clergyman of distinction in the Presbyterian Church, and Elizabeth Stewart, of Carrollton, a woman of fine education and exemplary traits of character. His education was carefully looked after by his parents and obtained in the common schools of his home and in those of higher grade in Lima, Ohio. He was only thirteen years old when he was able to enter the preparatory department of Miami University, at Oxford, Ohio, where he remained a year and then entered the freshman class. He was expecting to graduate, when the call for troops aroused his patriotism and though but fifteen years old he relinquished his studies and enlisted as a member of Capt. Dodd's university company, and in April took his first lesson of military discipline at Camp Jackson, Columbus, and served with his regiment during the year. Returning to the university he resumed his studies, completed the regular course, and was graduated in 1863. Mr. Brice, after teaching for awhile, went into the army again, reuniting a company and going back as captain. Being firm in the resolve to devote himself to the law, after the war he entered the law department of the Michigan University, and was admitted to the bar after being graduated from there. He has attained great distinction as a corporation lawyer, has been a leader in financial circles, and as United States Senator has done much good for the Democratic party.

CALVIN S. BRICE.

CUSHMAN K. DAVIS.

THE scholar in the United States Senate has appeared to advantage in the person of Cushman K. Davis, one of the senators from Minnesota. Mr. Davis was born in Henderson, Jefferson County, N. Y., June 16, 1838. While he was but a child his parents removed to Waukesha, Wis., where he attended the public schools and became afterward a student in Carroll College. He then entered the University of Michigan and graduated from that great institution in 1857, when only nineteen years of age. He studied law and began its practice in Waukesha, but at the beginning of the Civil war became a lieutenant in the Twenty-eighth Wisconsin regiment. He served creditably and was rapidly promoted, becoming assistant adjutant-general on the staff of Gen. Gorman, but in 1864 became incapacitated by typhoid fever and was compelled to leave the service. In 1865, with recovered health, he removed to Minnesota and resumed the practice of his profession in St. Paul, which city is still his home. A deep student and brilliant orator, he soon became widely known, both on the political and lecture platforms. He was elected to the Minnesota Legislature in 1867, and in 1868 was appointed United States attorney for Minnesota, which position he held for five years. In 1874 he was elected governor of the state on the Republican ticket, and served one term, declining a renomination. In 1875, and again in 1881, he was a candidate for United States senator, but in the then condition of Minnesota politics was each time defeated. In 1887 he was elected, and in 1893 was again chosen for the position. He ranks high in the Senate, both as statesman and as a man of extraordinary cultivation and scholarship.

CUSHMAN K. DAVIS.

IGNATIUS DONNELLY.

— —

A STRONG, vigorous personality, and an immense amount of energy, are among the characteristics of Ignatius Donnelly. He was born in Philadelphia November 3, 1831, and was graduated from the Central high school of that city in 1849. He then went to St. Paul, Minn., where he took up the work of journalism. In 1860 he was elected lieutenant-governor of that state, was sent to Congress in 1863, and made state senator in 1873. He is also an author, and his books are well known and bear the stamp of Mr. Donnelly's strong imagination. Among those most favorably known are "Caesar's Column," "Dr. Huguet," and quite a recent one, "The Golden Bottle." What might almost be called his life work is "Cryptogram," a claimed cipher conveying the information that Sir Francis Bacon was the author of the plays attributed to William Shakespeare. This assertion on the part of Mr. Donnelly has of course provoked much discussion and has not increased the estimation in which he is held by the great mass of thinkers; on the other hand it has secured quite a contingent of those who take the Bacon side of the controversy. It may be said of Mr. Donnelly that he has at least the courage of his convictions. Mr. Donnelly is an advanced thinker, and shows indomitable will in whatever work he undertakes, literary or political. Mr. Donnelly has also appeared upon the platform as a lecturer supporting his own views, especially as to the Bacon cipher. Even those who differ from him on that question admit he makes a very ingenious argument in support of his theory. Mr. Donnelly is very popular in his own state and has a large number of admirers throughout the country. His works are interesting and are possessed of much merit.

IGNATIUS DONNELLY.

CARDINAL JAMES GIBBONS.

MODERN history must include the names of great dignitaries of the Roman Catholic Church in the United States. The life of Cardinal Gibbons affords an example of what ability and acumen, supplemented by a power of application to an end, firmness of purpose, and a fixed regard for duty, may accomplish. James Gibbons was born in Baltimore, Md., in 1834. Of Irish parentage, he was taken for a time to his father's native country, and there began his first studies for the priesthood, to which he was destined, returning to take his theological course at the seminary of St. Sulpice in Baltimore. He was first assigned to a small church in the suburbs of Baltimore, but his talents, soon observable, carried him to a broader field. In 1868 he was made vicar apostolic of North Carolina, with the rank and title of bishop, and in 1886 was recognized as one fitted for the hightest dignity of the church. He visited Rome, and there, in the midst of an imposing ceremonial, received the red biretta from the hands of the Pope himself. The selection made was most satisfactory to the Roman Catholic Church in the United States. The cardinal's hat has become its new bearer well. The face, thoughtful, intelligent, almost ascetic in its expression, indicates the character of the man. He has tact, it may be great ambitions, but his great executive ability, his self-denial, his modesty and his attention to his duty are the qualities which endear him to the world. His influence is widely felt and his friends are not confined to those of his own church, and more could scarcely be said of any religionist than that, for religious antagonisms are generally the strongest of all. He represents the progressive and broad-minded spirit of the day.

JAMES GIBBONS.
497

JOHN B. GORDON.

A BRAVE soldier, loyal to the South, fighting to the last for "The Lost Cause," who, when the war is ended becomes a stanch supporter of the Union, such a man is Gen. John B. Gordon. He was born in Upson County, Georgia, February 6, 1832. His ancestors came from Scotland to Virginia in the seventeenth century, and were prominent in the days of the colonies. During the Revolutionary war they were prominent officers in the Continental army. General Gordon was educated at the University of Georgia. After completing his law studies he began practice with his brother-in-law, L. E. Bleckley, afterward chief justice of Georgia. In 1854 he married the daughter of Hon. Hugh Anderson Haralson, who represented Georgia in Congress for many years. In 1861 General Gordon raised and uniformed a company of men for the Confederate army and was chosen captain. General Gordon's war record was remarkable for bravery and audacity. At the battle of Sharpsburg, in 1862, he was severely wounded four times, but remained on the field with his men until the fifth ball struck him full in the face and knocked him senseless. He fought with stubborn valor throughout the war. He guarded the retreat from Petersburg, and at Appomattox Court House was put at the head of the four thousand troops that were intended to cut through General Sheridan's line, which was prevented by the surrender of General Lee. He was delegate at large to the National Democratic Convention in Baltimore in 1872; was elected United States senator in 1873, and again in 1879. In 1886 he was elected governor of Georgia, and was re-elected in 1888. In 1890 he was again elected senator. His career in Congress has been very brilliant.

JOHN B. GORDON.
497

JOEL CHANDLER HARRIS.

A DELIGHTFUL delineator of Southern life, with a keen appreciation of the negro character, Joel Chandler Harris is one of the most popular authors of the day. He was born December 9, 1848, in the little village of Eatonton, Ga. Before he was six years of age he had learned to read, and later he enjoyed the advantages of a few terms at the Eatonton Academy. When he was twelve years of age he decided to learn the printer's trade. He soon found an opportunity to do so in the office of a Colonel' Turner who was then publishing a weekly newspaper called "The Countryman." He found his position a congenial one, as Colonel Turner allowed him the use of his magnificent library. It was here that this country boy received his education. He began his literary career by sending anonymous communications to "The Countryman," which were printed. He afterward threw off his disguise and contributed a number of essays and poems which were highly praised by the publisher. At the close of the war he obtained employment on various newspapers in Macon, New Orleans, Forsyth and Savannah. In 1876 he became a member of the editorial staff of the "Atlanta Constitution." Soon after Mr. Harris went on the "Constitution" he was requested to furnish some negro dialect sketches, then becoming very popular. While on the Turner plantation he had often listened to the weird folk-lore tales of the negroes, and now decided to reproduce them. In a few weeks appeared the "Uncle Remus" sketches, which at once created a sensation. His later works are: "On the Plantation," "Daddy Jake," "The Runaway," "Uncle Remus and His Friends," "Balaam and His Master," and "Little Mr. Thimblefinger."

JOEL CHANDLER HARRIS.

EVAN P. HOWELL.

AN eloquent orator, a journalist of rare ability, and a patriot whose heart is full of love and devotion for his countrymen, Evan P. Howell is one of the most distinguished men of the South. Captain Howell is a native of Forsyth (now Milton) County, Georgia. At the age of twelve years his father moved to Atlanta. Here the son passed with distinction through the common schools of Warsaw and Atlanta, entering the Georgia Military Institute at Marietta in 1855. After completing a two years' course he went to Sandersville, where he read law until the end of the year 1858, when he was enrolled among the Lumpkin Law School matriculates, at Athens. A year later he began the practice of law, which was interrupted by the breaking out of the Civil war. He enlisted in the First Georgia Regiment as orderly sergeant and was appointed a lieutenant before the expiration of a month. He was promoted to the rank of first lieutenant, and before the second year he remodeled the company and became its captain. From service under General Jackson in Virginia he was transferred to the Western army in time to engage in the struggle at Chickamauga. In the retreat from Laurel Hill the sufferings of Captain Howell and his men were intense. He served until the close of the war and when the conflict ceased he returned to his home and began farming, which he carried on for two years. In 1868 he became city editor of the "Atlanta Intelligencer," but a year later he renewed the practice of law. He was elected to the State Senate in 1873 and was reelected for a second term. In 1876 he purchased a controlling interest in the Atlanta Constitution, and became its editor in chief.

EVAN P. HOWELL

JOSEPH JEFFERSON.

—

THERE are few actors on the American stage who have so succeeded as Joseph Jefferson in winning not only admiration but,
in a degree, the affection of the public. The nature of the parts in
which he has distinguished himself, notably that of Rip Van Winkle,
may have had something to do with this, but there is much in the
personal character of the man himself to win such regard. He was
born in Philadelphia in 1829, and when but three years of age figured
as the child in the drama of "Pizarro," then one of the most popular
plays. In 1843, after the death of his father, Joseph joined a company of strolling players who made their way to Texas and followed
the United States army into Mexico. On his return to the Northern
States the youth was engaged for minor parts in various theaters, and
in 1849 married Miss Lockyer, an actress. He continued the usual
life of an actor, drifting from place to place, and from 1850 to 1856
was employed as actor and stage manager in Philadelphia, New York,
Baltimore and Washington. After a trip to Europe, his health having
been affected, he became stage manager again, and in 1857 became
connected with Laura Keene. In 1858 he made a pronounced success
as "Asa Trenchard" in "Our American Cousin." In the early sixties he sailed for Australia, in which country his success continued,
and in 1865, after his return to this country, appeared, much against
his own inclination, as "Rip Van Winkle." Since that time his right
to be counted one of the great American actors has not been disputed,
and his reputation has been fully maintained in all the parts he has
taken. He is wealthy, and, when in retirement, spends his time as
painter, student and angler.

JOSEPH JEFFERSON.

ROBERT TODD LINCOLN.

INHERITING the name which his illustrious father made the synonym of wise leadership and patriotic devotion to his country, Robert T. Lincoln is one of the most modest and unassuming of public men. He was born in Springfield, Ill., in 1844, and was graduated at Harvard University. During the latter years of the Civil war he served as a member of General Grant's staff, subsequently taking up the study of law at Harvard. He was admitted to the bar in 1867, and began the practice of his profession in Chicago, which has continued to be his home to the present day. In 1868 he was married to the daughter of Hon. James Harlan, at that time Secretary of the Interior of the United States. As a lawyer he achieved success, confining his practice largely to the United States courts and to civil suits, leaving the other branches of the work to his partners. In 1880 Mr. Lincoln was chosen a presidential elector on the Garfield and Arthur ticket, and when President Garfield assumed the duties of his office he invited the young man to a seat in his cabinet as Secretary of War. He was the youngest cabinet officer that had ever served in that capacity up to that time, and he filled the office with marked ability for four years, being retained by President Arthur after Garfield's death. In 1889 President Harrison appointed him Minister to England, and he spent the next four years in London. Returning in 1893 he has since devoted himself to the practice of law in Chicago. Mr. Lincoln, though bearing a name the most potent with his party in summoning a sentiment of affection for its wearer, has not utilized the circumstance for his personal advancement. The son of Abraham Lincoln is a hard-working Chicago lawyer.

ROBERT T. LINCOLN.

THOMAS LOWRY.

NOT active in politics or literature, seeking fame of no sort, but working strenuously in a broad way for material ends, because his nature will not admit of any other course on his part, Thomas Lowry has become one of the foremost figures in the great Northwest. From a struggling young attorney he has become a millionaire and has set an example of daring in new fields, worthy of imitation by young men everywhere. He was born a little over fifty years ago, one of the great brood of young Illinoisans who saw the Prairie state in its infancy coeval with their own, and after the ordinary education of a youth of the region studied law at Rushville in the state named, and later removed to Minneapolis, Minn., to engage in practice. He succeeded very well, but it was not as a lawyer that he was destined to acquire most prominence. He was one of the men who recognized the great future of Minneapolis and St. Paul and who were shrewd enough to ride with their own fortunes on the wave of development of the twin cities. He had no money to speak of, but he borrowed it of Boston capitalists, purchased the rickety street car lines of the two towns and began their steady improvement. He struggled under a great load of debt, bankruptcy often stared him in the face, but his indomitable pluck and energy, his personal popularity and his financiering genius carried him through eventually, and he is now the owner of one of the greatest of urban transportation systems, as well as being deeply interested in different railroad companies and one of the heaviest of owners of real estate in both the cities named. He has never been a candidate for office, though he has served as a delegate to Republican national conventions. He is a remarkable man.

THOMAS LOWRY.

JOHN TYLER MORGAN.

BELIEVING implicitly in Democratic principles, Senator Morgan is one of the most consistent representatives of his party. He was born in Athens, Tenn., June 20, 1824. When nine years of age his parents removed to Calhoun County, Ala., and settled near the village of Jacksonville. In early life he attended school and later obtained an academic education. He studied law in Talladega and commenced its practice in 1845. He devoted fifteen years to the duties of his profession, acquiring a reputation throughout the state as an able and eloquent lawyer. In 1860 he was elected presidential elector, and voted for Breckinridge and Lane. In 1861 he was a delegate from Dallas to the state convention that passed the ordinance of secession. When the war broke out he enlisted in the Confederate army as a private. When the company was assigned to the Fifth Alabama Regiment, Mr. Morgan was appointed major, and soon after became lieutenant-colonel of the regiment. He was afterward commissioned as colonel, and returning to Alabama raised the Fifty-first Regiment. In 1863 he was appointed brigadier-general by Gen. Robert E. Lee, but refused the promotion in order to lead his old regiment, whose colonel had been killed. Later he was again commissioned brigadier-general and commanded a division, operating with Gen. James Longstreet in eastern Tennessee, and with Gen. Joseph E. Johnson and Gen. John B. Hood. At the close of the war he returned to Selma and resumed the practice of law. In 1876 he was a presidential elector on the Tilden and Hendricks ticket, and in the same year he was elected to the United States Senate. He was re-elected in 1883 and again in 1889. He is now serving his third term in that body.

JOHN T. MORGAN.

WILLIAM J. NORTHEN.

NO man has done more to advance the interests of Georgia than William J. Northen. An able, wise and trusted leader, he has won success equally as legislator, educator and governor. Mr. Northen was born in Jones County, Ga., July 9, 1835. The greatest and most successful part of his life has been identified with educational interests. He was graduated from Mercer University in 1853; began teaching school in 1854; assisted the famous instructor, Dr. Carlisle P. Beman, in the Mount Zion School, from 1856 to 1858, and then, on Dr. Beman's retirement, took control of the school, which he conducted with great success. When war was declared between the Northern and Southern States he enlisted as a private in the company commanded by his father, who was nearly seventy years of age. Immediately upon his return to Hancock County he again devoted himself to school teaching, continuing in this work until 1874, when his health became impaired and he began farming. His political career dates from 1867, when he was elected a member of the state Democratic convention, which was the first political body that assembled in Georgia after the war. He was a state legislator in 1877-78, and again in 1880-81. He was state senator and chairman of the educational committee of the General Assembly in 1884-85, and governor of Georgia from 1890 to 1894. As a practical and most successful farmer he has always taken a deep interest in agriculture. He has held both the vice-presidency and the presidency of the State Agricultural Society. The degree of LL. D. has been conferred upon him by Mercer University and by Richmond College, Virginia. He is now at the head of the Georgia Immigration and Investment Bureau.

WILLIAM J. NORTHEN.

ROBERT EMORY PATTISON.

PENNSYLVANIA has produced a great many men of force of character, and among those of recent activity Robert Emory Pattison, late governor of the state, takes no mean rank. He is a young man. He was born in Quantico, Md., in 1850, his father being a Methodist clergyman; who was later sent to Philadelphia, where the son attended the high school, graduated and became a law student in 1869. He began practice in 1872. In 1877 and 1880 he was elected comptroller of Philadelphia and his fearless administration of the office made the foundation of his political fortunes. He was nominated by the Democrats for governor and elected in 1882. Shortly afterward he sent a message to the Legislature recommending a policy of retrenchment and urging the modification or repeal of laws which resulted in the multiplication of useless offices. A storm ensued, but the policy of the governor was successful. His term expired in 1886, and in 1887 he was appointed a member of the Pacific Railway Commission, where his sturdy qualities were again made apparent. Again called upon by the Democrats, he was re-elected governor, and repeated the forceful administration of his first term. During the famous Homestead riots his judicial firmness of character was especially manifested. He recognized the fact that "a public office is a public trust," and his career was a shining example of loyalty to principle and honor. Without being a demagogue, he adhered strictly to the course he had marked out without regard to political influence or personal feeling. He was succeeded in office in 1895 by the Republican candidate, D. H. Hastings. With his youth, his admitted ability and his wide popularity in his party, his future, politically, may be counted most promising.

JOHN DAVISON ROCKEFELLER.

POSSESSING almost unlimited wealth, which he dispenses with the liberality of a prince to worthy objects, John D. Rockefeller is one of the most noted millionaires of the world. He was born in Richford, N. Y., July 8, 1839. In 1853 the family removed to Cleveland, Ohio. After completing his studies at the high school Mr. Rockefeller began his business career as clerk in the commission house of Hewitt & Tuttle. In fifteen months he became cashier, and before he was nineteen years old he engaged in the commission business in partnership with Morris B. Clark. By 1860 the firm of Clark & Rockefeller, with others, had established the oil refining business of Andrew, Clark & Co. In 1865 Messrs. Rockefeller & Andrews bought the interests of their associates in oil refining and established the firm of Rockefeller & Andrews. The firm of William Rockefeller & Co. was established in Cleveland, and a short time afterward the partners united in founding the firm of Rockefeller & Co. in New York, and two years later these companies were consolidated under the name of Rockefeller, Andrews & Flagler. In 1870 the Standard Oil Company was organized with a capital of $1,000,000, with John D. Rockefeller as president. In 1882 the Standard Oil Trust was formed with a capital of $70,000,000, which was afterward increased to $95,000,000. In 1892 the Supreme Court of Ohio declared the trust to be illegal, when it was dissolved. The business is now conducted by the separate companies, in each of which Mr. Rockefeller is a shareholder. Notwithstanding his great wealth Mr. Rockefeller is a man of simple manners and taste. He is best known as the founder of the University of Chicago, to which he has given $7,000,000.

JOHN D. ROCKEFELLER.
515

CLAUDE MATTHEWS.

PROMINENT in the politics of the West is the name of Claude Matthews, governor of Indiana. Recognized as a man of marked ability and unflinching integrity, he has commanded the respect of both parties. In fact, he is regarded as a presidential possibility. Mr. Matthews was born in Bethel, Ky., in 1845. He entered Centre College, whence he was graduated in June, 1867. In 1868 he removed to Vermillion County, Ind., where he engaged quite extensively in grain and stock farming. He has been quite prominent in the breeding of improved live stock. He organized the Indiana Short Horn Breeders' Association, and to him is due the formation of the National Association of the Breeders of Short Horn Cattle of the United States and Canada. In 1876 he was elected a member of the Legislature as a Democrat in a strong Republican county. In 1880 he was a strong candidate before the convention for lieutenant-governor, but withdrew. In 1890 he headed the Democratic ticket as candidate for Secretary of State, and was elected by a plurality of nearly twenty thousand. In 1892, although a candidate for re-nomination as Secretary of State he was requested to become a candidate for governor. He was elected by a plurality of nearly seven thousand. While governor he was confronted by many serious problems. In 1893, when the local authorities were helpless, he suppressed the Columbian Association at Roby, organized for the purpose of holding prize fights. The coal miners' strike of 1894 was broken in a short time by his decisive action, and the sympathetic strike of the same year interfered very little with the running of trains in Indiana. Governor Matthews lives a quiet life, devoting most of his time to the study of social questions.

CLAUDE MATTHEWS.

RICHARD OLNEY.

AN incident of the second administration of President Cleveland was the elevation to a position of public prominence of a man who was previously but little known outside of his own state. Secretary of State Olney comes from one of the oldest and most honored New England families. He was born in Oxford, Mass., in 1835, and graduated from Brown University with high honors in 1856. Two years later he graduated from the Harvard Law School, and began the practice of his profession with Judge B. F. Thomas, a descendant of Isaiah Thomas, the publisher of the "Old Thomas Almanac," and founder of the "Worcester Spy." In 1861 Richard Olney married Judge Thomas' daughter, thus uniting two of the oldest and most eminent families of New England. For many years Mr. Olney has been regarded as one of the ablest lawyers in Massachusetts, and his judgment in matters of public and party policy has been much sought after in recent years by the younger generation of Democrats in his state. He has twice declined the offer of a place on the supreme bench of Massachusetts, and has never sought office of any kind, although in 1874 he represented Roxbury in the state legislature, and was a candidate for attorney-general of the state in 1876, when the Democratic party was defeated. Since that time he has never aspired to public honors, but in 1893 he accepted the invitation to enter President Cleveland's Cabinet as Attorney-General of the United States. Mr. Olney is a man of dignified bearing, one who appreciates the responsibilities of the position he occupies. He was appointed Secretary of State by President Cleveland upon the death of Walter Q. Gresham. Judson Harmon, of Cincinnati, was raised to the office of Attorney-General.

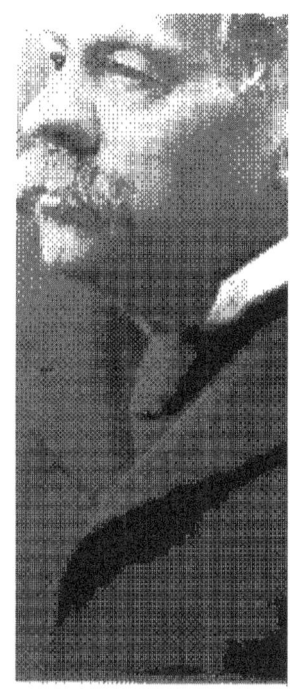

RICHARD OLNEY.

519

INDEX